tabula rasa

SHELLY REUBEN

tabula rasa

HARCOURT, INC.

Orlando   Austin   New York   San Diego   Toronto   London

Copyright © 2005 by Shelly Reuben

www.HarcourtBooks.com

Library of Congress Cataloging-in-Publication Data
Reuben, Shelly.
Tabula rasa/Shelly Reuben.—1st ed.
p.   cm.
ISBN 0-15-101079-X
1. Police—Family relationships—Fiction. 2. Children—Crimes against—
Fiction. 3. Arson—Investigation—Fiction. 4. Adopted children—Fiction.
5. Birth mothers—Fiction.   I. Title.
PS3568.E777T33 2005   2004025585

Text set in Minion
Designed by Linda Lockowitz

Printed in the United States of America

First edition

K J I H G F E D C B A

DEDICATION

TABULA RASA MARKS the end of a collaboration. Years ago, when I was doing research on arson, Charlie King was a supervising fire marshal for the New York City Fire Department. We met. We fell in love. We got married. From the first line I ever wrote about fire until publication of this book, Charlie King was part of it all. He taught me how to investigate fires, and he taught me how to think like a fireman.

I used to joke that as an author I had achieved the ultimate coup by marrying my research data. But what I had really done was marry my hero. We dated for two years; we were married for twenty-three. And every day of that time, I knew how lucky I was. I knew that I had married the guy who walks down Main Street at High Noon. The guy in the white hat. Honorable. Sentimental. Noble. Funny. And solid as a rock. Charlie King was good through and through.

I had been told that men like him didn't exist. He existed, and for twenty-five years, I had him. Charlie King died in July 2003.

He never stopped working. He never stopped helping, loving, and inspiring me.

This book is for Charlie.

ACKNOWLEDGMENTS

IN THE COURSE OF researching *Tabula Rasa,* I received invaluable assistance from Tom Schoff of the School of American Ballet, Diana Byer of the New York Theatre Ballet, John Magnus of the Joffrey Ballet School, Tammy Ellis of A Class Act School of Dance, and Donna Decker of the Decker School of Ballet, all of whom provided insights into the intricacies of being dancers, living, loving, and teaching ballet.

A special thank-you goes to Donna Decker for reading and commenting on my manuscript, and to Karla Jones and her parents, Lorraine and Bob, for sharing their perspectives on being a student dancer, a parent, and a state trooper. I was also exposed to much-needed knowledge when John Tucker guided me through the Professional Children's School in Manhattan, and José Morales gave me a tour and answered my questions about the Bedford Hills Correctional Facility. Access to this maximum security prison was made possible through the courtesy of Elaine Lord, superintendent and Paul R. Levine, first deputy superintendent.

Joseph P. Altieri was generous in explaining his duties as a senior parole officer, as was Rev. Anne Rebecca Elliot, executive director of Project Greenhope, when she permitted me to tour her halfway house. I am grateful to Paul Kluge of the Syracuse Police Department for sharing his knowledge of repeat fire setters, and to New York State Police Senior Investigator Michael C. Sweeney of Troop NYC, and Sgt. Jim Barnes of Troop C in Sidney, for helping me to understand the inner workings of the state police.

A tip of the hat also goes to Robbie O'Connell, chief of the Rawlins, Wyoming, Fire Department, who helped a stranger on the phone to equip an imaginary fire department with real apparatus. There are never too many good things to say about a fireman.

On a more personal note, I would like to thank my friend Laurel Rothman for reading an early version of my manuscript and for protecting it from all manner of danger, including airplane crashes, snow storms, and marauders. A warm thank-you, too, goes to Doreen Davis, for sharing her childhood photos, memories, and many cups of tea, and to Kathryn Kennison for a thousand good deeds.

The wonderful people at RLR Associates—Bob Rosen, ever "my boss"; Jennifer Unter, my incomparable agent; Tara Mark; and Walton Shepherd—are the literary agents who I once dreamed I might have. Sometimes I think I must have conjured up my editor at Harcourt, David Hough, in a dream as well. But David is as real as is his incredible, intuitive expertise, his toughness, his talent, and his kindness.

Last but not least in my bottomless thank-you bag are those for my mother, Ghita Reuben Olit; my sisters, Selma Holo and Linda Schwebke; and my brother, Chuck Reuben. You stalwart souls got me through a tough year and I love you. May all of your silver linings have silver linings.

TABULA RASA
(tab'ye le ra se), n

1. a mind not yet affected by experiences, impressions, etc.
2. anything existing undisturbed in its original
   pure state [1525-35. <L: scraped tablet, clean slate]

book one

Ladybug, ladybug, fly away home,
Your house is on fire, and your children will burn.

—ANONYMOUS

chapter 1

NOT ALL BABIES are created equal.

Some gurgle and coo.

Some cry.

Some demand unconditional affection. These are the ones whose tiny hands are drawn to your fingers like a magnet, and curl around them with a grip like a gorilla.

Then there are those other babies. The very rare, perhaps only encountered-once-or-twice-in-a-lifetime babies; they seem to have been born thinking, calculating, evaluating, making judgments.

These are the babies who stare.

You've seen one. Surely you have. Think back. It might have been on a bus or in a supermarket. A lone, strange child surrounded by adults murmuring the appropriate noises.

What a darling!

She has your eyes!

Such delicate ears! I forgot how small ears can be!

No one, however, will comment on the baby's beautiful smile.

The baby doesn't smile. Not at all.

And the baby doesn't cry. Not at all.

The baby stares.

You stare back, mesmerized by the tiny mind behind the tiny eyes.

Your eyes lock.

You are captivated.

Something is happening between you and this tiny, helpless infant.

The baby holds your eyes for five seconds. Ten seconds. A lifetime.

Then the infant releases your eyes and moves onto something else.

The bond is broken.

Your brain does a double take.

What just happened?

You walk away from the baby carriage. Away from the admiring adults.

Away. Away.

But feeling as though you had somehow made contact with an alien life force.

Of such stuff and substance was the baby who lived in the ugly house—for that is what the townspeople called it—just beyond the intersection of Mabel Newton Road and Route 18 in the village of Sojourn.

"SHE'S SO QUIET, that one. Sometimes I don't know if she's alive or if she's gone and died on me."

Words to that effect had been spoken on many occasions in the ugly house by Edith Tuttle, the mother of the infant, whom, from a discreet distance, we have been observing.

After giving birth to this child, Edith occasionally was

overheard making off-hand comments that indicated she was at least marginally aware that her new baby was in some respect different—more like a changeling than anything she and her husband, Wilbur, could have been expected to produce.

"Hell, there's so much to do around here, a body's got to make herself heard if she wants to get my attention. Never a peep out of that one, though. I swear, if it weren't for Gabe and Minna, it'd never get fed, never get its diaper changed. Them two fuss over her like they was her ma and pa instead of me."

The "Gabe" in question was Edith Tuttle's youngest son, Gabriel Cotter Tuttle. Gabe was a freckle-faced youngster with hair the color of apricot jam and eyes that crinkled when he liked you—and he liked everybody. Gabe was the kind of a boy who would be likely to carry around a toad in his pocket because he loved animals and to jump off the garage roof because he thought he could fly (he wanted to be an astronaut when he grew up). He had a voice like a golden thread stretched out in the sun, so pure and pretty that it inevitably doomed him to playing the angel whenever Christmas plays were performed.

Minna, his sister, was much plainer. She was the only one of Edith and Wilbur's children who hadn't been given a middle name. Minna was a sweet, nondescript child, tall and lanky for her age. She had long, mousy brown hair, blunt bangs, and a please-like-me smile that should have gone right to the heart of any adult who happened to cross her path, but somehow didn't.

It was Gabriel and Minna who got their sister up in the morning. Dressed her. Fed her. Bathed her. Loved her. Without them, she probably would have starved to death long before she had reached her first birthday. Because of them, she made it. But just barely.

When Edith Tuttle was enthroned against the pillows on her bed in the maternity ward, she had been given a form with an empty slot provided where she was to fill out her newborn's name. Instead, she wrote the words BABY TUTTLE, and told the nurse that she would think of a "real nice name" later.

But she never did.

BABY TUTTLE.

Sometimes Edith called her "the baby," almost in the same tone that a person would refer to "the refrigerator" or "the mail box."

Sometimes, she would refer to her youngest as "it," as in "did anybody remember to feed it?" or "I'm sure it was in the bedroom before I came downstairs."

Usually, she didn't refer to it at all.

Baby Tuttle was quiet, pensive, and judgmental. She had a habit of linking eyes with a chosen few adults.

And physically, she was precocious.

She was crawling at two months, walking at six, and climbing before she was eight months old.

Wherever she was, she wanted to be someplace else.

She was active without being hyperactive. A small, determined, ambulant universe unto herself opting to endure the ministrations of her brother and sister as if she knew that she had to be fed, clothed, bathed, and groomed in order to be launched.

A moment of docility was the price she was willing to pay for the reward of movement, freedom, self-determination, and escape.

And those who had seen her in action speculated that it was probably this particular characteristic, more than any instinct for survival or unconscious response to danger, that saved her life.

Yes. She did walk, tumble, toddle, or fall out of the ugly house's front door and down the steps to the gravel and dirt driveway.

Yes. She did flee the fire that killed Minna and Gabriel.

But she would have escaped anyway.

With or without the fire.

Because leaving the ugly house was the one ineradicable constant of her existence.

That is all that she had ever wanted to do.

chapter 2

BILLY NIGHTINGALE came from a family of extremists.

Billy's father, Mortimer, said that Billy's mother, Evelyn, never made statements, she only made sweeping statements. In turn, Billy's mother complained that Billy's father would work hard to locate the one brick wall in the middle of an open field so that he could get a running start to butt his head right up against it.

Nobody disagreed that Billy's sister, Annie, made Sarah Bernhardt look like a piker.

And all of the Nightingales, including the ranch hands, believed that Billy himself was going to be the star of his own epic disaster movie. Or at least he was, until he reached the age of fifteen, at which point he changed.

Sort of.

Both Billy and Annie were born in the town of Rawlins, Wyoming.

Annie was eleven years old when her English teacher gave her an assignment to write a composition about her family. She was told that she could describe their genealogy, their involvement in sports, their health, their histories—anything. As long as it was true.

This is what Annie Nightingale wrote:

HOW THE NIGHTINGALE GOT HIS NAME
Annie Nightingale—Grade Six

My mother came from Jolly Old England. She was born in Manchester. She had two parents and three sisters, except that one died when she was two days old, and three brothers. My mother's name is Evelyn. When she was seventeen years old, she got into a spectacular fight with her parents because she wanted to be an actress. They said you'd better not do it, because if you do, off with your head. So Evelyn journeyed to America and got a job with a bunch of other adventurous people who put on plays and sometimes sang songs and danced and did magic tricks.

Evelyn was very pretty and she had fabulous long red hair and beautiful blue eyes. In her job, she always got the part of the princess or the girl who got pregnant even though her boyfriend wouldn't marry her.

She went to a lot of different cities with her job, and one time she played Desdemona and got strangled sixty times in fifty-two days.

When she was twenty years old, she was in Cheyenne, Wyoming. It was five degrees below zero, and it was snowing so hard that Evelyn's group couldn't get out. They were stuck in the hotel.

It was late at night and some guys were playing music and some other guys who were ranchers from Elk Mountain were in town to make trouble and spend their paychecks, and one of the troublemakers was a gigantic man, over nine feet tall. He had wide shoulders like an ox and big hands like a monster. But he had a nice face, and his voice was low and soft and gentle, and Evelyn said it reminded her of a train whistle.

So this guy saw Evelyn sitting alone at a table with another girl, and the other girl said, "I hate this place. I hate snow. I hate winter."

Evelyn said, "It is bleak, isn't it?"

And the other girl said, "Yes. It's disastrous. There's nothing out there but snow, snow and more snow."

Evelyn looked out the window and didn't see anything alive. Not a dog or a cat or a mouse or a flower or a bird, and she sighed and said, "My kingdom for a Nightingale," because she used to like seeing those birds in Jolly Old England.

And that's when this nine foot tall guy comes over to her table and leans down, which he had to do because he was so tall, and he says, "Well, what do you know, Little Miss. My name just happens to be Mortimer Nightingale."

Well, pretty soon Mortimer asks Evelyn to dance, and pretty soon he tells her about the ranch where he raises cattle and sheep about twenty miles into the Medicine Bow Mountain Range, and pretty soon he asks her to marry him, and pretty soon she says yes, because she doesn't want to be an actress anymore.

And then they got married, and Mortimer said, "Guess what?"

And Evelyn said, "What?"

And Mortimer said, "I lied to you. When I heard you say, 'My kingdom for a nightingale,' I fell in love with you. So I changed my name. I did it right then at the dance hall. Just like that. So that you'd dance with me. But I changed it legally later on, so you really are Mrs. Mortimer Nightingale." Then my father looked at Evelyn and said, "Are you mad at me?"

And Evelyn said, "No."

And they lived happily ever after, which is good for me, because if Evelyn had said, "My kingdom for a milkshake," I could have been named Annie Milkshake, and if she hadn't said anything, I would have been Annie Koussevitzky, daughter of Mortimer and Evelyn Koussevitzky, which would have been a fate worse than death.

At the top of her paper, Annie's teacher had scrawled, "You really must learn to curb your imagination. Next time tell the truth!"

In all fairness to Annie, with the exception of her father's height and the color of her mother's hair, Annie had more or less stuck to the facts. In particular, those that explained how the Nightingales got their name.

About Billy, though, the thing that made him seem like a helium balloon drifting toward a sharp object, was his tendency to grab onto every new fact, idea, or piece of information that came his way and, on a minute by minute basis, try to literally reinvent the wheel...the toaster...his father's weed wacker...his mother's electric hair curlers...his sister's dolls.

When Billy was six years old he joyfully realized that he could insert his plastic rocket ships into the slots of the toaster, depress the lever for a countdown and...BLAST OFF!!!

P I N G.

Up those little buggers sprung, almost as high as the tops of the kitchen cabinet doors.

Billy's second countdown was equally successful, but by his third, the rockets had started to smolder a bit. On the fourth, the plastic melted and stuck to the red-hot coils on either side of the toaster's bread slot. There was a terrible smell, a small fire, and...

Billy's father's weed wacker was another experiment.

Billy had been studying South America in his seventh grade history class when he learned that Argentinean cowboys used an intriguing weapon made of a long cord and heavy balls at the end, called a bola. It was used for throwing at and entangling the legs of cattle.

Fascinating, Billy thought, looking at his father's weed wacker. *It* had a long cord, and if he drilled a hole through a croquette ball, he could attach it to the cord, and, instead of manually swinging a bola over his head, he could use the cord of the weed wacker to . . .

One window was broken and one wall demolished before Billy's interest in South American ranching practices was put to rest.

Billy joyfully disemboweled radios and television sets. He encased the metal prongs of his mother's electric hair rollers in clay and plugged them in, convinced that his makeshift kiln would produce a candelabra capable of holding twenty-four variously sized candles. Instead, his experiment resulted in a lump of plastic-fused clay that looked like the larva of a prehistoric bug.

For a while, Billy's sister's dolls fascinated him, particularly the intricacies of their arms and legs. After surgically removing the hooks and rubber bands that tethered their limbs to their torsos, he reattached them with a wire spring, a wind-up key, and an ON/OFF mechanism, and created what he called a "Disco Doll." In fact, it came closer to resembling a manic depressive mannequin crossed with a threshing machine, and after seeing it, Annie renamed it the "Psycho Doll."

By the time Billy Nightingale hit his teens, he was spending most of his time fiddling with automobile engines, with an occasional chemistry class–inspired foray into making explosives out of cow manure.

Five months after he blew up the outhouse behind the shearing shed, thereby confirming to his satisfaction that high nitrogen–content fertilizer mixed with diesel oil and detonated with a blasting cap really *does* explode, Billy's entire outlook changed.

And, as he explained to anyone who would listen, it wasn't even anything that he *did.*

At mid-day on August 25 during the hottest, most sun-scorched Wyoming summer that anyone could remember, the main barn on the Nightingale ranch burned down. Billy was three hundred feet away at the time, on his way from the house to the corral when he saw a few stray wisps of smoke that looked more like dust from a tractor than anything else. But when the "dust" kept coming out of the barn and the tractor didn't, Billy knew that something was very wrong. Within seconds the wisps turned into billows, and the gray smoke started to turn black. Billy ran to the house, got on the phone, and called the Elk Mountain Fire Department. Twenty minutes later, all five pieces of equipment and all fifteen volunteer firemen were on the scene.

Billy personally played no part in extinguishing that fire. He did, however, observe the strange ballet of men and machinery, and as flames punched angry orange fists through doors, windows, and openings in the roof, Billy decided that if life and the vicissitudes of fate were theater, then fire and the catastrophes, collapses and rampages associated with it had to be grand opera at the very least.

Billy Nightingale watched the flames... enthralled. He observed every phase of fire-fighting operations... fascinated. And after the Elk Mountain Volunteer Fire Department wetted down every last cinder and took up their hoses, he approached Chief Warren Buffer... inquisitive.

He pointed to an ancient piece of apparatus. "What's that?"

"A 1957 Chevy pumper."

"Pretty old, huh?"

"Prehistoric, Billy. But it works just fine."

"What about this one?"

"Another dinosaur. 1950 International Quick Attack. Holds 250 gallons of water.

"It did the job, though. Huh, Mr. Puffer?"

"It sure did. This one over here is a 1,500-gallon tender with a 500-gallon pump; and this is a six-by-six multifueler of a military design with a 1,000-gallon tank capacity. It has a 150-gallon pump on the end. Old equipment, but good. And good men using it."

Billy nodded. "You saved my dad's barn."

"Saved some. Lost some. Contents are pretty bad. Tractor's gone. Whole tack room's a mess, and the interior isn't going to win any beauty prizes."

"What do you think started the fire, Mr. Puffer?"

"Well, Billy. We were wondering if you did."

"Me?"

"Thought you might have been tinkering around again. Another one of those experiments you learned in school. Maybe something went wrong."

"No, sir, Mr. Puffer. No sireee. Not me. Not this time."

"You sure, Billy?"

"Sure as I'm standing here."

"Swear it?"

"Double swear it."

"All right, then, son. Let's go inside and have a look around."

TAKE THE ORDINARY and blur every straight edge. Transform every surface into jagged rectangles suggestive of an alligator's rugged hide; dampen it; blacken it; permeate it with the unmistakable odor of a just-fought fire. Then step into it. Look. Poke. Prod. And hope what's left of the sodden mess will give up some of its secrets about where the fire started— how and why.

"We're pretty sure we can eliminate arson," Chief Puffer told Billy's father later. "Nothing looks fishy, and I didn't see any evidence that a flammable liquid was used. All the outlets looked okay, too, so I don't think that it was electrical. Near as I can figure, the fire started somewhere in the vicinity of this stall here, but I can't for the life of me figure out how. Sorry, Mort. This one's just plain got me stumped."

Chief Puffer listed UNDETERMINED on the Elk Mountain Fire Incident Report as the cause of the fire in the barn—a cause that satisfied the fire department, satisfied Chief Puffer, and satisfied Mort Nightingale. It did not, however, satisfy Mortimer Nightingale's insurance company. They read the Incident Report, hired a private investigator, asked him to go to Elk Mountain, and told him to root around their policyholder's life for something incriminating so that they could turn down the claim.

He did, and they did.

"How?" Mortimer asked his claims representative. "Why?"

"We believe that your son started the fire."

"That's stupid."

"Is it?"

"Damn right it is."

"Well, Mort. Just five months ago, Billy set off an incendiary device that caused an explosion in . . ."

"Kid stuff."

"Billy is only fifteen years old, so nobody's saying the fire in your barn wasn't kid stuff. But arson is arson, and not you or anybody else in your family can collect on this insurance policy if any one of you deliberately set fire . . ."

Mortimer hung up on him.

Then he called in the big guns. This was something that, despite having lived his life on the open range, he was entirely capable of doing. For Mortimer Nightingale had not lived his *entire* life in the Elk Mountain area of the Medicine Bow Mountain Range. During World War II Mortimer Nightingale had served in the United States army. As an infantryman he had shared trenches with one Delmore O'Shaughnessy, with whom he had been exchanging Christmas cards ever since. In the intervening years, O'Shaughnessy had become a fire marshal in the Bureau of Fire Investigation for the City of New York. Recently, he had been promoted to the rank of deputy chief.

Mortimer Nightingale picked up the phone and made what was for him a highly uncharacteristic long distance telephone call.

chapter 3

DELMORE O'SHAUGHNESSY had only been out of New York City twice since the war. Once, to give a lecture on pathological fire setters at an International Association of Arson Investigators convention in Atlantic City, and again to attend his sister's wedding in Poughkeepsie, New York. In order to visit his old war buddy in Elk Mountain, he had to fly direct from LaGuardia to Denver and change planes there for the short hop to Laramie.

From the window of his plane, Delmore O'Shaughnessy, whose idea of the west had never extended beyond New Jersey, saw spacious skies and amber waves of grain; he saw majestic purple mountains and vast fruited plains. And this child of the Lower East Side—this man who had fought and investigated fires in Manhattan's claustrophobic tenements and cramped luxury skyscrapers—was dumbstruck by the realization that this country, his country, was so big, so formidable, and so very much like the words of the song.

O'Shaughnessy was even more amazed after he arrived at the Laramie airport. He stood at the door of the plane, looked up, and saw how the sky sprung from horizon to horizon like some wild and crazy war hoop. Never before had he seen a sky so unencumbered by either skyscrapers or enemy aircraft.

"God damn gorgeous," he said, his eyes glued to the heavens as he started down the stairs. His friend Mortimer Nightingale was waiting for him there when his foot hit the tarmac. They collected his luggage, and as they walked to Mort's truck, they spoke softly of years gone by and of different skies...ones from which bombs had fallen. Two hours into the trip from Laramie to Elk Mountain, they had finished with the past and were discussing the fire in the Nightingale barn and why Mortimer had asked his old friend to come.

DELMORE O'SHAUGHNESSY was a man of middle height, middle age, and middle weight. He had blue-gray eyes, thick white, southern-senator hair, and big calloused hands. He chain-smoked menthol cigarettes, carelessly tossing his stubs wherever he was standing, and talked non-stop, particularly when he was inspecting a fire scene. Occasionally, he interjected Yiddish phrases into his monologues to make a point, a habit he had picked up when he was sixteen and worked for a pickle vendor at the Essex Street Market.

When Delmore O'Shaughnessy looked at people or objects, his eyes latched onto them like suction cups on a window pane.

As he was being introduced to Billy, the fifteen year old felt those eyes latch right onto him.

"Come here, kid," the older man commanded.

The youngster stepped forward.

He was, O'Shaughnessy noticed, tall, gawky, angular, and eager. His face was full of freckles, there was dirt under his fingernails, and his hair was the color of dandelions. All of which confused Delmore O'Shaughnessy. He had no trouble understanding or anticipating the moves of fifteen-year-old boys who carried lead pipes and used switchblade knives. Ones who wore farm overalls, sheared sheep, and drove tractors, however, were as foreign to him as creatures from another planet.

"So you're the alleged perpetrator," the older man said gruffly, wondering if teenagers in Wyoming spoke English.

Billy looked down at his shoes.

"Some *schlimazel* in Connecticut thinks you burned down the barn because a year ago...maybe less...you burned down something else. A smoke house. An outhouse. Some house."

Billy's head jerked up quickly. "That was an accident. I was conducting an experiment and..."

"Yeah. Yeah. Tell it to the judge. Anyway, past history doesn't equal motive, and even if it did, motive doesn't tell you *bubkas* about how a building burned down. Only a *putz* investigates a fire by looking at a suspect's past."

Billy gave a quizzical look. "Is that good?" He hadn't understood a word that O'Shaughnessy had said.

The fire investigator laughed. "Well, kid. It isn't good, and it isn't bad. It just is." He craned his head to peer through the barn door. "Tell you the truth, I never did a barn fire before. We don't get a big call for cattle-ranch investigations on the upper East Side. Not that it matters, because a building is a building, and fire doesn't care if it's taking down a Burger King or the Taj Mahal. It does what it's going to do no matter what you, some *meschugana* insurance agent, or Smokey the Bear has to say about it." O'Shaughnessy looked down at his young companion for a response, but Billy's face had gone completely blank.

"Hey. Kid. Am I boring you?"

"No, sir." Billy said fervently, too nervous to know what to say or how to react.

"All right, then. Follow me."

Deputy Chief O'Shaughnessy led his friend's son into the same old barn that Billy had known his whole life, familiar in terms of size and shape, but alien because of the dampness, the darkness, the haze of smoke, the charred wood, and the strange smells.

"See this," O'Shaughnessy said, pointing to a accumulation of burned boards on the floor. "It's dropdown fire. Probably part of the ladder to the loft." He walked to a tatter of fabric hanging from a nail on a wall. "And this *schmatte* here is what's left of a blanket." He flipped it over. "See. Red. Green. And some fuzz left on the other side." He led Billy to the office at the front of the barn, turned the knob and pulled the door forward. "If it had been opened at the time of the fire," he ran a finger along the clean edge where the door had hugged the frame, "all this would be black." He turned to Billy. "Are you getting it, kid?"

Billy opened his mouth to answer, but hesitated when he realized that he still didn't know what to say.

O'Shaughnessy crossed his arms over his chest, stared, and waited.

Finally, Billy stuttered, "Geee... getting what?"

"Getting that what I'm doing here has a purpose. It's what I get paid for. What do you think that purpose might be?"

"To help me and my dad?"

"The taxpayers of the City of New York wouldn't pay me a penny to help you and your dad. Try again."

"To... to.... to look for stuff?" Billy offered without confidence.

"Good guess. Where?"

"At a fire?"

"What kind of stuff am I looking for?"

Billy shuffled his feet, bit his lip, and shrugged.

"Listen, kid," O'Shaughnessy said. "What I do is I'm a fire marshal. I investigate the origin and cause of a fire. It's my job to find out where a fire started and figure out what set of circumstances were at play to make that fire happen. *Farstaisch?*"

"Sort of."

"Sort of isn't good enough. Come here."

Billy walked to where the fire marshal was standing.

"Look down."

Billy looked down.

"When you're doing a fire, kid, the first thing you want to locate is the lowest point of burning. Why do you think that is?"

The fifteen year old hunkered down and stared at the ground. For about a minute he didn't say anything, but his hands did a pantomime of opening a match book, striking a match, and holding it out in front of him. After he did this twice, he shifted his eyes up to Delmore O'Shaughnessy and said, "When you start a fire in a burn barrel or fireplace... no matter where you start it, after you strike the match, the flames burn up from there."

"Yeah. Go on."

"Okay." Billy squinted around the thought forming in his mind. "Fire starts at the bottom of wherever it is, like at the bottom of a match. And it climbs. So, maybe that's why you look for the lowest point of... what did you call it?"

"The lowest point of burning. And excellent, Billy. You nailed it. Fire burns up and out. I know you were imagining striking a match just now. Think how it flares out from the bottom in more or less the shape of a V. The lowest point of that V is the lowest point of burning. Got it?"

"Yes, sir."

They moved deeper into the barn. "What you're looking for at any fire scene are burn patterns. Remember those two words, kid. Burn patterns. They're the diary the fire writes in the floors, walls, and ceiling of a room. Without them, all the charred wood and collapsed beams in the world don't mean a thing. With them, you can figure out where a fire started and how. Sometimes, you can even figure out why."

Although Chief Warren Puffer had identified the area of origin right after he had helped to extinguish the fire in the Nightingale barn, the how and why of the fire had eluded him. The fire chief had showed Mortimer the stall where the fire had started and pointed out that there was nothing over, under, next to, or around the area of origin that could have been the ignition source. No electrical outlets. No frayed wires. No appliances. No fixtures. No equipment. No machinery. And no carelessly discarded cigarettes, despite the trail of them that the fire marshal was now leaving in his path.

Just clumps of hay in the middle of an empty stall.

Delmore O'Shaughnessy entered that same stall, knelt beside the same shallow depression in the floor, and beckoned Billy over. "See this?" He fingered a few fragile stems of ash. "This is where it started. Right here on the floor. The hay caught fire first, burned for a while, and set fire to the wood framing here. After these boards and beams got underway, the flames shot right up the wall to the hayloft. From there the fire communicated to the rest of the barn and vented out through the doors, windows, and roof."

Billy looked toward the interior of the barn. He could see a charred saddle at the entrance to the tack room, and he thought he could make out a collapsed beam to the left of a dented pail. But he was barely able to differentiate individual shapes in the fluctuating shadows of the dark structure. There was the corner of a harness poking out from a pile of rags ... a grimy black window pane ... a light fixture dangling by a single wire ... one leg of what looked like a broken three-legged stool. And slowly ... slowly ... Billy saw burn patterns emerge from the debris in the same way that, as a child, he had seen monster faces materialize in books of frightening puzzles after he had connected all the dots.

"The problem with this fire," O'Shaughnessy said, standing up, "is the ignition source."

He crossed a narrow corridor, walked into an alcove about six feet away, and stopped at an ancient kitchen table under a double-hung window. Despite a light coating of soot, the table and its contents had been untouched by the fire. Blinding sunlight streamed through the window panes, highlighting a clutter of rusty nails, pliers, hammers, tea tins, convex mirrors, and old gardening tools.

"*Tchotchkes*," O'Shaughnessy said absentmindedly, his eyes moving to an object, evaluating it, logging it into the appropriate slot in his brain, and then moving on to another one. There was an assortment of glass jars spread out along a window sill behind the kitchen table. Some were empty, and some were filled with nuts, bolts, screws, washers, brads, and nails. Halfway up the window, another shelf displayed an empty circa 1950 milk bottle, a cheap crystal vase, a jelly jar half-filled with shiny liberty dimes, and a small, round fish bowl.

Sunlight streamed through all of the items on the shelves, making them sparkle and shine despite a spattering of grime and dust. It streamed aggressively, like a predatory animal. Relentlessly, like a pummeling fist. And hotly, like the blast from a pizza oven.

Delmore O'Shaughnessy grabbed his chin with a sooty fist and nodded toward the window.

"There's your culprit," he said.

Billy turned to the shelves. He saw bottles. He saw knick-knacks. He saw nails. He turned an enquiring eye to the fire marshal.

"Solar heat," O'Shaughnessy explained. "Most often, it happens in rural areas. It's rare now, but it didn't used to be. Back when I joined the department, fires like this were taught in all of the old instruction manuals. Now, you can't find one written up anywhere. It still happens, though."

"What still happens?"

O'Shaughnessy pursed his lips thoughtfully. Instead of answering, he said, "Kid. Did you ever use a magnifying glass to burn ants?"

Billy hesitated before admitting, "Yes, sir."

"Well, it's the same principle here. Radiant heat from the sun came through this window. It turned the fish bowl or the milk bottle or maybe a piece of broken glass into a lens. Then, just like your magnifying glass, the lens concentrated all of the solar energy into a focal point of light, directed it toward the middle of the stall, and kept on shining there until the hay reached ignition temperature and burst into flames."

He looked at Billy Nightingale. "Does that make sense to you, kid?"

Billy didn't answer right away.

He continued to follow O'Shaughnessy around the barn, watching the fire marshal take photographs, tentatively asking him questions about how fire burned, and gaining more and more confidence as the explanations began to make sense to him. Later that same afternoon the fire marshal led Billy back to the alcove opposite the stall and told him to look again at the miscellaneous bottles and objects on the shelf. Billy watched and waited. He waited and watched. And then, at just about the same time of day when the fire had initially occurred, he saw a shaft of sunlight stream through the milk bottle on the shelf and continue across the room to the middle of the stall in exactly the same way that O'Shaughnessy had described it. It jabbed into the spot where the fire had originated as precisely as if it had been the point of an angry finger.

Billy turned to O'Shaughnessy. He nodded. "Yes, sir. It makes sense to me now."

"Glad to hear it, kid," the older man grinned. And he slapped Billy Nightingale affectionately on the back, not knowing that he had so impressed the teenager that Billy would spend the rest of his childhood waiting, planning, scheming, and saving so that one day he could go to the Empire State and do what he would have to do to become a New York City fire investigator.

Like Deputy Chief Fire Marshal Delmore O'Shaughnessy.

The man who had become his hero.

chapter 4

ANNIE NIGHTINGALE looked like an elf.

She was two years older than her brother, but other than their shared "take no prisoners" attitude toward life, she did not resemble him at all. Billy was tall and fair. Annie was slim and tiny. She wore her hair in a jagged pixie cut that perfectly offset her catch-me-if-you-can features.

Annie's nose was straight, her eyes were amber, her hair was brown, and her smile was joyous. She always painted her lips with vivid red lipstick, and she often wore a beret. When she dressed up, she looked chic, confident, and sexy. When she dressed down, she wore blue jeans, a western shirt, and moccasins.

Annie Nightingale loved admiration. She was never humble or self-effacing, she gloried in compliments, and she didn't argue when somebody called her a flirt. Before leaving Wyoming to go to college, she had turned down four proposals of marriage from three different boys—one of whom had proposed twice—without giving any of them a reason why. Annie considered it great fun to be adored. Adoration was inconsequential, perhaps. But inconsequentialities were high on Annie's list of "Things that Are Important."

If asked to list five additional things that were important to her, Annie would have replied, "*my* freedom, *my* parents, *my* brother, *my* health, *my* happiness, and *my* future." If you tried to explain to her that she had listed six things instead of five, she would have just smiled beatifically and said, "*I* get six."

When Annie was seventeen years old, she left Elk Mountain to attend the Constance Gill College of Liberal Arts and Sciences on Manhattan's upper East Side. Constance Gill was perfect for a girl with vacillating career objectives because it allowed her to take advantage of everything the city had to offer. Journalism majors worked as interns at the *Daily News* or the *Wall Street Journal*; art students audited courses at the Metropolitan Museum of Art; English lit majors were encouraged to visit the Morgan Library and the Lincoln Center Library for the Performing Arts. The school's guest lecturers included Noble Prize–winning writers, scientists, and politicians, and among its alumni were the prime minister of a small nation, an Academy Award–winning costume designer, and the only woman who had ever beaten an IBM computer at chess. As a school, Constance Gill offered more opportunity than it did restraint, but even in its academically unconventional atmosphere, Annie Nightingale's advisor had to swallow hard when Annie announced brightly, "I don't see that I've done anything particularly heinous" after she had chosen to major in five subjects instead of just one or two.

"It took me all summer to narrow it down to five...I mean, don't *you* want me to learn absolutely everything? *I* certainly do."

Annie played the piano brilliantly, but had turned down a scholarship to Julliard because she had no intention of becoming a concert pianist.

She loved journalism and particularly enjoyed gossipy human-interest stories... "but I could never, never interview someone who had just been burned out of his house. I mean, *I couldn't!*"

When Annie was growing up in Elk Mountain, she had found her grandfather's vintage box camera and enlarging equipment stored in the attic, set up a darkroom in the basement, and taught herself to take and develop pictures. Before she graduated from high school, she won three national photo contests; and thirty-two of her landscapes were exhibited at the Laramie Museum of Art. But... "I don't think that the *Daily News* would be willing to wait around for me to develop my old black and whites, and I don't want to switch to a 35mm Nikon. I just *don't.*"

Annie Nightingale always had a good reason to acquire a new skill and an even better one not to practice it. After several combative sessions with her academic advisor during which she had complained many times to the poor woman, "Why are you *persecuting* me?", Annie finally pared her list of majors down to two. Eventually, at the age of twenty-one, she graduated from Constance Gill with a bachelors degree in fine arts and public relations. Her first job was at the Paris Noel Abbot Gallery on Madison Avenue.

It was a glamour job. A job where everyone that Annie met was rich, famous, and effete. Annie's work required her to travel to France, Spain, Portugal, Greece, Great Britain, Japan, and Germany. She was invited to only the best parties. And after five raises, four promotions, and three marriage proposals from individuals with flaccid muscles and large portfolios, Annie was driven to exclaim in a manner reminiscent of her mother many years before, "My kingdom for a cowboy!"

Such was Annie's state of mind two weeks before her twenty-fifth birthday. It was mid-March, she had just returned from Palm Springs, and it was eleven o'clock in the morning on one of those meteorologically impossible days when breezes exist for the sole purpose of disrupting our routines, interfering with our equanimity, and transporting us into rhapsodies of misadventure.

By 11:05 AM, Annie had flung open her boss's door, marched into his office, and announced, "I'm not here."

Noel Abbot the Third, accustomed by now to the eccentricities of his assistant, raised his head and smiled vaguely. "Excuse me?"

"I'm not here, today, Noel. I called in sick."

"You look positively beaming to me, darling. Is it contagious?"

"Terminal."

"I see. And if I'm not being too personal, your specific malady is...?"

Annie leaned over her boss's desk and whispered conspiratorially, "Spring fever." Then, before he could react, she flounced out of the room.

A few minutes later, she emerged from beneath the canopy over the entrance to the gallery on 53rd Street and Madison Avenue. She was wearing a frothy summer frock to match her frothy summer mood. A slim gold belt accentuated her narrow waist, gold loop earrings jostled gaily from her ears, and sling-back high heels lent a chorus girl sexiness to her legs. She strode up Madison Avenue, feeling very much like a peacock at a party of barn swallows, awake, exhilarated, and, as they would have said back on the ranch "ready for bear."

As she walked, Annie's full focus was on nothing but her surrender to the day. She moved briskly, like a brightly painted pony that had escaped from a carousel. She smiled at everybody and nobody. Happy to be alive. Happy to be happy. By the time she got to 86th Street, Annie's happiness had increased, but her pace had slackened off. Sling-back heels, it became evident, were not designed to be worn by exhilarated women mortally consumed by spring fever.

She spotted a French bistro in the middle of the block ahead. It had small, bright green tables dotting the sidewalk that seemed like early harbingers of spring. Annie sat at a table close to the street, slipped off her shoes, ordered iced coffee, and watched the world go by, waving at tourist busses on their way to Harlem and winking at children on their way to school. Like her brother, Annie Nightingale was a great absorber of life. Unlike Billy, she had no desire to analyze its component parts, solve its problems, or unravel its mysteries. She was thrilled just to plop herself down in the middle of the *sturm und drang* and soak it up, as lazy and contented as a glutton in a bake shop.

And like a glutton, Annie sipped her coffee, gloried in the sunshine, and observed the comings and goings of the people passing by. There were two giggling teenagers who had braces on their teeth, walking side by side with knapsacks on their backs; there was a sour-faced nanny wearing an orange jumper and pushing a purple polka dot baby carriage; there was a double-decker city bus advertising a celebration down in Battery Park; there was a trio of arguing nuns wearing habits and gesticulating vehemently as they crossed the street; and there was a dark blue and yellow New York State police car.

An impeccably groomed, silver-haired lady walked slowly up the avenue. Annie smiled at her and she smiled back.

"I want to look just like you when I grow up," Annie called out.

"Bless you, child," the old lady responded, and continued to walk up the block.

A group of school children dressed in navy jumpers with bright blue blouses skipped and cavorted down the sidewalk behind their teacher, a flustered young woman who was walking backward and counting heads. There was a dark, brooding delivery man on a battered bicycle who looked like the beneficiary of an Aztec curse. And then, again, moving more slowly this time, there was that same dark blue police sedan.

Annie finished her coffee and watched as the car circled the block two more times. After its last circuit, instead of continuing around the corner, it pulled up to the curb no more than ten feet away from where she was sitting.

She watched as the window rolled down.

She waited as the driver, clearly a man, unfolded what she assumed was a map. In doing so, he raised his left hand, revealing that he was not wearing a wedding ring. Annie sipped at her empty coffee cup and studied the broad shoulders and what appeared to be the tall, well muscled, physique of the driver. He had a high forehead and thick black hair. At first, she couldn't see his face, but then he turned, looked at her, and caught her staring at him.

He stared right back.

He had dark, amused eyes, and big, irregular features that included a nose you would never see hovering over a brocade sofa in an art gallery. It was a Mount Rushmore, damn the torpedoes, full speed ahead sort of nose.

As they continued to stare at each other, Annie saw the narrow, slow-to-smile lips that had probably never sipped mineral water or tasted sushi begin to smile at her. His big, galooty hands looked as steady holding the map against the steering wheel as her father's hands did holding the reins of a horse.

Annie slipped her sling backs on her feet and got up.

"Hi, there, cowboy," she said as she sauntered over to his car. "Are you lost?"

His dark eyes twinkled.

"Yep," he said. His voice was deep. Low.

"Where are you headed?"

"John Jay College of Criminal Justice."

"Are you taking a course there?"

"Nope. Giving one. Guest lecturer from the New York State Police."

"Are you a state trooper?"

"Yep."

"Well, trooper. You're on the wrong side of town. This is the East Side. You want to be about thirty blocks south of here, on the West Side."

"How do I get there?"

"The hard way or the easy way?"

"Easy way."

"I get in your car and take you. Unless it's against regulations."

"Regulations?" He shrugged. "Never learned the word."

Annie discovered during the short drive to John Jay that her trooper's name was Sebastian Bly. He was twenty-seven years old, had never been married, and was stationed in Sidney, New York, which was a four hour drive from Manhattan—three hours at "trooper speed."

Annie helped Trooper Bly find a parking space, accompanied him to a small auditorium to listen to his talk on law enforcement, and agreed to join him for dinner. They wandered down Forty-seventh Street—or was it Forty-fifth?—until they happened upon a romantic Italian eatery with red checked table cloths and wine bottles coated with dripping candle wax. In the years to come, they regretted that they hadn't written down the name of the restaurant because neither one of them could remember where it was located.

Four weeks later, they were married.

A year after that Sebastian admitted to Annie Bly *nee* Nightingale that on the day they met, he had not been lost.

"What do you mean you weren't lost? I saw you circle that block at least three times before you pulled over."

"Still, I wasn't lost."

"If you weren't lost, then what were you?"

"Devious."

"Huh?"

"Yep. Devious and cunning. I saw you sitting at that table with no shoes on, and you were as pretty as a picture. Half a minute later I made up my mind to marry you. Then I drove around that block two more times before I thought to pull up to the curb, take out my map, and pretend to be lost."

"What if I hadn't come over to your car?"

"No chance of that."

"But..."

"Annie, give it up. I saw you. You saw me. We found each other. It was destiny. Meant to be. Resign yourself. We're just plain stuck being lucky."

chapter 5

ONE YEAR INTO Annie's marriage, Mortimer Nightingale decided that there was profitable fossil fuel to be had somewhere on the five hundred square acres at the northwest corner of his ranch. Playing his hunch, Annie's father commissioned a seventy-two-page mineralogical report from a geologist at the University of Wyoming; then he sent copies to wildcat oilmen and strip miners in Wyoming, Colorado, and Montana.

While other excavations on other ranches in the Elk Mountain area yielded nothing but dinosaur bones, the Nightingale ranch yielded oil, copper, and coal. This bonanza had relevance for all four Nightingales because for the first time, they would have money. Money to play with. Money for new furniture. Money for an indoor swimming pool, a new fireplace, a Steinway piano, vacations to Hawaii, and "Whatever the hell else we want to buy," to quote the *paterfamilias* in a moment of euphoria.

It was important to Mortimer and Evelyn that Billy and Annie take pleasure from their increased bank account, so the parents transferred a percentage of the mining profits to their children. This gave Billy the ability, on a fireman's salary, to buy a two bedroom garden apartment in a brownstone on Manhattan's upper East Side.

Annie, too, made good use of her money.

Sebastian's parents had long wanted to sell their farm on Willow Keep Road in Fawn Creek and retire to Florida, and Annie and Sebastian had long wanted to acquire the house and the adjoining two hundred acres. So the first thing Annie did with the money from the mining lease was to buy both. For cash.

Four weeks later, they moved in.

The second thing she did concerned her employment. After marrying Sebastian and moving to Fawn Creek, Annie had worked as a reporter for the *County Courier and Gazette*, a weekly newspaper serving three towns on Route 7. With pen and steno pad in hand, Annie attended tractor pulls at the county fair, church quilting bees, raffles that raised funds for the local SPCA, and meetings at the town hall. Annie liked what she was doing but hated to get up at seven o'clock every morning to be at her desk by nine. Her nature rebelled against routine, and working five days a week for the same company, in the same city with the same people made, as she explained to Sebastian, her "brain go gluey." So, armed with the new option of being a lady of leisure, Annie quit her full-time job and continued to work for the *County Courier and Gazette* on a freelance basis.

The third thing Annie did with her new-found wealth had as much to do with patience as it did with money. She and Sebastian waited, and waited, and waited, and when the duplex on the second and third floors of Billy's townhouse finally became available, they bought it to be their Manhattan pied a terre.

And so, when the fire occurred that involved that intense and unsmiling infant whose mother had not bothered to give her a name, Sebastian and Annie Bly were married and living on Willow Keep Road in Fawn Creek; Billy was already a New York City fireman; and all three were happier than one would think that anyone had a right to be.

chapter 6

STATE TROOPER Sebastian Bly was twenty-eight years old. He loved his job, and wanted to keep doing it for as long as he could. As far as he was concerned, he was starring in the movie version of his own life, and even the bad times were good.

Sebastian was sitting behind the wheel of his patrol car, finishing up some paperwork; and Billy Nightingale, who had gotten permission to accompany him, was in the passenger seat. It was the first of May, and they were in the third hour of what had started out to be an uneventful eight-hour tour when the radio suddenly crackled to life.

"Immediate assistance requested by the chief of the Sojourn Fire Department," the dispatcher said. "He's got two DOAs and wants to know how long it will it take you to get there."

"Tell him thirty-five minutes," Sebastian said.

It took him twenty-three.

Trooper speed.

SEBASTIAN AND BILLY arrived in Sojourn at 11:48 AM. They easily found the house they were looking for because the fire trucks were parked in the street.

As their car slowly approached, Billy's throat went dry.

"Jesus Christ," he said. "What a nightmare."

The structure they were looking at had bow windows, elaborate cornices, a mansard roof, and a square cupola. It had once been painted white and was probably built by the town judge or banker over a century before. All of the paint had faded, the wood siding looked soft, spongy, and repellent, and the entire exterior had turned mushroom black. Whoever was living there now had draped dirty bedsheets over all but two of the ground floor windows. The other two windows, near the side entrance door, were covered by disintegrating shades.

Two small bicycles, one shiny and new and the other one rusty and lacking a front tire, lay in the middle of a patchy front lawn that had become a dumping ground for old tires, hub caps, and dented fenders. There was one crumbling hitching post on either side of the driveway and a battered oil drum at the edge of the grass a few feet from a broken hand-tiller. Both the house and the yard reeked of malice, and the new bicycle in the center of the lawn looked like bait, as if it had been put there to lure children into a quagmire of decay.

Sebastian and Billy got out of the car and walked over to the guy from the Sojourn Volunteer Fire Department who was wearing the chief's hat.

"Welcome to the ugly house, boys," he said somberly. "I never liked the damned place. Now I hate it. I'm Otis Quick. Today we lost two."

"I know," Sebastian said.

"The boy was eleven. The girl was nine."

"Didn't know that."

"It's always worse with children."

"Amen to that."

For a while, nobody spoke. Then Billy said, "The ugly house. Does everybody call it that, or just you?"

"Everyone. Except for the Tuttles. They live here."

"So," Sebastian jutted his head toward the fire scene. "What have you got?"

OTIS QUICK HAD been chief of the Sojourn Volunteer Fire Department for over fifteen years and, other than the two years he served in Korea, had lived in this town his entire life. He owned the Chrysler dealership in Cassandra, a seventeen-minute drive from his house in Sojourn, and he knew everybody in town. Those he didn't know personally, he knew about because Otis Quick was not adverse to gossip unlike most middle-aged men with similar backgrounds. Before and after fighting a fire he would both receive and transmit choice tidbits of information with perfect equanimity. And when he was ready to leave the scene of a fire he could tell you not only what he had done but could also tell you what everybody else at the fire had done, seen, or heard.

He told Sebastian Bly and Billy Nightingale that the fire in Edith and Wilbur Tuttle's house was unusual in that nobody had ever called it in. The day before the fire an aerial ladder the town had ordered was delivered to the firehouse, and because the day of the fire was a civic holiday Chief Quick decided to call in his volunteers to familiarize them with their new piece of equipment.

As part of their training exercises, he got into the bucket of the extension ladder, and told his lieutenant raise him up.

The ladder stretched upward. Twenty feet ... forty feet ... eighty feet ... one hundred and ten feet off the ground. When it reached the top of its extension, Otis stayed put for a few minutes to enjoy the view. He turned south and saw the fairgrounds. He turned west and saw the river. He turned north and saw the Huckleberry Cider Mill. But when he turned east, toward the intersection of Route 18 and Mabel Newton Road, he noticed that something was wrong. On one side of that intersection was the building that contained the post office and the Sojourn General Store. On the other side was the Tuttle house. Both were no more than five hundred feet west of the Sojourn Volunteer Fire Department.

Since volunteer firemen are rarely on the premises when an alarm is called in, it would have taken at least fifteen minutes on a normal day for them to respond to a fire, even if that fire was only five hundred feet away. First the call comes in. Then volunteers have to get to their cars or trucks. Once they are inside their vehicles, they have to drive to the firehouse or to the fire scene.

The siren on top of the fire house blares.

Telephones jangle to life.

"Where's Chuck?"

"Taking a bath."

"Well get him out of the bathtub. We've got a fire to put out!"

Volunteers push aside wives, lovers, children, and meals. They jump into pickup trucks like cowboys leaping onto horses to chase the varmint who has just run off with the blue-eyed gal. Adrenalin pumps, speed limits are broken, and not a second is wasted. Even so, by the time the apparatus has arrived flames are shooting out the windows, smoke is seeping through the roof, and the structure is fully involved.

On any other day and at any other time, the Tuttle house would have resembled the remains of a giant campfire.

That this did not happen was entirely due to Otis Quick being in the bucket of his new aerial ladder at the time.

Mere seconds after he saw smoke, he and his men were on their way.

To quote from Chief Quick's Fire Incident Report:

```
10:35 AM. We entered through the side door and
stretched a line up the staircase to the second
floor. We entered the rear bedroom on the second
floor, observed the closet area on fire, and saw
a kerosene heater. We used a fog nozzle because
we didn't want to drive the burning kerosene all
over the bedroom. Simultaneously the ladder com-
pany broke the bedroom window on the second floor
to vent the smoke so we could advance with the
hose line. Fireman Rossetti raised a portable lad-
der to the second-floor window and conducted a
primary search. He stumbled upon two children
lying in their beds. He picked them up and handed
them to Fireman Jones, who was in the bucket of
the aerial ladder. Both firemen started CPR imme-
diately on the children while the bucket was being
lowered to the ground. Despite their efforts, it
became evident that the children were gone. As
soon as the fire was declared under control, I ra-
dioed the state police dispatcher that there were
two DOAs at the scene, and I requested the assis-
tance of a state trooper and the coroner.
```

Two small bodies were laid out in the grass on the far side of the driveway and covered with faded bath towels. Bly turned away from the bodies and said to Otis Quick, "The parents. Where are they?"

"The father's in New Jersey, visiting his mother in a nursing home. He's on his way back now. Edith is across the street. Albertina Hipkiss has a picnic table in her backyard, so I sent Edith with Albertina to get her away from . . ." He indicated the bodies of the dead children.

"Edith is . . ."

"Edith Tuttle. The husband is Wilbur Tuttle. This is their place."

"Do you know them?"

"Everyone knows the Tuttles. Wilbur can fix anything mechanical with a wad of chewing gum, a can opener, and his wife's hair spray. Edith babysits."

"Where was Edith when the fire started?"

"Downstairs in the cellar. She heard the sirens and came up. Said she didn't know the house was on fire."

"What was she doing in the cellar?"

"Looking for mason jars. She said she wanted to can some peaches and make blueberry jam."

"Blueberry season isn't for . . . what? Four or five months?"

"Uh huh."

"How is she reacting to all this?" Sebastian jerked his head in the direction of the children.

Otis Quick shrugged. "Tears. Lots of tears. Like I said, I sent her to her neighbor's across the street. Albertina used to be a district nurse. She's good with grief, and she's got a lot of friends. Pretty soon all of the church ladies will be there fighting over who can do more for Edith and Wilbur. You'll see."

"Do the Tuttles have any family hereabouts?"

"Don't know of any."

"What about a place to stay?"

"One of my boys called Harold Draper. Harold's our Red Cross Disaster Services coordinator. Nice fellow, but he's not good at delegating responsibility. He'll be here in . . ." Otis

Quick glanced at his wrist watch. "I'd say, within the hour. He'll take care of Edith."

Sebastian's eyes drifted away from the fire chief. First, he looked at the ugly house and studied it for a minute or two. Then he looked at the two small bodies covered by faded towels in the grass. He turned back to Otis.

"Do me a favor?"

"Name it."

"Tell me when the Red Cross guy arrives."

"Not a problem."

"And keep Mrs. Tuttle across the street. I want to talk to her."

"Done," Otis said.

"Thanks." Sebastian turned to his brother-in-law and gestured towards the house. "You're the expert," he said. "After you."

chapter 7

BEFORE BILLY NIGHTINGALE'S twentieth birthday, he had joined the International Association of Arson Investigators and the National Fire Protection Association. He also had subscribed to *Fire Engineering, Fire Technology,* and *Fire House Magazine.* He read the *Fire Chief's Handbook* and the *Fire Protection Handbook* as if they were page-turners instead of dense, tedious, and complicated tomes. His idea of a vacation was to accompany Delmore O'Shaughnessy to abandoned warehouses and derelict apartment buildings when the deputy chief was investigating a fire.

Billy moved to Manhattan shortly after he turned eighteen, and he lived with his sister until he could afford to get a place of his own. The year he arrived, he did two things. First, he took the test to become a New York City fireman. Next, he enrolled in the John Jay College of Criminal Justice. At John Jay he took a double major in fire science and criminal forensics, graduating two months before his appointment as a probationary fireman.

Billy was twenty-six years old when he accompanied Sebastian to the fire in the ugly house. He had spent the past four years at busy firehouses in Brownsville and Red Hook, responding to hundreds of working fires and being exposed, as Deputy Chief O'Shaughnessy had planned it, to so many "worst case scenarios" that there would be little that could trip him up or surprise him. Under the deputy chief's tutelage Billy had already investigated over two hundred suspicious fires and was about to be transferred to the Division of Fire Investigation as O'Shaughnessy's driver and aide in anticipation of his appointment as a provisional fire marshal.

"Did you bring your flashlight?" Billy asked Sebastian.

"Yep."

"Okay. Follow me."

The dim vestibule of the ugly house was oppressive with the smells of smoke and waterlogged debris. Overcoats, sweaters, and raincoats had been stuffed into a doorless closet among a mangle of wire hangers, winter boots, and hats, and everything was covered with soot. Billy pocketed his flashlight and yanked the shades off the double windows in the small entrance area. Then he strode out of the foyer into the living room and tore the bed sheets off the windows, letting bright spears of sunlight streak across the room to a dilapidated green sofa on the opposite wall. Two unmatched arm chairs were on either side of the sofa. One, brown tweed. The other, bright orange with what looked like grape jelly stains on the seat. A coffee table in front of the sofa stood across from a television set on a dented metal stand. There was a built-in bookcase to the right of the sofa, its shelves bare except for three romance novels, two matchbox cars, a TV remote control, and a bottle of hand lotion. Almost blocking the entrance from the living room to the dining room were a floor lamp with a bare bulb and a small playpen. There were no pictures on the walls and no plants on the window sills.

Billy slowly did a 360 degree rotation of the room, looking up, down, and all around, until he had observed its every object, aspect, and angle.

Then he and Sebastian entered the dining room through a wide opening where four tarnished brass hinges were all that was left of two French doors. Six wood-look chairs with brown corduroy cushions surrounded a large dining-room table, and a huge china cabinet filled with plastic Christmas decorations and unmatched crockery took up most of one wall. On top of the china cabinet was a stuffed beaver who appeared to be sniffing a nearby bouquet of plastic daffodils.

The kitchen, just off the dining room, had suffered the most overhaul damage. The sink was filled with dirty dishes, and on top of the counters were cigarette stub-filled ashtrays, four crumpled packages of Newport Lights, an empty milk carton, cereal boxes, a toaster, and a bowl of yolk-smeared egg shells. All of the cupboards were open and displayed the usual assortment of boxes, cans, dishes, glasses, and bowls. The stove was encrusted with old food and there was a clutter of pots and pans on the floor. The firemen had torn holes in the walls, and a ceiling fan dangled by a single electric wire overhead. Just off the kitchen, a door that had been broken either before or during the fire fighting operations blocked the entrance to the cellar.

Billy yanked it out of the way, flicked on his flashlight, and followed the light beam down the stairs. First, he held the light on two shelves suspended over a slop sink, where twenty or thirty empty mason jars were gathering dust. Then he swung it around the basement, shining it on the fuse box, the water heater, and a monolithic oil burner.

Billy shone his light up to the ceiling and illuminated a

string of cloth-covered wires intersected by white ceramic orbs.

"What's that?" Sebastian asked.

"Knob and tube wiring. It must have been put in when the house was built, and this house is as old as God. I've only seen knob and tube wiring in a text book."

"Is it safe?"

"You mean did it start the fire?"

"Yep."

"Not unless some idiot spliced it into new BX or Romex cable."

"Did that happen here?"

Billy shrugged and led Sebastian back up the stairs. They crossed the narrow kitchen passageway to the flight of steps leading to the second floor. Billy stopped for a moment at the top of the landing. He took a long and hard look at the smoke blackened door to the room where the two children had died.

"Shouldn't we..." Sebastian began.

"Not yet," Billy said.

He turned off his flashlight and walked into the bathroom. A grimy, age-stained tub sat under a small window that had been painted shut decades before. Thin, unmatched towels hung from a rod over the tub. Two more towels and a balding terrycloth robe drooped from a hook behind the door. A bar of cracked, gray soap sat on a crumpled wash cloth on the sink, and five tooth brushes, two large and three small, had been stuck into a glass next to it. The shelf above the sink was cluttered with disposable razors, a rusty shaving cream can, a hair brush entangled with strands of brown, red, and gray hair, a pile of bobby pins, and an ashtray filled with lipstick-stained cigarette butts.

Sebastian followed Billy down the hall to the front of the

house. They opened the door to the closet of the master bedroom, the floor of which was buried in oil-stained work boots, worn women's mules, and scuffed brown slip-ons. Shoe boxes, an electric blanket, and two emaciated pillows were crammed onto the shelf of the closet. A battered blue plastic bowling ball bag and an old hair dryer with a gray plastic hood were squashed in between the pillows.

The master bedroom itself contained an unmade queen-sized bed covered with a faded blue floral comforter. There were blond night tables on either side of the bed, with dime store table lamps and butt-filled ashtrays on each. A folding metal chair outside the closet had a large, flesh-toned bra hooked over the backrest, and a pair of boxer shorts folded on the seat. The blond dresser at the foot of the bed matched the night tables and the headboard. Spread out on top of the dresser were a lipstick tube, a can of hair spray, a jar of Vaseline, another ashtray, a saucer containing pennies and buttons, a book of matches, a New Testament Bible, and a thin vase containing a red plastic rose. Behind the vase was a small white jewelry box decorated with embroidered pink rosettes.

Billy walked across the room and opened what he thought would be a second closet door. Instead, he found a girl's bedroom containing a neatly made up twin bed covered with a ruffled pink bedspread. Teddy bears were neatly arranged along the top of a two-drawer dresser, and on a tiny night table was a stack of children's books. There was a small student's desk under the room's one dusty window, and beyond that was another door leading to what had once been a walk-in closet, but was now a minuscule nursery, complete with crib, changing table, diapers, and a diaper pail.

Billy stared at the crib, leaned down, and lifted the lid off the diaper pail.

Then he and Sebastian retraced their steps through the child's room, the master bedroom, and the hall, back to the room that they had not inspected at the top of the stairs. The room where the fire had started and the two children had died.

He studied the door.

"Do you see this?" He asked Sebastian.

"Yep," the state trooper answered, not knowing what he was supposed to be seeing.

"The door jamb is clean, and the paint is still white on the edge of the door. There's no char and no oily black residue like there is on the rest of the door. Do you know why?"

"Nope."

"Because a seal was created between the door and the door jamb. That seal kept the fire inside the room and it kept the paint clean."

"Which means?"

"It means that the door was closed at the time of the fire."

"Is that important?"

Billy switched on his flashlight and motioned his head towards the inside of the room. Then he somberly repeated to Sebastian the two words that he had said before.

"Follow me."

chapter 8

GABRIEL TUTTLE's bedroom was obviously a boy's room. There was a rocket-ship pattern on the bedspread, a poster of an Apollo rocket on the wall, and plastic models of spaceships dangling from the ceiling. A baseball mitt, a stack of Spider-man comics, worn sneakers, and dirty socks were all jumbled together on the floor. There were two beds in the room.

One child had died in each.

The larger of the two beds consisted of a maple headboard with a twin mattress; it was the one with the rocket-ship bed-spread. The smaller was more of a cot, made up with sheets that had once been white and a yellow waffle-knit blanket. The covers on both beds had been tossed aside, exposing the ghostly silhouettes of the two children who had died there.

Everything else was coated with an oily film of black soot. That there had once been colors on the walls and patterns on the fabrics could only be detected from random bits and pieces that had been protected from the fire.

There were three windows in the room. Fireman Rossetti had entered from the east window, the one overlooking the backyard. He had conducted his primary search and handed the little girl and then the little boy through this same window to Fireman Jones in the bucket of the aerial ladder.

The other two windows faced north. Water had streaked in an ugly, irregular trajectory through viscous soot on all of the unbroken glass panes.

A sodden heap of shirts, jeans, books, and lamps were matted to the floor of the bedroom. Pencils, a spelling bee medal, a radio, and an autographed picture of test pilot Chuck Yeager had been transformed into filthy relics by the urgency to put water on flames, ventilate, evacuate, and stop the spread of fire.

On top of a small dresser to the left of the bedroom door was a portable television set with a rabbit-ear antenna. The bed and cot had been positioned against opposite walls, so that both could face the television. Next to the TV was a shallow alcove. Someone had mounted a rod across the alcove, hung a heavy curtain from the rod, and turned it into a makeshift closet.

Firemen had thrown some of the clothes from the closet to the floor, where they became charred remnants of the shirts, shorts, sweaters and pants they had once been. The rest had been yanked off the pole and tossed out the window to fall, still burning, to the yard below. Immediately in front of the closet, so close that it must have been touching the fabric of the closet curtain, stood a kerosene heater.

When Billy Nightingale and Sebastian Bly stepped into Gabriel Tuttle's bedroom, the heater was the first thing that they saw.

BILLY BLINKED ONCE. It was like the shutter clicking on a camera. He walked to the center of the room, turned, looked back at the closet, and blinked again. With each blink, he seemed to be making a permanent record of what he saw.

"The fire started here," he said to Sebastian.

Bly nodded.

They returned to the closet. Billy put one hand on the kerosene heater and gently tilted it back. Unlike the flooring in the rest of the room, the patch of wood underneath the heater was clean.

"This hasn't been moved since the fire," Billy said, allowing it to tilt back to the upright position.

The kerosene heater in question was about twenty-four inches tall and sat on a twenty-inch-square base. The base was oversized to provide stability and to prevent the heater's safety guard from coming into contact with the wall. Most of the white paint on the outer cylinder of the heater had been oxidized by the flames and had turned to rust. The filler cap was still in place, but the plastic control knob and fuel gauge had melted away completely.

A congealed knot of something that looked like an incinerated body part had adhered to the top of the heater and was recognizable as burned material only because loose strands of fabric had escaped from the globule in the same way that hair escapes from a bun. A burn pattern resembling a sloppy "V" or a wide "U" was evident on the side and back of the alcove's walls. The lowest point of the burn pattern was on the floor in the charred remains of curtain fabric and clothing.

Almost all of the fire had been confined to the closet area.

"Some moron put the heater right up against the clothes in the closet and killed his own kids," Billy said, his voice tight with anger. "God, I hate idiots."

Sebastian hunched forward over the kerosene heater. "I thought these things are supposed to be safe."

"Safe is a relative term. Your kid can walk fifteen blocks to school and live forever. But if you don't teach him to look both ways before he crosses the street, you might as well be sending him through a field of land mines."

Sebastian jerked his head towards the closet.

"Exactly what happened here?"

"What happened is that the aforementioned moron put the kerosene heater too close to the curtain and the clothes inside the closet. In a small enclosed area like this the ignition temperature for cotton and most synthetic fabrics would have been reached in minutes—which is why every warning label on every space heater sold in this country tells you to position it at least three feet away from combustibles." Billy's hand clenched into a fist. "And that's what our imbecile didn't do."

For a moment Sebastian thought that his brother-in-law was going to punch the wall in frustration. Instead, he asked, "What time is it?"

"Five to twelve."

Billy turned away from the heater. His eyes rested on the two empty beds.

"When was the fire called in?"

"Before 10:00 AM. I'll get the exact time from Chief Quick."

"What day is it?"

"Monday. May first."

Billy squinted. "It's a beautiful, sunny Monday morning, Sebastian." His voice was still low and the expression on his face still angry. "Why where those children in bed?"

"No school. It's a holiday."

"And the girl's room is down the hall. Why was she sleeping in this bedroom? Why was the door to the room shut? And if it's the first of May, why were they using a kerosene heater?"

"Because it was cold last night. It's only about fifty-five degrees now."

Billy ignored him.

"Even if there was a good reason for them to be sleeping in the same room, for the heater to be on, and for the door to be shut, that still doesn't explain why two normal, healthy children would be in bed at nine or ten o'clock in the morning. And if they were in bed, why were they asleep? Why didn't either of them smell smoke or yell bloody murder when they saw flames? Why didn't they hide or run for a window? *Why didn't those two kids try to escape?*" Billy's eyes darted to the bureau, the windows, the debris on the floor. Then he looked straight at the nightstand midway between both beds and pointed at a small, sooty glass bottle.

He strode across the room, crouched, and made out the word, "L-u-l-l-a ... Lullabide."

"What is it?" Sebastian asked, following him.

"It's an over-the-counter antihistamine for children. Colds. Coughs. The flu. One of the guys in my engine company took his family to Disneyland last month. His six year old is scared to death of flying, so the kid's doctor told Danny to give him this Lullabide."

Sebastian looked blankly at Billy.

"The generic name is diphenhydramine hydrochloride. I looked it up."

"What for?"

"Same reason I looked up the weight of a sperm whale's tongue. Same reason I looked up the height of the Chrysler building. I hear something. I see something. I get interested. Anyway, if you give a little kid a few tablespoons of this stuff, it puts them to sleep. Danny's kid slept all the way from La-Guardia to Los Angeles. Out like a light." Billy looked down at the bottle of antihistamine. "We need evidence bags."

"In my car," Sebastian said.

"Good. And get my camera, too. It's on the floor in the backseat."

"Okay. But what are you thinking?"

"I'm thinking that I missed something."

"What?"

Billy closed his eyes and held up his hand. "Shush, I'm thinking. It's coming to me. It's coming to me." His eyes popped open. "Okay. I got it."

"Got what?"

"The toothbrushes. How many were there?"

"Hell, Billy. I don't count toothbrushes."

"There were five. Five toothbrushes. And how many people live here, Sebastian?"

"A mother, a father, and two kids. That's four."

"Right. So why was there a fifth toothbrush? And the two kids. How old were they?"

"One was nine. The other was eleven."

"So why was there a playpen in the living room?"

"The chief said that Mrs. Tuttle babysits."

"There's a crib in that little room upstairs. A crib. A changing table. Diapers. A diaper pail. Another child lived here, Sebastian. A baby. I'm sure of it. And we've got to find it. Maybe it's still alive. Maybe it's hurt. Maybe..."

Sebastian grabbed his brother-in-law's shoulder. "Slow down, Billy. Let's think this through. Babies don't use toothbrushes because they don't have teeth. And we already searched every room in the house. You did. I did. So did the chief. I know you're a fireman, and you guys can't stand to lose anybody, but..."

Billy shrugged off Sebastian's hand.

"Just get the evidence bags. And my camera. Then go talk to the mother. But don't mention the missing child and..."

"There is no missing child."

"Ask her to describe exactly what happened before and after she found out about the fire. Where was she? What time was it? Where were the kids? Draw her out. Get a sense of her. Charm her, Sebastian. Win her over. Get her to tell you everything she wants you to know. Then make her tell you everything that she'd never want you to find out."

Sebastian snorted. "Yeah. Sure. And while I'm outside tormenting some poor woman whose son and daughter just died, what are you going to be doing?"

Billy's eyes glinted. "Me, Sebastian? I'm going to find that missing kid."

chapter 9

UNLIKE BILLY NIGHTINGALE who, in his own mind, had already arrested, tried, and convicted Edith Tuttle for causing the deaths of her children because she had left a kerosene heater too close to combustibles, Sebastian Bly was instantly able to come up with half a dozen scenarios that let him view her with a sympathetic eye.

As he walked across the road, he considered that she might have been planning to move the heater away from the closet curtain when the phone rang and then had forgotten to reposition it when she got back to the room. Or one of the Tuttle children might have put the heater smack up against the closet curtain after their mother had gone to the basement. Or Mrs. Tuttle could have turned off the heater and put it away in the closet, but her son or daughter might have felt a chill and turned it back on.

To Sebastian, people were just people. The good ones did their best. But life being what it is, their best sometimes wasn't good enough.

And so it was in a forgiving frame of mind that Sebastian approached Edith Tuttle and Albertina Hipkiss at the picnic table in the backyard of the house across the street.

"Ma'am," he said to Mrs. Hipkiss. "If you'd excuse us for a minute."

Albertina shot Sebastian a reproving glance and continued to murmur words of support and sympathy to Edith. Sebastian shrugged inwardly and took those extra few minutes to stand by silently and observe.

Edith Tuttle had a square face with small, symmetrical features and two soft chins. Her fiercely noticeable orange hair hung lankly an inch or two below her ears. Her skin was flushed and shiny, her eyes were watery beige, and her eyebrows and lashes were so light they were almost invisible. If she had ever possessed distinguishable breasts, hips, or a waistline, they had long since disappeared into each other, giving her torso the look of a tightly filled laundry bag.

She wasn't crying when Sebastian took a step toward her, but Edith Tuttle's face had that pinched look that a child's face gets before a good bawl.

"Ma'am," the state trooper repeated, this time making the word sound more like a command than a request.

Realizing that her temporary reprieve was over, Albertina Hipkiss hurriedly added, "Edith, dear, Reverend Detweiler assures me that he's on his way," before she gave Sebastian what could only be described as a "tut tut" look and disappeared into her house.

Sebastian introduced himself, pulled out a pen and note pad, and gradually eased the fire victim from reluctant monosyllables and robotic responses to coherent sentences and fluid speech.

"What's your full name, please?"

"Edith Muriel Tuttle."

"How old are you?"

"Thirty-seven."

"What was your daughter's name?"

"Minna."

"Age?"

"Nine."

"Your son?"

"Gabriel . . . Gabriel Cotter Tuttle."

"How old was he, ma'am?"

"Eleven."

"Can you tell me what happened? We'll take it slow and easy, from the time you got up."

No response. Just a bovine, unintelligent stare.

"When did you get up this morning, Mrs. Tuttle?" Sebastian asked again, clearly enunciating each syllable.

"Early. Before seven. About six-thirty."

"You're doing real well, ma'am. Now, tell me about your husband. Was he with you this morning?"

"No. Wilbur went to New Jersey. His mother's in an old people's home there. He spent the night in a motel. Someone called and told him about the fire."

"So you were alone this morning?"

"Just me and Minna and Gabe. They was both sick."

"Go on, Mrs. Tuttle. Tell me more about Minna and Gabe."

"Well, last night, Gabriel had the sniffles, and this morning the both of them seemed feverish so I took their temperatures. Minna was 100 degrees and Gabe was up to 102. So I put 'em right back to bed."

Sebastian looked across the street at the ugly house. "Is Gabriel's room in the back?"

"Second floor. Across from the bathroom."

"And Minna's?"

"Her room's on the other side of the house. But I put her in with Gabe on the cot, for company's sake so they could both watch TV. Gabe's got a television set but Minna don't, so it only seemed fair."

"There was some medication on the night table in Gabriel's room..."

"Lullabide. Good for runny noses. Colds. Flu."

"Did you consult with a doctor about their condition, Mrs. Tuttle?"

"Waste of time. Any fool mother knows what to do when her kids get a cold."

"Would you mind going over the sequence of events for this morning? You say you got up at six-thirty. Then what?"

"I went to check on Gabe. I felt his forehead, and he didn't look so good. Then I went to Minna's room, and she was sick, too. So, like I said, I took their temperatures, and the both of them had the fever. They say feed a cold, starve a fever, but they don't tell you what to do when you got both, so I figured scrambled eggs, tea, and toast. Something light."

"Then what did you do, Mrs. Tuttle?"

"Well, most days, Mrs. Doxey drops off her girl Darla before eight so that she gets to the elementary school on time."

"Who's Mrs. Doxey?"

"Beth Doxey. She's a teacher's aide. Darla's her daughter. Two-and-a-half-years old. I babysit her from eight til two, but today, with school being off, Darla didn't come. That's why Wilbur went to visit his mother, having a free day and all. And after I got Gabe and Minna arranged in Gabe's room, I..."

"Excuse me a minute, Mrs. Tuttle, but can I ask you a few questions about your house?"

"This ain't my house. Me and Wilbur rent."

"How long have you been here?"

"Eight years, give or take."

"Who owns the house?"

"Mr. Elkstrom."

"Say again?"

"Elkstrom. Lucas Elkstrom. Used to live here. When his wife died, I never met her myself, Mr. Elkstrom tried to sell, but you know how it is around here ever since the typewriter plant shut down. With all them people put out of work, you can't give a house away. Mr. Elkstrom wanted to go to Miami, Florida, to live with his daughter, so he decided to rent the house to us. Works out good all around because Wilbur don't need no one to fix the plumbing or mow the grass. He can do all that hisself. And Mr. Elkstrom gets his rent money."

"Do you have any insurance on the house?"

"I don't know nothing about no insurance. All I know is that I can't go back to living there. Not after..."

"One more question about the house, Mrs. Tuttle. How was it heated?"

"There's a big old oil furnace in the cellar. I don't have nothing to do with it. That's Wilbur's department."

"Who pays the fuel bill? You or the landlord?"

"We do."

"Did you have the furnace on last night?"

"Didn't make no sense to heat a whole house that's empty except for Gabe's room. So...I...so...if Wilbur'd a been here, none of this would have happened. I've always been a fool with machinery. Can't turn a screw. Can't change a light bulb. Can't even drive a car. But...but..."

"Did you bring the kerosene heater into your boy's room?"

"It was already in there from yesterday. Wilbur set it up."

"Did he position the kerosene heater by the closet?"

"No. He put it in the middle of the room."

"And you moved it?"

"Minna complained she was too hot, and Gabe said he was too cold. So I moved it to Gabe's side of the room."

"In front of the closet?"

"Yes, sir. Moved it and then shut the door to keep in the heat. And if I hadn't a done that...if...if..."

"Mrs. Tuttle, why don't we take a short break. Your friend can make you a cup of coffee or tea, and we can talk more later."

Edith Tuttle looked anxiously across the street. "But... but..." Tears began to stream down her cheeks. "Minna... Gabe... *my children.*"

Sebastian shook his head and, as kindly as he could, he said, "There's nothing you can do for your children now."

chapter 10

BILLY NIGHTINGALE believed in atmosphere. He believed in haunted houses, and he was convinced that molecules of good and evil live on in a structure long after the inhabitants have gone. He believed that atmosphere is similar to burn patterns and that you can read it in the same way.

When Billy first moved to New York City, he and his sister were apartment-hunting at a building on East Twenty-ninth Street, standing outside the manager's office and getting ready to ring the doorbell. A second before his finger touched the buzzer, Billy and Annie exchanged a "this place gives me the creeps" glance and dived for the door. A few minutes later Billy stopped at the firehouse on East Twenty-seventh Street to ask about the area. The fireman on house-watch told him where the pharmacy was, where not to buy pizza, and who gave the best haircut. Then he cautioned, "But stay away from..." and he gave the address of the building that Billy and Annie had just been to.

"Last Wednesday a woman was raped and murdered in the lobby."

Billy Nightingale believed in happy houses, sad houses, and repressed houses. Not too long ago, a Manhattan lunatic asylum built in the 1890s was gutted, rewired, refitted, and modernized. It had new plumbing, high-tech lighting, and a million-dollar security system. *Architectural Digest* featured one of the beautiful new condominium apartments in a six-page spread, and by all accounts, the building was the "in" place to live. Billy wouldn't have moved there if he had been given the penthouse free because he was absolutely certain that over the years, the bricks, I-beams, and floor joists had absorbed the agony of the incarcerated inmates, and that in the dead of night, the whole building would scream.

Which is why, even before they had pulled into the driveway of the ugly house, he knew with absolute certainty that something was wrong.

The atmosphere was bleak in the converted closet off Minna's bedroom. Billy had returned to the makeshift nursery immediately after Sebastian left because he wanted to study the area where he had seen the crib. As with the other rooms in the house, there were no pictures on the walls, no dangling mobiles, and no Disney posters featuring Cinderella or Winnie the Pooh.

The battered white crib took up most of the space, its sides decorated with peeling decals of Miss Muffet on her tuffet, Jack Horner in his corner, and a dispirited cow leaping over an unsmiling moon. The plastic mattress was covered with a baby blanket as old and tired as the crib itself, and a small dresser nearby held a few tiny undershirts, a pile of clean diapers, a little sweater, and some baby socks. There were no rattles, no pacifiers, no teething rings, no teddy bears, and no rubber ducks in evidence.

Lean pickings.

Billy left the nursery and began to prowl restlessly through the rest of the house, pausing every few seconds to listen for a whimper, a cry, or a rustle of movement. His eyes scanned dressers and desk tops for family photographs or souvenirs.

Nothing.

Except for the childish touches in the boy's and girl's bedrooms, the house had all the warmth of a cheap motel.

In the living room Billy stopped for a moment to examine the playpen. It was toyless, joyless, and empty. He rubbed his jaw with the fingers of his left hand, thinking. He was still hovering around the edges of the same thought when he walked back through the living room to the hall and out the side door of the house to the splintered platform that served as the first of the three steps leading to the dirt and gravel driveway below.

Billy sat down on the top step.

He was thinking about how he could interject himself into an investigation that was clearly outside his jurisdiction. He was thinking about insurance claims and arson, and the absence of any indication that a flammable liquid had been used. He was thinking about previous fires and how many, if any, the Tuttles may have had.

And because he was thinking about everything except the missing baby, Billy Nightingale heard a sound. Then he heard a series of sounds. The sounds turned into a meandering trickle of soft syllables that burbled like water music. Billy got to his feet. He tiptoed down the last two steps to the driveway, crouched, pulled out his flashlight, and began to crawl, slowly and silently, under the platform where he had been seated. He heard a soft whimper of fear. He reversed the beam of the light and flashed it against his own face, not knowing if he was crawling toward a rabid raccoon, a skunk, or a missing child.

"Don't worry, sweetheart," he murmured into the darkness under the stairs. "I'm the guy in the white hat, and I'm going to save you. Stay were you are."

Slowly he inched forward. Slowly he began to rotate the flashlight away from his face. A little to the right. A little to the left. And...

Brown eyes.

Enormous. Intense. Alert. Frightened. Intelligent.

Billy looked into them.

They stared back at him.

He reached forward and held out his hand.

A small, unloved baby who never cried and who didn't have a name reached back. The palms of her hands and her knees were bleeding from having crawled on gravel and climbed down splintered stairs. Billy dropped his flashlight and grabbed her.

The fingers of her right hand curled around Billy's index finger, held it tight, and wouldn't let go.

He raised the little girl up to his face, kissed her gently, and said, "There's nothing to be afraid of, sweetheart. You're safe now. Your Uncle Billy is here."

chapter 11

THE CONSCIENTIOUS ladies of Sojourn were always at their best in an emergency. When the Otselic River overflowed and swept the Badgers' house off its foundation, it took them less than four hours to accumulate a truckload of essentials and locate three neighbors willing to take the family in. A day later they had organized a pancake breakfast, the proceeds from which would go toward rebuilding the Badgers' home.

They were at it again when record-setting blizzards devastated the area north of Buffalo, causing tree trucks to split down the middle from the weight of the ice and leaving towns without heat, hot water, and electricity for eight days. The dedicated ladies of Sojourn not only organized a food, clothing, and book drive, they also got their husbands to take a fleet of pick-up trucks to Toronto packed full with warm blankets, flashlights, paperback novels, candles, cans of soup, condensed milk, boxes of breakfast cereal, candy bars, and disposable diapers.

Up until the "tragedy that took those two poor angels," which was how the locals referred to the Tuttle fire, the most recent occasion on which the community-minded Sojourn matrons had conspired was the ramp they built for Elwood "Pete" Singleton's wheelchair. But that was two months before Christmas and six months before the fire in the ugly house. Since then, there had been no organized charitable activity in town. No floods, no fires, no tornados, not even a toxic chemical spill. The Tuttle fire gave the hard-working ladies of Sojourn the opportunity to roll up their sleeves and do what so many people in upstate New York did so willingly and so well.

Help their neighbors.

The fire in the Tuttle house had started sometime after ten o'clock on the morning of May first. By twelve noon, Albertina Hipkiss, her daughter-in-law Cheryl, and the Sertoma Society, who were also responsible for putting up Sojourn's Christmas tree lights, had the Tuttles completely boxed in by good deeds. They had already been supplied with doughnuts, jars of instant coffee, clean clothes, serviceable pillows, fresh blankets and bed linens.

The local cleric, Reverend Detweiler, was on call, and so was Mr. Fogel, who ran the Riverside Funeral Home.

The ladies of Sojourn, experienced in all aspects of human misadventure, knew that in the face of such a tragedy, the Tuttles would be desperate but not destitute. Wilbur Tuttle had a good job as shop foreman of Bova Auto Repair in Cassandra, and he made extra money on weekends overhauling cars in his driveway. So it wasn't the long-term survival of the Tuttles that concerned their friends and neighbors. The concern was getting them through the next few days. And the major part of that burden would fall not on their shoulders, but on those of the American Red Cross.

At 12:45 in the afternoon, two hours after the Tuttle fire was extinguished, Harold Draper, the disaster services coordinator of the Chenango County Red Cross, turned into the driveway of the ugly house on Mabel Newton Road.

chapter 12

AFTER ARRIVING AT the scene of a natural disaster, a Red Cross representative will ask the distraught survivor of a hurricane, earthquake, tornado, fire, or flood to fill out a Disaster Registration and Case Record Form 901, providing his name, age, and social security number. The form asks who is the head of the household, does he own or rent his home, does he have property insurance, who insures him, who lives with him, their names, ages, sexes, and so on. Form 901 also wants to know if anybody was injured, hospitalized, missing, or deceased; if the survivor has access to money; and if he has a place to spend the night.

Once the form has been filled out, the victim is given a comfort kit containing toothpaste, a disposable razor, shaving cream, tissue, deodorant, shampoo, and a washcloth. He will be issued vouchers to buy necessities from local merchants; and if he has nowhere to go, the Red Cross will put him up at a local motel. All of this is accomplished at no expense to the victim and without his having to manipulate and retain a drawer full of paperwork.

Through a system of vouchers he has been provided with food, warmth, comfort, clothing, and shelter. He rests, he regains his sense of equanimity and humanity, and after a few days, he is able to continue on his own.

Years later, if this same individual decides to search back through his receipts and records to refresh his memory of Red Cross involvement in his personal catastrophe, he won't find a thing.

If he is a certain kind of a person, he will forget that the encounter ever occurred.

American Red Cross records, however, tell a different tale. And regarding the fatal fire that took place in the so-called ugly house, the interviews conducted and the forms retained by disaster services coordinator Harold Draper were comprehensive indeed.

chapter 13

JUST AS BILLY NIGHTINGALE was backing out of the crawl space underneath the Tuttle's stairs he saw Sebastian Bly walking towards him, eyes wide with astonishment. Billy lowered himself onto the bottom step, settled the baby on his lap, and looked at the tiny hand still wrapped around his forefinger. Then he looked at his brother-in-law and shrugged.

Sebastian sat down beside him and shrugged back.

Both men stared at the baby.

She was small for her age, weak from her ordeal, cold, hungry, and wet. Billy slipped out of his jacket and wrapped it around her. The infant followed him with her eyes—eyes that seemed to absorb his every flicker of expression with desperate intensity.

Sebastian raised an eyebrow at his brother-in-law.

Billy responded, "She's in love with me."

The state trooper looked back at the baby. There was a fringe of long, orange eyelashes around her enormous brown eyes. Her nose, lips, and ears were delicate and perfectly formed. Her skin was dead white. And she was small. So small and fragile.

"I don't know how people can stand to have babies," Sebastian said quietly. "They're so...breakable."

Billy's voice was hushed with awe. "Once you've got one, it's yours forever. And once it's yours, you've got to do right by it." He shook his head. "That's a terrible responsibility."

The baby blinked. She blinked again. Her eyes opened slowly. And closed slowly. Opening and closing. Slowly. Slowly. Finally, they stayed closed. She was asleep.

"What do we do now?" Sebastian asked.

"Let me think a minute." Billy studied the face of the sleeping infant as if she were a pool of flammable liquid or a burn pattern. With the forefinger of his free hand he softly touched a scratch on her cheek. Then he looked up.

"Sebastian," he said. "This wasn't an accidental fire."

"Come again?"

"On the surface, it looks like a fire that started because some idiot put a kerosene heater too close to a closet full of clothes, but I don't believe it. Why put the heater there? There isn't a plausible explanation. There isn't even an implausible explanation. And another thing. Why didn't Edith Tuttle tell Chief Quick that Marmalade was missing?"

"Who's Marmalade?"

Billy indicated the baby in his lap. "I just named her."

Her hair was, in fact, the color of marmalade jam.

Sebastian returned to the question. "Maybe Edith forgot."

"Forgot a whole baby?" Billy snorted. "Yeah, sure."

"She could be in a fugue state."

"What's a fugue state?"

"Something like temporary amnesia."

"Is that how she seemed to you?"

"I don't know. I don't think Edith is a bad person. Just

stupid. One of those people stuck in a rut who will never get out. I feel sorry for her."

"Save your sympathy and tell me what she said. Exactly."

Sebastian took out his note pad. He read off his questions and Mrs. Tuttle's answers.

"Was she crying?" Billy asked.

"On and off."

"Crocodile tears?"

"They looked real to me."

"Where is she now?"

"Across the street with Harold Draper."

"Harold who?"

"The Red Cross guy."

"Would Harold let Edith leave without telling us?"

"No. I asked him not to."

"Good," Billy said. The baby in his arms made a soft twittery sound like a music box on the verge of winding down.

"She's a pretty little thing, isn't she?" Sebastian said.

"Marmalade?" Billy rocked her gently in his arms. "A future Miss America." The baby whimpered. To the state trooper and the fireman it sounded like an inconsolable sigh. "Poor Marmalade," Billy cooed. "What a rotten coming-out party you had." He looked at his brother-in-law. "She's hungry and scared. She has scratches on her arms, hands, and knees, and she needs to be taken care of. Now. But I don't trust any of the gullible ninnies in this town to do it right. And I sure as hell don't trust Edith Tuttle. What Marmalade needs is..."

Sebastian snapped his fingers. "Annie!" he said firmly. "She needs my wife. I'll call her. She can borrow baby things from the people up the road. Then I'll call my sergeant and tell him to contact Child Protective Services."

"Have him run a background check on Edith Tuttle."

"On both of them. Edith and Wilbur."

"Good," Billy said. He looked worriedly down at the small human bundle in his arms. "What if neither of them has a criminal record?"

"If they're clean and if the fire was accidental, then Marmalade can go back to her mother and we can all go home."

"I'm not going to let that happen."

"How are you going to stop it?"

"This was an incendiary fire, Sebastian. A multiple homicide. Deliberate and premeditated. The murder weapon was a kerosene heater and...and I need your help to get the murderer."

"Name it."

"Do you think you could lose Marmalade in the welfare bureaucracy for a while?"

"How long is a while?"

"As long as it takes us to solve this case."

Sebastian stared down at his shoes for a few seconds. "If Annie gets here before the Child Protective caseworker does, I might be able to do it."

"Do what?"

"Convince Edith that under certain circumstances giving up your child is the right thing to do." He glanced at the baby. "I never saw a baby this quiet before. Was she crying when you found her?"

"No. She was staring at me." The infant's eyes popped open. "Like she's staring at me now. But no tears."

"I don't get it," Sebastian said. "All babies cry."

"Well, this one doesn't. Not Marmalade. Not my poor little orphan."

"She isn't an orphan."

Billy Nightingale raised his head. He looked across the street at the tidy two-story home where Edith Tuttle sat drinking tea, garnering sympathy from her neighbors, and receiving succor and sustenance from a representative of the Red Cross.

The expression on his face hardened.

"She will be if I have anything to say about it."

chapter 14

HAROLD DRAPER had come to the American Red Cross from his job as the regional sales manger for Bosack's Incorporated, a chain of retail department stores flourishing in the rural northeast.

During his childhood, Harold's personal gods had been those who trekked into the Heart of Darkness to heal wounded natives in feverishly exotic lands. In his fantasies, he got Africa mixed up with Ecuador and Dr. Schweitzer mixed up with Dr. Dooley, but one thing about which he was never confused was what he wanted to do.

Harold's dream, when he was asleep beside his beloved wife, Phoebe, or awake and charting adding machine sales in his seven regional stores, was to help people. At Bosack's, he was the one who initiated the fund drives to pay for poor children's doctor bills, and he was the one who set up a bottle bin in the parking lot to collect nickel deposits to pay for new uniforms for the high school marching band, and he was the one who talked the department store bigwigs into sponsoring the girls softball team's trip to Cleveland for the All-Star Playoffs.

His biggest commitment, however, was to the American Red Cross. For twelve of the seventeen years he had worked at Bosack's, he had single-handedly organized the annual blood drives. Because, other than his wife and his daughters, the Red Cross was Harold Draper's first love. He had always known that someday he was going to work there, and as soon as Phoebe was able to add her weekly salary to their joint checking account, he told Bosack's that he was quitting.

Three weeks and a twenty-five percent pay cut later, his new job was services coordinator for the Norwich office of the American Red Cross.

Harold was deliriously happy.

When his team distributed food and blankets or doled out coffee and doughnuts to firemen and members of the National Guard, he experienced an emotional high similar to that of leaping tall buildings at a single bound. Harold was always on call, and he was about as anonymous as a billboard. So when disaster struck in the middle of the night, the firemen, county sheriffs, state troopers, and local police chiefs all knew to call Harold at home instead of calling the Red Cross office in Norwich.

In his personal appearance and demeanor, Harold Draper looked more like a portabello mushroom than a hero. He had a monkishly fringed bald head, a too-thick neck, and he was five feet four inches tall. But his appealing puppy-dog eyes and gentle mouth had a way of attracting old ladies, blood donors, and children the way that silk attracts lint.

Everybody liked Harold Draper.

Many people underestimated him.

A few underestimated him during a disaster.

After talking to Mrs. Tuttle and taking down as much information as she seemed capable of conveying, Harold decided that the Red Cross would provide Edith and her husband with temporary overnight accommodations and that he would drive Edith to the motel. He also made arrangements for someone to be waiting for Wilbur at the ugly house.

If on some level Harold noticed during the interview that Edith Tuttle had not asked what was to become of the bodies of her children, Harold did not think about it consciously at the time. He did notice, however, that Edith seemed oddly familiar with Red Cross jargon and procedures. She had asked for her Comfort Kit by name, and she seemed to know that Harold should be referred to as a disaster action team member rather than as a volunteer. She also knew much more about the emergency voucher system than Harold would have thought credible or possible. All of which made him vaguely uncomfortable—if not out and out suspicious—in her presence.

When State Trooper Bly rapped his knuckles against the jamb of Albertina Hipkiss's opened kitchen door, Mrs. Tuttle had just finished signing the Red Cross release of confidentiality form.

"Sorry to interrupt," Sebastian said.

"That's all right. We're finished here." Harold removed the confidentiality form from Edith's hand and gathered up the rest of his paperwork. "I'm taking Mrs. Tuttle to the Twilight Motor Lodge in Cassandra, Sebastian. I'll wait for her outside."

"Thanks, Harold. I'll just be a few minutes."

Sebastian pulled up a chair opposite Edith Tuttle and noticed that the rims of her eyes had turned bright red and her cheeks had taken on a vibrant pink glow. Edith's shoulders were more erect despite the shudder from an occasional sob. And the soft swell of her double chins seemed to have achieved an odd, almost pugnacious, dignity.

"Mrs. Tuttle, you and your husband are in for some tough times ahead," Sebastian said without preamble.

Edith nodded and dabbed at a teary eye with a crumpled napkin.

"You've got the funeral to plan and what with having to live out of a motel room and all, I thought it would be easier on you and Mr. Tuttle if you let me arrange for Child Protective Services to take your daughter off your hands."

Edith's head snapped up. A startled expression of fear flitted across her face. "My...my what?" she said sharply. Furtively. Then, almost as quickly, her features rearranged themselves into a look of motherly concern. "My baby! My poor little...how is my..."

"She's being well taken care of." Sebastian cut her off. "And if you give me your consent, I'll see that Child Protective Services keeps on taking care of her."

Edith's eyes narrowed. She studied the state trooper's face. Suddenly, she seemed to be evaluating options and calculating.

She said nothing.

"You and Wilbur are going to be very busy," Sebastian plowed on. "You'll have funerals to arrange. Relatives to call. Cards to write. At a time like that, a baby could be a burden."

Edith nodded.

She nodded again, a little less anemically. Slowly, dramatically, she manufactured two tears.

"Like you say, it's gonna be real tough for me and Wilbur, living out of a suitcase and not having no home. Babies and funerals don't mix, and we still got a lot of crying left to do.

So, I suppose it wouldn't do no harm if she stayed with someone else. Just for a while." Edith rose arduously to her feet. "I guess I'll be going now."

Trooper Bly also stood up.

"One more thing," he said.

She stopped.

"Her name," Sebastian asked. "What's her name?"

"Whose name?"

"I have to tell Child Protective Services what to call her. What's your baby's name?"

"Oh, that." Edith Tuttle laughed. "Me and Wilbur...we never got around to giving her an official name. We just call her Baby."

chapter 15

AT EIGHTY-FOUR years of age, Mrs. Albertina Hipkiss had been a widow for six years. Other than being a housewife, mother, grandmother, great grandmother, and district nurse, she was a former president of the Ladies Auxiliary of the Central New York Fireman's Association and department president of the Women's Relief Corps. She had joined the Girl Scouts when she was ten years old and had been a Girl Scout leader for over fifty years. She was a founding member of the Sojourn Historical Society and a past president of the Sertoma Club.

She also sang alto in the Presbyterian church choir.

Other than being a local heroine of sorts, Albertina was an unabashed busybody. Over the course of the years her shoulder had served as a weeping post for many a man, woman, and child because Albertina had a disconcerting habit of being there—wherever 'there' might be—whenever a crisis occurred. Edith Tuttle, she believed, needed help. Which is why Albertina initiated an activity known locally as a "telephone tree." This required her to call certain people on a list who in turn would call other people on a different list and so on, until every innocent bystander within a radius of ten miles of Sojourn had been alerted to Edith and Wilbur's terrible tragedy and told what they were expected to do. These activities included organizing a pancake breakfast, starting a clothing drive, notifying newspapers, and contacting local charitable church groups.

While Billy Nightingale, who had been given sanctuary in Mrs. Hipkiss's kitchen, studied the unfamiliar territory of the baby on his lap, Albertina spun the rotary dial on the old telephone in her living room with the zeal of a gambler playing roulette. Annie, who had arrived only moments before, said, "Give me that washcloth over by the sink, Billy."

"I can't. Marmalade won't let go of my finger."

She knelt to study the link. "How long have the two of you been latched together like that?"

Billy glanced around the kitchen for a clock. "I found her just after one. It's three o'clock now. My finger is turning blue."

Annie heated a soft towel in the microwave oven, draped it over the kitchen table, lifted the baby off Billy's lap, and put her on top of the towel. She changed the soggy diaper, cleaned her, and powdered her. Then, one leg at a time, she threaded the baby's legs and feet into borrowed pajama bottoms and booties.

"Tell her to let go of your finger," Annie said. "I have to put a top on her."

Billy leaned his head forward and said sternly, "Marmalade. Release my finger. At once."

The baby stared at him, her eyes fluid beacons of adoration.

"Okay," he continued, unphased and unflappable. "On the count of three, I'm going to pull and you're going to let go. One. Two. Three."

Billy tugged at his finger. A tenacious little fist moved right along with it.

"Good job, Billy," Annie laughed. She reached over, unwrapped the baby's fingers, one by one, and in a motion so rapid that neither man nor child realized what was happening, Annie slipped the pajama top over the baby's head and reaffixed her fingers to Billy's other hand.

"Now, we have to feed her," Annie said confidently. She plopped the one year old on Billy's lap. "I assume you don't mind."

And so it went. The baby was accommodating to a fault, except when Billy seemed to be pulling away. Then a look of despair filled the already dark pools of her huge brown eyes and stayed there until she was certain that she was once again in absolute possession of the treasured digit, at which point she would relax.

Annie studied the baby's small, intense face and commented, more to herself than to her brother, "She doesn't laugh. She doesn't smile. She doesn't cry. Have you ever seen her cry, Billy?"

"Not since I've known her."

"I never took Babies 101, but even a blathering idiot would know that this isn't normal."

Billy didn't respond.

"What are you thinking?" Annie asked.

"About what it would be like not to laugh or cry. Not to have anything to smile or laugh or cry about." He engaged the baby's attention. "Marmalade. Marmalade. Marmalade. Why are you looking at me with the eyes of a sad old woman? What are you thinking? What do you want?"

Annie sighed.

"Billy, it isn't healthy to be so . . . so . . . still. We have to do something."

Her brother raised a hand to show Annie that his finger remained entrapped. "I'm doing my bit for the war effort."

"I mean something else."

"Like what?"

"I don't know. Make her laugh."

"That would be like trying to get a bug out of a glass paperweight."

"Then make her cry."

"Make her cry by doing *what* to her? Her siblings are dead, her house burned down, her mother abandoned her, her body is beat up from climbing over splintered steps and gravel, and she hasn't got a name. If all of that doesn't make her cry, short of beating her, I don't know what . . ."

The doorbell rang.

Albertina Hipkiss walked to the front door, opened it, pointed the newcomers toward the back of the house, and returned to her command post by the telephone. Sebastian Bly entered the kitchen first. A tall, harassed-looking middle-aged woman stalked in after him.

"Hello," she nodded curtly to Annie. "Hello. Hello," she jerked another two rapid nods at Billy Nightingale and the baby on his lap. She flung a battle-scarred three-ring binder on the table and dropped a scuffed purse that looked like an oat bag on the floor.

Her hair was short and blond, and it radiated away from her face as if it were being forced back by gale winds. Her forehead was high and bony, and she had a big nose that dominated her long-jawed, mannish face. The image she projected was that of a no-nonsense, liberated, take-charge woman. It took all of Annie's strength of character and resolve not to punch her right in her big, arrogant, no-nonsense, take-charge nose.

"My name is Lucille Brundage, but don't call me Miss

Brundage and don't call me Lucy. Lucy makes me feel like an ape. You may call me Lucille." Her eyes darted from Annie to the baby to Billy. She turned around and addressed the state trooper. "My office told me you needed someone here from Child Protective Services. Posthaste. This, obviously, is the child. I don't know who the rest of you people are, but this baby doesn't look threatened to me. What am I supposed to be protecting her from?"

Sebastian Bly indicated an empty chair at the table. "Would you like to sit down?"

"I'm quite capable of finding my own seating arrangements should I care to sit. Which I do not. Please explain the situation as succinctly as possible with regard to the needs of the child so that we don't waste any more of my time."

Sebastian looked at Annie, who rolled her eyes, and at Billy, who shrugged. Then he leaned against the kitchen counter and related as little as he could about the circumstances in which he had found the baby, while Lucille Brundage listened with her lips jammed together, upper against lower like the front and back covers of a sociology text.

After Sebastian had finished, she said, "Bottom line, you don't want to give the baby back to its mother."

"That is correct," Sebastian said, adopting her tone.

"Where is the mother?"

"The Red Cross is placing her."

"With friends? With family?"

"At the Twilight Motor Lodge."

"Well, that's homey," the Child Protective Services woman said sarcastically. "Is there a father?"

"He's on his way back from New Jersey."

"How does this baby-snatch thing sit with the mother? As a rule, we don't like to take children away from their homes."

"She doesn't have a home. It just burned down."

Lucille Brundage scowled. She crouched down and stared none-to-nose into the baby's face.

"What's its name?"

The baby flinched. Either from proximity to the case-worker's breath or from the cold belligerence of her tone.

"She doesn't have a name."

"She looks clean. Smells clean. Her clothes are clean. She doesn't look hungry. She isn't crying. Where did she get all of these scratches and bruises?"

"Escaping from the fire."

Lucille Brundage stood up. "Well, as long as the mother's not making a stink, Child Protective is amicable to helping you out. Except for one thing."

"What?" Sebastian asked.

"I don't have anywhere to place her. My families are already full up and..."

Annie leaped to her feet.

"We'll take her," she said, almost shouting. She took the baby from her brother and held Marmalade in her arms. With the baby's hand still firmly connected to Billy's finger, the three of them looked like a human Tinker Toy.

The social worker frowned at the outburst and turned a haughty nose to Annie.

"Who are you?"

"My wife," Sebastian answered.

"And we'd be happy to take care of the child," Annie added.

Lucille turned to the other man in the room, dissecting Billy Nightingale with her eyes.

"Who is he?"

"My brother, my brother-in-law," Anne and Sebastian said at the same time.

The social worker nodded curtly, yanked a form out of

her binder and a pen out of her purse, and began to write furiously. When she got to the bottom of the form, she snapped, "What did you say her name was?"

"Meredith," Annie shot back. "Her name is Meredith."

"How many Rs?"

"One. We're going to call her Merry."

"I don't care if you call her Albert Schweitzer," the caseworker said as she slammed her notebook shut. She flipped it against her chest, snatched up her purse, flung it over her shoulder, and strode out of the room. After the door had closed behind her, all three adults looked blankly at each other. Then, collectively, they let out a sigh of relief.

Annie, still holding the baby, who was still holding Billy's finger, dropped back into her seat. Sebastian pulled out a kitchen chair, spun it around, and straddled it. "I thought you hated children," he said staring speculatively at his wife.

"I can't stand them."

He lowered his eyes to the baby in her arms. "Last time I looked, that thing you're holding was called a child."

"She's different," Annie asserted smugly.

"Uh huh," Sebastian nodded. Then he stopped nodding. "How is she different?"

"She's surly. I like surly things. They remind me of me."

"Okay. Surly. I get it. So why are you calling her Meredith or Merry?"

"Yeah," Billy joined in. "Why don't we just call her 'Surly,' or 'Marmalade'? I still like 'Marmalade.'"

"The name is a talisman," Annie answered. "A magic charm to turn this grim, miserable little sourpuss into a merry creature. Like her name. We're going to surround her with happiness and joy and options. Mostly options, because to have choices is the most important thing in the world. Literally, figuratively, cognitively, and philosophically, we are going to give this child a new chance. You know. Fresh start. Blank slate. Tabula rasa and all that. We're going to..."

"Hold on a minute," Sebastian said. "You're talking like you expect to keep her."

Annie looked up. She smiled at her husband.

He shook his head. Then he shrugged and smiled back.

Billy poked his sister on the arm. "Hey, Annie, do you still want me to make Marmalade cry?"

"Cry or laugh. Yes."

"Forget laugh. I tried that."

"What are you two talking about?" Sebastian asked.

"Your wife here is convinced that if Marmalade doesn't cry, she won't have a normal life."

The state trooper contemplated the orange-haired infant and said, "It isn't right for a baby not to cry."

"Well, I can make her cry," Billy said. "I could have done it all along. I just didn't want to."

"How?"

Billy gently uncurled Meredith's fierce, tenacious fingers from around the forefinger of his right hand. Then he stood up, gave the baby an apologetic shrug, and walked quickly out of the room. And for the first time in her short, lonely, emotionally-bereft life, this child who had never laughed, never smiled, and never cried, let out a wail so loud that it could be heard by the volunteer firemen stashing their gear at the firehouse over two thousand feet away.

She howled. She wept. She sobbed.

And she never saw Billy poke his head around the corner, wink, and say to his sister, "Piece of cake."

chapter 16

TROOPER SEBASTIAN BLY stared at the slender forms of Gabriel Cotter Tuttle and Minna Tuttle on the metal gurneys in the morgue of the Binghamton General Hospital. What made their deaths so heart-wrenching, he thought, wasn't the damage to their corpses but rather the lack of damage. After the thin layer of soot had been washed away, all that was left was clean, supple skin. No blood. No bruises. No bloat. No gore. Just sweet faces on two apparently sweet kids. Gabriel, had he been alive, looked as if he would be ready to pound a fist into a catcher's mitt and shout, "Let's go. Throw the ball."

Minna, her long brown hair splayed behind her head like a lost Ophelia, looked more studious and intent as if, could she be magically reawakened, she would press her nose against the pages of a book and inhale an intoxicating stream of words.

Death, Sebastian said to himself, is always a thousand times worse when the deceased looks a heartbeat away from being alive. He told the morgue attendant that he would come back later, fervently hoping that the forensic pathologist would be done with the autopsies before he returned.

The previous day seemed to Sebastian to have been arranged like a flawed TV miniseries, with a beginning and a middle, but no end. After Annie left with the baby, Sebastian drove with Billy to the C-Troop station in Norwich to report in. He told his sergeant about the fire, about the Tuttles, and about why he and Annie had assumed custody of the Tuttle baby. Then he asked Billy to explain to Sergeant Thunder why he considered the fire to be incendiary and how he thought the investigation should proceed.

Sergeant Horace Thunder had met Billy Nightingale a few years earlier and had a grudging respect for the young fireman's capabilities. Based on the results of the criminal histories he had run on Edith and Wilbur Tuttle, however, he was less than impressed with either man's opinion of the fire. Wilbur, apparently, was so clean that he had never even been cited for a traffic violation, and Edith didn't drive a car. No arrests, no convictions, and no hint of suspicious activity for either of them. Ever.

"Game's over," Sergeant Thunder said. "Your theory struck out. Everybody go home."

"Can I say something?" Billy Nightingale asked.

"No."

"Sebastian and I are convinced that the fire was arson."

"And I'm convinced that if I flap my wings fast enough, I can fly. But that doesn't make me right either."

"I have reasons, Sergeant Thunder."

"You don't have suspects."

"Yes, I do."

"Skip the suspects and give me the reasons."

"Okay," Billy said. "I'll start with the fire itself. The most successful arsonists don't slop gasoline all over and they don't attach sticks of dynamite to fancy timing devices. They succeed because they never introduce anything foreign to a fire scene. Everything a fire marshal finds there has a legitimate reason for being there."

"Like the kerosene heater?"

"Like the kerosene heater. A really smart arsonist uses available materials when he's setting a fire. That's why he doesn't get caught. But sometimes, Sergeant, a dumb, crude, and unsophisticated fire setter will act the same way. I've seen it happen before, and I think that's what we have here. A sort of an idiot savant of arson. Someone stubborn and mulish, with a single focus, who figured out that by keeping it simple and only using what's already in the room, no one will puzzle it out."

"I asked for reasons," Sergeant Thunder said. "You're giving me a theory."

"You want reasons? Okay. Here are your reasons. One, the kerosene heater was too far inside the closet to have been put there accidentally."

"Not if the Tuttle woman is as stupid as you say she is."

"I said that she might be an idiot savant. Not an idiot. Stripped down to its essentials, a kerosene heater really isn't much more than a lit match with a fuel source and a few safety features, and even a ten year old knows that you don't put a lit match into a closet full of clothes. So the fire in and of itself stinks. Two, the conventional response to fire is to run or hide, which is why children are usually found huddled against a window or curled up in the fetal position under a bed. What children don't do at ten o'clock in the morning on a day where there's no school is sleep through a fire. Not even if they have colds, and particularly not when there are two of them in the same room."

"Maybe the kids were overcome by carbon monoxide before they could..."

"That's another thing I don't like." Billy cut off Thunder.
"If those kids were sick enough to be in bed, then they were
sick enough for their mother to want to be able to listen for
them if they needed help. So reason number three is why was
Gabriel's bedroom door shut?" Billy stood up and started
pacing. "Reason number four."

"Is what?"

"The mason jars."

"What about 'em?"

"Edith Tuttle told the fire chief that she was down in the
cellar looking for mason jars when she heard the fire engine
sirens approach her house. When we checked the cellar, the
first thing we saw were dozens of mason jars on a shelf at the
bottom of the stairs. They were at eye level. Helen Keller
couldn't miss them."

"So?"

"So why did Edith have to look for them?"

"Thin," Sergeant Thunder said. "But point taken. Is that
all?"

"No. I've got one more thing. There was an infant."

Thunder turned an inquiring eye to Trooper Bly.

Sebastian nodded. "Same baby, Sergeant."

"What about it?"

"At about 1:15 this afternoon, I found her hiding in a
crawl space under the stairs to the Tuttle's front door, " Billy
said.

"Is that relevant?"

"Yes."

"When were the other children found?"

"Right after the fire department got there. The apparatus
arrived at 10:35 AM. Within five minutes, the bodies of

Gabriel and Minna Tuttle were found in Gabriel's bedroom. By 1:15 PM, which was over two hours later, Mrs. Tuttle still hadn't told anyone about her missing baby. That's not normal."

Thunder grunted. "Nothing about this fire is normal. How did the Tuttle woman react when you told her that you'd found the child?"

"I didn't tell her," Billy said. "Sebastian did."

"Well?" Thunder turned to the state trooper.

"Edith looked like I'd caught her stealing someone's laundry."

"Not relieved?"

"Not relieved. Not grateful. Not happy. Not normal."

"What else?" Sergeant Thunder glared, first at Billy Nightingale, and then at Sebastian Bly.

"The Red Cross," Sebastian said.

"What about 'em?"

"The Tuttles don't have tenant's insurance, so we can't check with insurers about previous fire claims, and there's no mandatory reporting system for volunteer fire departments in New York state, so we can't backtrack to see if the Tuttles had other fires anywhere else in the county. All we've got going for us is the Red Cross."

"Like I said, what about 'em?"

"Harold Draper thinks he can help us."

"Who the hell is Harold Draper?"

"The Red Cross services coordinator who interviewed Mrs. Tuttle."

"So?"

"So he told us about disaster registration cards."

"This better be good."

"It is. Every Red Cross fire victim has to fill out a disaster registration card. It's called a 901 form. It lists the date of the fire, the address of the fire, the victim's name, age, social security number, and so on. The Red Cross keeps these cards in a master file. Harold thinks that the 901s in the Binghamton office go back fifteen or twenty years, which means that if the Tuttles had any previous fires, and if they were obliging enough to have had them in Chenango County, and if the Red Cross responded, and if the Tuttles accepted their help, there will be a record of it."

"That's a lot of 'ifs.'"

"Not that many."

"This Harold guy says he's going to give you these hypothetical 901s?"

"He will if you can get the district attorney to issue a subpoena. Tomorrow, on my way to Binghamton General, I can drop off the subpoena at Red Cross headquarters and pick up the 901s."

"If there are any."

"If there are any," Billy agreed.

"Then what?" Horace Thunder asked.

"We prove that the Tuttles have a history of setting fires and that gives us probable cause."

"Probable cause for what?"

"A search warrant."

"What are we searching for?"

"I'll think of something."

"You said the Tuttles don't have property insurance?"

"They're renters. What they don't have is tenant's insurance."

"So why set a fire? What's the motive? It can't be profit."

"I'll think of a motive."

Sergeant Thunder remained silent for a few thoughtful seconds. Then he turned to Sebastian and said, "Give me the phone number for the district attorney."

chapter 17

CHARLOTTE WASHINGTON was a sixty-year-old black woman
with blue eyes, high cheek bones, and a long Modigliani
neck. She had bride of Frankenstein hair, which she kept in
check by wearing it short and tight to her head, and she
dressed in classically tailored suits that emphasized her slim
figure and dramatic height. At six feet two, she claimed to be
the Red Cross's tallest employee and added that if she had
been compensated by inches instead of experience, she
would also be its highest paid.

As the Red Cross disaster services director for the southern tier, Charlotte was in charge of all branch offices in En-
dicott, Binghamton, and Johnson City, as well as the chapter
offices in Delaware, Otsego, Chenango, and Broome coun-
ties. She was Harold Draper's boss and outranked him, not
only because she was his immediate superior but also because she liked to boss people around. In this context, Charlotte liked to tell a story about an Academy Award–winning
actress who had worked for a much-hated and often vilified

studio head during Hollywood's golden years. This gruff and inelegant individual exercised total control over every aspect of movie production and, as a consequence, was resented by many of his equally egomaniacal but subordinate production personnel, particularly his directors.

After the studio head's death a tabloid reporter approached the Academy Award–winning actress for a quotation.

Much to his surprise, instead of adding her bit to discredit the dead mogul, she said, "He may have been a tyrant, but I liked him. I like tyrants. They get things done."

Charlotte Washington got things done.

She broke rules, defied bureaucrats, courted the media, wrote articles, and marched in Memorial Day parades. She did anything and everything, including organizing blood donor "singles weekends" and senior citizen baseball games to publicize, popularize, and promote the image of the American Red Cross.

"I was born in a small town on the Mississippi River," she explained to the dozens of reporters who had interviewed her over the years. "When I was fourteen years old, it started raining in Clydesville and after about ten days it seemed as if the deluge would never stop. By the time the rescue workers got to us, our house had been knocked off its foundation, all of our possessions were being swept downstream, and we were perched on the roof of the Clydesville elementary school.

"The Red Cross took us in, fed us, clothed us, and sheltered us until we could get back on our feet. Then they disappeared from our lives like the Lone Ranger at the end of a movie. It took me a while to admit it to myself, but ever since that day I've known that the Red Cross is where I belong and that what I am doing is what I have always been destined to do."

Charlotte graduated from college with a masters degree in clinical psychology and went to work at the outpatient clinic of the Roosevelt Psychiatric Hospital. After about two years there, she said, "To hell with all this," and applied for her first job at the American Red Cross.

During her thirty-five-year career there, she had worked on or developed programs for the full spectrum of Red Cross services, including human tissue collection for medical transplants, volunteer training, and providing assistance to members of the American military. Now, at her professional peak, she was being considered to replace the organization's regional director, who was retiring at the end of July.

Harold Draper had already returned to his office from driving Edith Tuttle to the Twilight Motor Lodge when he telephoned his supervisor. Somewhat nervously he related the circumstances surrounding the fire and the information he had shared with the state trooper, and he expressed his concern that he might have said too much.

"Nonsense, Harold," Charlotte Washington said. "You behaved superbly. If one can't relate one's suspicions to a state trooper, to whom can we relate them?"

"But a lot of people are suing for breach of confidentiality nowadays, and looking back on my conversation with Trooper Bly, I'm not sure what I was allowed to tell him."

"Would you rather be sued for not having protected a member of the public when you had the opportunity to do so?"

"No. I wouldn't."

"Well, Harold, life has its risks. Choosing to do the right thing is one of them. I can assure you that the events you've set in motion are both appropriate and necessary."

"Thank you for saying that, Charlotte."

"No thanks are necessary. The mission of the Red Cross is to improve the quality of human life. Aiding and abetting a potential menace to society doesn't fall within the purview of that mission. Nor is it in the public's best interest for us to harbor arsonists. Don't you agree?"

"Yes, I do."

"I believe that your instincts and experience have served you well. Certainly, many of the things that this Tuttle woman told you also strike me as being odd. When will your friend from the state police be delivering the subpoena?"

"Sometime tomorrow afternoon."

Charlotte Washington looked at her calendar.

"May 2," she murmured. "Good. I'll be here all day."

"Do you want me to come in?"

"No, Harold. Ida Suss will help me. You remember Ida, don't you?"

"Indeed I do. Please give her my regards."

"I shall. I will also ask her to locate the Tuttle's previous 901 forms, if there are any, and to make photocopies of them anticipatory to handing them over to the state police. You may rest assured that I'm behind you one hundred and fifty percent. It's possible, indeed probable, that your evaluation of the circumstances surrounding the fire may, in the future, save other human lives."

"That's what I was thinking," Harold Draper said slowly, sadly. "Two children died today. Beautiful kids. Just beautiful."

"Exactly. One can only hope and pray that there have not been others."

CHARLOTTE WASHINGTON's prayers were not answered.

Ida Suss burrowed into drawer after drawer of file cabinets, searching through 901 forms that went back as far as twenty-two years. Ida was eighty-five years old and had been with the Red Cross for sixty of them, twenty as a volunteer, forty as a paid employee, and the last fifteen as Charlotte

Washington's personal assistant. She was as small as a hobbit and as relentless as a dunning agency trying to collect an overdue bill.

When she finally pushed the last file drawer shut and walked into the disaster services director's office, Ida was holding four 901 forms in her hand.

Charlotte looked up.

"Bad news, Ida?"

"Terrible, Charlotte. Just terrible." She laid the forms on her boss's desk and shook her head. "Those poor little children. Those poor, poor dears."

Charlotte Washington studied the four pieces of paper. On each was the name of at least one dead child. In all, six Tuttle children had died, not including Gabriel and Minna Tuttle.

chapter 18

ADDED TO THE *bare bones of the 901s found in the Red Cross files were facts gleaned by investigators from old newspaper clippings and from interviews conducted with firemen, neighbors, and others living in the towns where the children had died. Also incorporated was evidence uncovered as a result of subpoenas and search warrants issued by the New York State Police.*

JUNE CASSIDY TUTTLE

June Cassidy Tuttle was born on December 5, eleven months after Edith and Wilbur were married. Mrs. Cornelia Vesper, age sixty-two, lived across the street from the ramshackle grey farmhouse on Route One in Kipplebrook, New York, where the Tuttles moved after their wedding. She remembered Mr. and Mrs. Tuttle and their baby.

June was a sweet girl. I babysat her on more than
one occasion. She wasn't a particularly happy
child, but she was engaging. Sweet. I always liked

having her around. There was something homey about her. Like a well-kept kitchen or a freshly ironed tablecloth. If she had lived, I'm sure as anything that she would have grown up to be a housewife. She was always following me around the kitchen. If you can spare a few minutes, I'll show you a snapshot of her. Ever since Aaron died... Aaron was my husband... I've had a lot of time on my hands. Too much time. So one week, I up and bought myself half a dozen photo albums, and I finally organized all of my pictures. They're arranged by date. Let's see now, the Tuttles had that horrible fire after the big flood when the Dexter Road Bridge collapsed, but before Albany tried to put in the nuclear waste dump. If I count backward, that'd put it about... goodness. To think that eighteen years have already gone by! The snap of June should be on this page. Here it is. My, wasn't she a dear little thing? My heart went out to Edith when that baby died. She was so broken up, I thought she'd never get over it. The town did what it could to help, but...

The child in Mrs. Vesper's photo album was wearing a white dress with embroidered red trim on the collar, pockets, and sleeves. Although June's eyes were hidden in shadow, the sun glinted off her honey-brown hair. She had a button nose and as Mrs. Vesper had said, a sweet, shy smile. The photograph showed June in the arms of a much younger and slimmer Edith Tuttle. The mother held the baby slightly away from her body. The expression on Edith's face was unreadable.

"THERE WAS NEVER any doubt that the cause was electrical," said Isaac "Ike" Miller, who had been a member of the

Kipplebrook Volunteer Fire Department eighteen years ago. He hunched over a coffee cup in the kitchen of the fire station with an old manila folder labeled TUTTLE opened on the table in front of him.

I was just a pup at the time and had never seen anyone dead before. I hated it so much, I almost quit the department that same day. But I stayed. Like they say, it's a dirty job, but somebody's got to do it. I was going to take a glance over the file before you came, but the truth is, I don't have to. You always remember the ones where someone died. Particularly the children.

The alarm came in at 11:00 PM. A passing motorist saw smoke coming from the second floor of a farmhouse and stopped at the public phone in front of the library. He told the operator where the fire was, asked her to notify the fire department, and then he just kept on going.

Our response time was good. Only six minutes. But the baby was already dead when we arrived. The parents suffered smoke inhalation, but they didn't have to stay the night in the hospital. The fire chief back then, Burt Tinker, called the Red Cross, and they put up Edith and Wilbur in a motel. Gave them food, clothing. The usual. There were donations from the people in the town, too. I don't recall the details of who gave what, but I remember how generous everybody was and how surprised we were when the Tuttles just up and left. One day they were there. Cordial. Not overly friendly, but polite. The both of them were always polite. Edith looking kind of faded and sad, as if an ill wind might come along and blow her away. Wilbur walking around town like someone had hit him over the head with a two-by-four. Then, the next thing you know, they're gone. No forwarding address. No nothing. And you'd better believe that some of the noses on some of the ladies in this town were bent out of shape, what with the charitable efforts they'd gone to and trying to make them feel that Kipplebrook would always be their home. But most of us didn't think that way. We believed that the Tuttles up and left because they just couldn't stand to live in the town where their baby died.

What did you say? You want to know the cause of the fire? You mean I didn't tell you yet? Lord, I can run off at the mouth. Well, the cause was electrical. No doubt about it. That fire started inside the baby's bedroom wall, on the second floor. Years before the fire, no one knew exactly when because the house had been bought and sold so many times, but sometime in the past, someone did a sloppy job of sheet-rocking a wall, and drove a nail right into the electrical wiring. Then, what with time passing and the house expanding and contracting the way old houses do, that nail worried itself through the protective plastic sheath over the wiring until it got clean through to the wires themselves. You know what happens when a steel nail comes into contact with an energized electrical wire. Spark. Short circuit. And fire.

Like I said, it started in the baby's room. We tried mouth-to-mouth when we got there, but one look and we knew it was too late. No, we didn't have the state fire marshals in. Back then there weren't any. But Burt Tinker, our chief, said that there was no question in his mind it was an electrical fire. Burt was a licensed electrician and had an electrical contracting business, and if Burt said it, I believed it. Great guy, Burt.

Nope. You can't get in touch with him. Leastwise
not unless you have an Ouija board. Burt died five
years ago.

SHERWOOD LYON TUTTLE

Three years and one month after the death of June Cassidy
Tuttle from carbon monoxide inhalation, Sherwood Lyon
Tuttle died. He was two years old at the time. By then Edith
and Wilbur had moved to Hopewell Falls, New York; Edith
was twenty-three years old, Wilbur was twenty-two, and
Hopewell Falls was over fifty-five miles north of their first
home in Kipplebrook.

According to photographs found in an old edition of the
North Chenango News, the Tuttles were renting a small wood-
frame house at 571 Wanda Street at the time of their second
fire. The first floor consisted of a living room, an eat-in
kitchen, and two bedrooms. The only bathroom in the house
was on the second floor, next to an unfinished attic that
could easily have been turned into a third bedroom, but was
used to store junk. A covered porch ran along the front of the
house. About thirty feet west of the porch was a detached
garage.

The article accompanying the photos in the *North
Chenango News* reported that at the time of the fire, Wilbur
Tuttle was working at Ernie's Overhaul Garage, about six
miles away, in the village of Shelton; Edith was home, frying
bacon for breakfast, and Sherwood was strapped in his high
chair. After the fire, Sherwood's body was found about four
and a half feet from the stove.

Fire Chief Tom Pratt was quoted as saying that nobody
could have predicted or prevented the tragedy.

"Mrs. Tuttle," he said, "knocked over a coffee pot and

spilled hot coffee on her arm." She had told Chief Pratt that she thought she turned off the flames under the bacon before rushing upstairs to the bathroom to run cold water over the burn and to apply antiseptic spray.

Apparently she had not.

The bacon continued to fry, the fat bubbled and spattered, and after thirty-five or forty seconds, the bacon grease caught fire. Edith told the fire chief that a roll of paper toweling had been mounted on the wall near the burner where the bacon was frying, and Chief Pratt concluded that after the paper towels ignited, the fire spread to a dish towel draped over the back of a chair next to the stove. The flaming towel then set the kitchen curtains on fire. That fire communicated to the walls and ceiling, and within minutes, the entire kitchen was involved.

Edith Tuttle also claimed that by the time she smelled smoke and heard her baby crying, the heat and flames were so intense that it was impossible to reenter the kitchen and save him. And since the only telephone in the house was in the kitchen, she had no option but to run up the road to her nearest neighbor to call in the fire, which delayed the fire department's response time even more.

Sherwood Lyon Tuttle was declared dead at the scene.

Other than Edith, there were no witnesses to the fire, and other than the perfunctory autopsy performed at the Norwich hospital, no official inquiries were made. Edith and Wilbur Tuttle suffered no injuries and were not hospitalized. They did, however, accept the temporary shelter offered to them by the American Red Cross.

A week after the fire, there was one last newspaper reference to the Tuttles in a half-page ad placed by the Hopewell Falls Volunteer Fire Department. It announced that on June 26, a pancake breakfast would be held at the fire station and that the proceeds from it would be used to help pay for Sherwood's funeral.

Despite numerous inquiries, investigators were never able to locate anyone in Hopewell Falls who remembered either the Tuttles or their fire. The Volunteer Fire Department keeps its records for three years and then throws them away, and the house that had once stood at 571 Wanda Street was bulldozed only a week after the fire.

In the Hopewell Falls cemetery, though, there's a small stone, engraved with the birth and death dates for Sherwood Lyon Tuttle. The grave is overgrown and has obviously been neglected for many years.

RACHEL HADLEY TUTTLE, FIONA LEE TUTTLE, AND ROSE DANUBE TUTTLE

The third Tuttle fire occurred five and a half years after Sherwood's death. Rachel Hadley and Fiona Lee Tuttle, twins, were five years old at the time, and Rose Danube Tuttle was four. Alisa May Tuttle was only two and a half years old, but she survived the fire.

By then Edith and Wilbur, aged twenty-eight and twenty-seven respectively, had moved to Lucky Junction, the nicest town in which they had lived so far. Their two-story, white-clapboard rental was inside the town limits, hooked up to village water and sewer, and within walking distance of Mabel's Country Cupboard, the post office, and the town hall. The volunteer fire department was next to the Department of Public Works storage facility, where Wilbur was employed as a mechanic and heavy equipment operator.

Mabel Boggs, aged fifty-six, owned Mabel's Country Cupboard and lived behind the store. She remembered the Tuttles well. Her first recollection wasn't of the fire, but of the dazzling array of hollyhocks that grew between the sidewalk and the entire length of the Tuttle's front porch.

They were every color you could think of. Reds the color of convertible sports cars, and pinks as bright as the lipstick thirteen-year-old girls wear at the mall. The white hollyhocks reminded me of Father Jessup's surplice, and the yellow ones put to mind melted butter on a thick pile of fresh-made buckwheat pancakes. But it wasn't Edith who planted those hollyhocks. No sir. She never had a way with plants. It was Mrs. Woodrow. She owned the place. Mrs. Woodrow sure did love those flowers. Treated them better than most people treat their kids. They grew taller than most children, too. Taller than me. Taller than you.

But it isn't flowers you came here to talk about, not that there were any at the time of the fire, since it happened on Christmas. December 25. Not a day easy to forget. Back then, I guess it was ten years ago by now, there weren't any lights along Main Street. My place is at 20 North Main Street. Edith and Wilbur lived two blocks west, at number 44.

Now, of course, we really spruce up the town for the holidays, and it doesn't cost us a penny, because Lucky Junction has a benefactor. Remember the Episcopal church you passed by on the way in? The one with the stone façade and the round stained glass window? Well, it went up for sale a few years back, and who should buy it but Larchmont Fowler. Sounds like a made-up name, doesn't it? What Larchmont does is sell antiques. He turned that old Episcopal church into an antique store. Emporium is what he calls it. And he's well on the way to turning Lucky Junction into the showcase of Chenango County. We already have one bed and breakfast up and running since he's been here. Hell, next thing you know, I'll have to throw out all of my Maxwell House coffee and start serving cappuccinos and croissants.

Anyway, it's Larchmont who brought the Christmas lights to town, and he's the one who pays for them, too. Every year. One side of the street to the other. Back then, though, before Larch Fowler, Lucky Junction was pretty bleak-looking around Christmas time. A few of us tried to relieve the gloom by putting our trees in the living room windows so that they'd shine out on Main Street.

My personal preference is a tree decorated with those tiny white lights. I think they're called Italian lights, but the Tuttles used the old-fashioned kind we all grew up with. You know, the big red, blue, yellow, and green lights. Bright colors. Like the hollyhocks. From the year they moved in, right up until the fire, they always strung up those very same lights. Not too imaginative, but it did the job.

Probably killed them, too. Those four Tuttle children. Two redheads, a blond, and a brunette. Although I believe that one of them survived.

The night of the fire? Of course. How could I forget it? Sirens blaring up and down Main Street, and fire engines coming from as far away as Norwich and New Berlin. I should know. I was up all night handing out free coffee and doughnuts. More than ten fire companies in all, once they got through the snow. But by then, it was already too late. Too late, that is, for the children.

The way Mabel Boggs remembered it, the snow started to fall before sunrise, at about five o'clock in the morning. By 7:00 AM, you couldn't see your own hand inserting a key into your own car door. If you had a flashlight and your headlights were on, maybe you could see your fingertips. But just maybe.

The employees of the Lucky Junction Department of Public Works, Wilbur included, had been plowing and spreading ash since six o'clock in the morning. Their first priority was Route 12, which had to be kept open because it connected directly to the hospital and the state police.

Many people who had lived in Lucky Junction at the time remembered the fire well. The volunteer fire department records, as well as follow-up reports by the local sheriff, newspaper clippings, and witness statements were made available to state police investigators. All sources agreed that North Main Street had not been plowed prior to the fire.

Edith Tuttle related a warmly domestic tale of eager children unhappy with the dreary light filtering in through a relentless curtain of snow. Rachel and Fiona, the five-year-old twins, along with their four-year-old sister, Rose, had pleaded with their mother to turn on the Christmas tree lights, which she ordinarily would not have done until after dark.

"But it *is* dark," the children insisted. And insisted. And insisted. Until, or so Edith Tuttle later stated, they wore down her resistance and she plugged them in, admonishing the girls to treat their new toys gently, or "all of them will be broke before the Christmas boxes is even throwed out." Then she carted Alisa May, her youngest, up the stairs to tend to a cut the child had gotten on the jagged edge of her highchair tray.

That was at about 8:15 AM.

By eight-thirty, Edith Tuttle, wearing an overcoat and galoshes and desperately clutching Alisa May to her chest, was across the street, pounding on the door of Ray Beverly's ground floor apartment.

"Help! Help!" she screamed. "Help! Help! Fire! My children!"

Of course, with nineteen inches of snow already on the ground and most of the roads still unplowed, the fire department's response time was not the answer to anyone's prayer. After Ray Beverly calmed down Edith enough to find out what had happened, he tried to get into her house to rescue her children. The Clifton brothers, all of whom were separated from their wives and living together in the apartment above Ray's, also tried to get past the wall of fire to save the girls. But the combination of combustibles, including gift boxes, wrapping paper, and plastic toys, as well as the delayed arrival of the fire apparatus, made their attempts futile.

Three days later, after fire department personnel had sifted through the debris, the overall consensus was that the cause of the fire had been electrical. Wilbur Tuttle told the fire chief that he had run the cord to the Christmas tree under the carpet, so the children wouldn't trip over it, and the chief theorized that, old as it was, friction from walking over the cord might have caused the wires to fray, and...

But nobody really knew.

The Christmas tree had been set up in an alcove overlooking Main Street, at the front of the Tuttle's living room. Rachel, Fiona, and Rose Tuttle were in that alcove, between the tree and the window, playing with their new dolls. That is where their bodies were found. It was general knowledge that the Christmas tree had been up for about three weeks prior to the fire, that it must have been as dry as kindling, and that it lighted up like a bonfire, imprisoning the children in the alcove and preventing their escape.

The fire was declared accidental. The cause: faulty Christmas tree lights.

No autopsies were ever performed. To do so, the fire chief said, would be like strapping a safety belt around an already dead child. "Anyway," he added. "We already know how those Tuttle children died. Let's just have the funeral director do what he has to do to spare the parents anymore pain, and get those kids into the ground as soon as we can."

Being a good man who had wasted no time in getting things done, the chief also telephoned the Red Cross. The disaster team members who responded had never seen the Tuttle's previous 901s, and they knew nothing about their earlier fires. They provided Edith and Wilbur with food, clothing, and shelter. For a third time.

Because the Tuttles had no property or life insurance, the leading investigators concluded that the couple had no conceivable motive to set a fire. But no one asked why Edith had taken the time to put on her overcoat and boots to go across the street instead of trying to rescue her children, or why she hadn't used the telephone in her kitchen to call for help. Nor did anyone verify that there was, indeed, a jagged edge on Alisa's highchair and a cut on her finger.

Even if arson had been suspected, the investigators would have been reluctant to interrogate the obviously grief-stricken Tuttles since they assumed that no parent, particularly a mother, could ever set a fire that would kill her own child. Or, in this case, her own children. Plural.

A memorial service for the Tuttle children was held in the Frank Sweeney Funeral Home, which also handled the burial arrangements. Both the service and the internment were paid for by the good people of Lucky Junction.

At the service, Sandy Solomon, owner of the local nursery school, read aloud a short poem she had written about her young students, describing them as flowers in a garden.

She compared Rachel Hadley, the shorter and more serious twin, to a bouquet of violets and Fiona Lee, older by seventy seconds, to a bright yellow sunflower. When she got around to Rose Danube Tuttle, it was obvious to all present that the four year old had been her favorite. Rose was like a rose, Mrs. Solomon said. A child so pure and lovely that one would have wished she could have been placed forever under a protective dome of fireproof glass.

Of those involved in fighting the fire at 44 North Main Street, most were still alive when Sebastian Bly and his colleagues conducted their investigation. Many no longer lived in Lucky Junction, but with the names, addresses, and telephone numbers provided by Mabel Boggs, who always kept her Christmas card list up-to-date, a surprising number were located and interviewed.

All remembered the deaths of the children and the generosity of the townspeople who had rallied around the Tuttles, bringing them homemade food, companionship, moral support, clothes, money, friendship, and even the promise to help them build a new house come spring.

They also remembered being stunned and hurt when, after the funerals and after the hundreds of acts of kindness, the Tuttles had packed up their meager belongings and disappeared. So negligible had been the ripple of their departure from Lucky Junction, it was as if they had hitched a ride on an itinerant moonbeam and just drifted away.

Now you see 'em. Now you don't.

A tune that Edith and Wilbur had played before.

ALISA MAY TUTTLE

The fire that killed Alisa May Tuttle occurred one year and four months after the fire in which her three sisters died.

Very little is known about it.

Edith Tuttle was thirty years old, Wilbur was twenty-nine, and they had moved to a big house in a small town called Primrose. The entire Primrose business district consisted of one building. The tenant on the east side of the building was the Do Wop Café. The space on the west side was leased by the United States Postal Service.

It was one of those if-you-blink-you-miss-it towns.

Edith and Wilbur Tuttle rented a house up the block and across the street from the Do Wop Café.

Other facts about Primrose included its population of three hundred, its lack of a bank or a church, and the absence in town of the flower after which Primrose was named, although Queen Anne's lace and milkweed grew in abundance. It also had no volunteer fire department.

When questioned, Postmaster Morgan Thorp remembered the Tuttles only because they left no forwarding address when they moved out.

Dottie Nichols, the owner of the Do Wop Café, said her memory of them centered around an incident involving a four-year-old child. One cold Monday evening at the end of March, a customer drew the girl to Dottie's attention because the child had been wandering around alone in the Do Wop's parking lot for more than twenty minutes, dressed only in a pair of pink panties and a powder-blue T-shirt.

Dottie said the girl's name was Alisa.

She brought her inside, threw an old sweater around her shoulders, and gave her a bowl of rice pudding, which she ate as though she hadn't eaten for a week. About fifteen minutes and two pudding bowls later, an orange-haired woman sauntered—that was the word Dottie used—into the Do Wop Café. Without being the least bit agitated or alarmed, the woman reclaimed the child, explaining that she and her husband lived in the big white house up the road and that when she had been chasing some chicken in her driveway, her daughter Alisa had wandered away.

The woman grabbed the little girl's hand, threw a casual "thanks" to nobody in particular—"the way you'd thank a stranger for holding a door open," Dottie said indignantly—and then departed without returning the sweater or offering to pay for the three servings of rice pudding.

After that, Dottie forgot about the incident until two weeks later, when she was awakened in the middle of the night by the wail of sirens less than a block away.

Dottie sent her boyfriend at the time, it was either Gordy Lewis or his brother Sim, to find out what had happened. About an hour later Gordy or Sim came back with the news that the big white house where the chicken always ran loose in the driveway had gone up in flames. He said one of the firemen, a guy named Larry, told him that everybody had made it out safely, except for a four-year-old child named Alisa.

Alisa was dead, and the girl's mother seemed to be taking it pretty hard.

"Did the mother have red hair?" Dottie asked.

"Orange," he answered. "Like a pumpkin."

When asked if she recalled any other details about the fire, Dottie said she remembered the mother going off with someone from the Red Cross and that Sim or Gordy had told her that the dead girl's father was off on a fishing trip up north. Near Plattsburgh. Or at least that's what Sim said that someone else had said.

Two days later Fireman Jeffrey Randazzo of the Oxford Volunteer Fire Department stated that the fire had been "accidental in nature." Fireman Randazzo, who had taken a five-day course in fire analysis at the State Fire Academy in

Montour Falls, interviewed exactly one witness—Edith Tuttle—and did a fifteen-minute walk-through of the house. His analysis of burn patterns consisted of looking at a kitchen drawer, which was open, and observing a box of matches beside Alisa's body. He concluded that four-year-old Alisa had somehow gotten into the drawer where her parents kept their matches and that she had been playing with them at the time of the fire.

No criminal charges were ever brought against the Tuttles. The tragic, bereaved Tuttles.

Nor did anybody question the validity of Fireman Randazzo's findings.

Alisa May Tuttle was buried in a small, plain coffin the day after she died. Her plot in the Primrose Cemetery is marked only by a cheap brass plaque. The Tuttles, instead of waiting around for weeks after the death of their child as they had done in the past, disappeared immediately upon internment.

Primrose is a cold town. A poor town. A mind-your-own-business town whose sunny name belies its indifferent nature. The residents, by and large, showed up at their jobs, paid their bills, and went their own ways.

Nobody had cared about the Tuttles when they lived there.

People cared even less when they left.

After the fire in Primrose none of Edith and Wilbur's children died for eight years and one month. Then, in the town of Sojourn, the lives of Minna and Gabriel Tuttle ended after they inhaled a deadly mix of toxic chemicals and carbon monoxide.

Edith was twenty years old when her first child died in a fire; she was only thirty-eight when her last two children died—thirty-eight years old, and easily capable of having five or six more babies, all of whom, had they been born, would probably have perished, too.

Over a period of eighteen years, eight Tuttle children had died in five fires. Edith and Wilbur Tuttle had been accused of setting none of them.

They were victims of a terrible and implacable fate.

At least, that is how they were perceived at the time.

SUCH WERE THE FACTS unearthed by State Trooper Sebastian Bly, his fellow investigators, and his brother-in-law. Facts that had become attainable only because Ida Suss had found four 901 forms in the bulging back files that had not yet been disposed of at the offices of the Southern Tier Headquarters of the American Red Cross.

Incriminating as those facts were, there were more yet to come.

chapter 19

DR. ARISTOTLE PAPPAS was a forensic pathologist at Binghamton General Hospital. Being the son of a medical examiner and the husband of an assistant district attorney who prosecuted felony assault and homicide cases, Dr. Pappas was familiar with death. As a consequence of his education and experience, he could perform autopsies with the cool detachment of a micro surgeon. As a consequence of his temperament and personality, he had never been able to take the death of a child in stride, and when his stride was broken, Dr. Aristotle Pappas noticed things.

Things that other people missed.

Aristotle Pappas, "Ari" to those who knew him, was a tall man who had been a tall boy. He played varsity basketball from his sophomore year of high school until his graduation and had been dubbed "String Bean" in the local newspapers. LEAN AND MEAN STRING BEAN CREAMS VISITING TEAM was one of the more memorable headlines of his high school career. As an adult, he was slightly myopic and extremely amiable, with a narrow face, a high forehead, and thick black hair. He was tenacious without being ambitious and was perfectly content to spend the rest of his professional life cutting up bodies in the basement of Binghamton General Hospital.

It was Aristotle Pappas who had performed the autopsies on Gabriel and Minna Tuttle.

As he had hoped, Sebastian Bly arrived too late for the actual autopsy, and when he took a seat across from Dr. Pappas in his office, he noticed that instead of a blood-spattered lab coat, Ari Pappas was wearing a button-down blue shirt with a cheerful yellow bow tie. His pants were perfectly creased, his shoes were flawlessly shined, and Sebastian had a perfect view of his high forehead as he hunched over a legal pad on his desk.

The pathologist looked, Sebastian later told Annie, more like a successful stock broker than like a man who dealt all day in blood and gore. Annie, who had often written news stories about trials at which Ari Pappas testified, had a perfect explanation.

"His wife dresses him in the morning."

But Sebastian had a different theory. He saw a gentle and tidy man functioning in a world of chaos and unexplained death, and he wondered if the pathologist's immaculate appearance wasn't a way of affirming life, the way it should be, away from an autopsy table's unrelenting gore.

The forensic pathologist looked up, but before he could say anything to Sebastian, the state trooper cautioned, "In words of one syllable, Doc. Please."

Ari Pappas removed his eyeglasses and rubbed his eyes.

"What do you want to know? The cause of death or what killed them?"

"Is there a difference?"

"There is in my mind."

"Tell me both."

"All right." He returned the eyeglasses to the bridge of his nose. "In layman's terms, both children died as a result of carbon monoxide inhalation. That's the simple explanation. The one I don't accept."

"Why not?"

"Because I don't like the locations and positions in which the bodies were found, I don't like the circumstances of the fire, particularly that the kerosene heater had been situated inside a curtained closet, and I don't like that the bedroom door was shut. Most of all, I don't like Mrs. Tuttle's failure to report or apparently even notice the absence of her one remaining child. Because of these and other factors that have to be explained with words of more than one syllable, I am convinced that what killed the Tuttle children was the diphenhydramine their mother administered to them."

"Diphenhydramine as in Lullabide, right?"

"That's right. And you are to be complimented for locating and bringing me the bottle. If you hadn't done so, there's a possibility, remote I admit, that I wouldn't have looked for the drug in their blood. As it is, I found there was enough of that sedative-laced antihistamine for both of those children to have slept through the London Blitz, let alone a bedroom fire."

"What about flame impingement? I didn't see any when I looked at the kids, but what do I know? Were either of them burned?"

"No."

"Bruises? Fractures? Evidence of cuts? Wounds? Battering?"

"None."

"How about their general health? I mean, before they died?"

It was the pathologist's answer to this question that was so hard for Sebastian to accept when he later explained it to his wife.

"Annie," he said, slowly and carefully, as if each word had to be extracted with pliers from a part of his mind that didn't want to give it away, "Dr. Pappas said that before Gabriel and Minna died, they were perfectly healthy."

Annie stared blankly at her husband.

"So? I don't get it."

"So, Gabriel and Minna never had the flu. They didn't have colds. They didn't have one mosquito bite between them. There was no inflammation in their lungs, no mucous in..."

"Skip the details, Sebastian, and tell me what's really bothering you?"

He looked down at the ground.

Annie reached out and took her husband's hands. She held them for a moment and then pulled forward, which had the effect of making his head lift up and his eyes meet her eyes, as if she had pulled the lever on a mechanical man.

"Come on, sweetheart. Talk to me."

Sebastian grimaced. He took a deep breath and said, "Aristotle Pappas believes that Mrs. Tuttle deliberately killed her own children."

"I understand that. I understood it yesterday. Wasn't that Billy's idea all along?"

"Yep. It was. But it's easy for Billy. He just buckles on his holster, slaps his white hat on his head, and goes after the bad guy. Billy's a cowboy. It's the justice that matters to him. Not the evil."

Annie lifted a finger and tapped it thoughtfully to her lip.

"You're right," she said. Then she added, almost apologetically, "That's Billy. And me, too, Sebastian. We're both shallow, picturesque, and passionate. Evil isn't real to us. It's an abstraction. Like a trillion dollars or the International Date

Line. We know it's out there, and our intellects tell us that it exists. But deep down ... deep, deep down, we still don't believe it."

"Aristotle Pappas believes in evil."

"Exactly what did he tell you, Sebastian? Break it down for me."

"He told me that Edith Tuttle. That's the mother ..."

"I know that."

"That she drugged Gabriel and Minna with diphenhydramine and that she gave each of them enough to 'render then unconscious.' Those are the words Dr. Pappas used. He said that Edith wanted them to be immobilized, but alive when she set the fire, so they would inhale the toxic fumes that would kill them and look like the victims of an accidental fire."

Annie scrutinized her husband's face.

"I still don't get why your reaction today is so drastically different from what it was yesterday."

"I know something today that I didn't know yesterday."

"Which is?"

"Annie," Sebastian paused for a long moment before continuing. "Let's say there's a woman. Any woman. Anywhere. I'll call her Sally. Sally's having a real bad day. Maybe she's pissed off because her husband is sleeping with his secretary, or maybe she's mad because she just got fired or evicted from her apartment. Maybe Sally's kids won't stop screaming at each other, or her mother-in-law moved in and picks on her twenty-four hours a day. Whatever it is, something, or a string of somethings, happen, and Sally flips out, tosses a match, and sets a fire. I don't like it, but I can understand it. People lose it all the time. Husbands. Wives. In-laws. Outlaws. Last week, we had a history teacher who threw a dictionary stand out the window of his third period class, and this is a guy who never so much as yelled at his students before. Three weeks ago, a priest slugged a blind man at a newsstand for giving him the wrong change. Flipping out is part of the human condition. It's wrong, it's bad, and it's dangerous, but it's what people do. After they come back to their senses, most of them have the good grace to feel terrible about what they've done and to be ashamed.

"But that's not what happened here. Edith Tuttle waited until her husband left town. She put both of her children into one room, drugged them, and put a kerosene heater against flammable material. She closed the bedroom door to keep the flames and toxic fumes inside. Edith Tuttle is no Sally. She didn't flip out like the history teacher or the priest. Every move she made, every tear she shed, and every lie that came out of her mouth was premeditated."

"So, what's the problem?" Annie asked, genuinely baffled. "You're the good guy. She's the bad guy. Arrest her, convict her, and send her to the electric chair. I can accept that. Why can't you?"

"Because . . ." Sebastian shook his head like a child rejecting the notion that there is no Santa Claus. "Because I just plain don't want to believe that a mother, any mother, could coldly and deliberately murder her own child."

Sebastian Bly was not alone.

The National Center for the Analysis of Violent Crime at the FBI academy in Quantico, Virginia, studied thirty-nine cases of mothers who, cumulatively, murdered fifty-six of their own children. *Women used methods that required less direct involvement in the actual death,* the report stated. *The most common cause of death was fire.*

Who are these women? Where do they come from? What do they do?

Wanetta Hoyt suffocated five of her offspring, claiming that they had died of SIDS or Sudden Infant Death Syndrome. During the long period before her arrest, she reveled in the sympathy she got from family, friends, and her community, all of whom praised her for her courage in the face of tragedy.

We have great difficulties acknowledging that mothers are capable of consciously harming their children, wrote Herbert A. Schreier and Judith A. Libow in an article for the *Saturday Evening Post. Even when mothers are known to have killed their children, they may be treated more leniently.*

Although Marie Noe of Philadelphia confessed to suffocating only four of her ten children, she was arrested and charged with having murdered eight of them over a period of nineteen years. Thirty-six years before her arrest, *Life* magazine had described Marie Noe as heroic, stating, *Courage in her lexicon counts more than tears.* Her husband was never at home when the children died.

Researchers . . . studied twelve mothers, one grandmother, and one father proven by video surveillance to be suffocating their children, the Schreier and Libow article continued. *Two of the mothers and the father had likely killed a child previously. All of the women were given probation, but the man was jailed for life.*

Marybeth Tinning of Syracuse, New York, gave birth to nine children. Her first three died within two months of each other. Eventually, all nine mysteriously perished. Of the nine deaths, only the last was investigated. It had not occurred to any of those who came into contact with Marybeth that she might be killing her own children. Not, at least, until she was arrested for the murder of her fourteen-month-old daughter, Tami Lynne.

Six hours after she was arrested, she confessed.

But it had taken nine deaths and fourteen years to arrest her.

Why?

Because, like Sebastian Bly, nobody wanted to believe that a mother could kill her own child.

chapter 20

WHEN ALL WAS said and done, after defense lawyers and pros-
ecutors had warehoused their police and fire department
records, their ambulance reports, and their investigative doc-
umentation of electrical wiring, Christmas tree lights, kitchen
matches, and kerosene heaters... after all of the analysis had
been made and all of the experts had been consulted... after
the means and methods of understanding Edith Tuttle had
been considered, argued, hashed and rehashed, what it came
down to in the end was the scrapbooks.

The original search of the ugly house had yielded nothing sinister. Wilbur Tuttle's bowling ball bag had contained
only a bowling ball, and his boxes of trout-fishing flies had
held only an assortment of decrepit feathers, hooks, and
beads. Edith's sugar bowls contained only clotted sugar, and
her handbag only a crumpled tissue, a ballpoint pen, a small
coin purse, an address book, a shopping list written on the
back of an envelope, a tube of lipstick, and a comb.

But the scrapbooks...

Billy Nightingale was the one who couldn't and wouldn't give up. Five hours after beginning their futile search of the ugly house, he slammed his open palm against his forehead and exclaimed, "Of course!"

Sebastian looked up from the desk he had been searching. "Of course what?"

"She took it with her."

"Took what?"

"Letters. A diary. Incriminating photographs. A how-to manual on setting fires. I don't know what, but whatever it is, Edith took it with her." He walked over to Sebastian. "Show me the search warrant."

The state trooper handed it to Billy.

"How broad a search does this allow us?" His eyes traveled over the document. "Do we have the right to go through their possessions now? I mean right now. Wherever the Tuttles are?"

"You mean in their motel room?"

"I mean does it cover their personal effects? What they're wearing. Holding. Carrying around with them."

"I have to check with my sergeant."

"Good. Do it. If it's not covered, how long will it take us to get a new search warrant?"

"If the judge is in his office, right away."

TWO HOURS LATER, Sebastian directed the manager of the Twilight Motor Lodge to unlock the door to Room 27. Wilbur Tuttle was at Bova Auto Repair at the time, putting a rebuilt carburetor into an old Ford Falcon, and Edith Tuttle, accompanied by Albertina Hipkiss and Albertina's daughter-in-law, Cheryl, were at the local funeral parlor, making arrangements for Gabriel and Minna's memorial service and burial.

It took Billy only four minutes to find what he was looking for, tucked in the bottom of an old leather suitcase underneath a neatly folded flannel nightgown and an unopened
six-pack of white cotton ankle socks. There were two scrapbooks in all. Each was of the five-and-dime variety, with an
embossed ivy border and the word MEMORABILIA scrolled
across the center of a shiny cardboard cover. The thinner
scrapbook was dark blue. The thicker one was bright green.

Billy laid both of them on top of the only table in the
room and dragged over two heavy chairs. Then, page by page,
they went through them, as scrupulously as if the scrapbooks
were infinitesimal hair follicles found at the scene of a crime
in danger of contamination.

The blue scrapbook contained news clippings about fires
that had occurred over a period of twenty years. Fires that
seemed to have no connection to each other or to the Tuttles.
The article on the first page described a fire in the kitchen at
the home of Angus McNulty, a well-loved character who had
survived with third degree burns over fifty percent of his
body. Angus was a bachelor, a retired dairy farmer, and a volunteer fireman. After he sold his last cow, he moved into a
bungalow across the street from the firehouse and indulged
in his passion for making doughnuts. Angus liked to sift the
flour, cream the shortening, roll out the batter, cut it, and
then throw it into a deep fat fryer for five minutes. He
claimed that his artery-clogging doughnuts were to a chicken
barbecue what hot dogs were to a baseball game, and just
about everyone who had ever attended a fire department
fund-raiser agreed.

The first article in the blue scrapbook described the fire
that had occurred in Angus's kitchen while he was frying
doughnuts in a large pot of boiling oil. Angus was still in the
intensive care unit of the hospital when the news story came

out, so very little was known about the events that had preceded the fire, other than the boiling oil was thought to have
caused it.

One subsequent article concerned Angus's medical condition, and other article described a pancake breakfast sched-
uled by his friends to help pay for his skin grafts. But there
were no more details about the fire.

The second series of newspaper clippings in the blue
scrapbook related details of a fire that took place on December 5 in a split-level house. Nobody died in that fire, and the
sole witness, seventeen-year-old Janice Whitman, was able to
confirm what the burn patterns in the gutted living room
suggested—that the fire was caused by an electrical short in
an old string of Christmas tree lights. Follow-up stories had
been neatly scissored and taped into the blue scrapbook, but
added little to what was already known.

The next series of news clippings in the scrapbook described a fire on the top floor of a six-family apartment
building. Nora Incantalupo and her two children, Maria, age
five and Tomas, age seven, occupied Apartment 3-North. At
about 9:00 PM on Saturday night, Nora left Maria and Tomas
alone and went to O'Malley's Bar. Four hours later, Mrs.
Lopez, who lived in Apartment 3-South, called in the alarm.
Everybody got out of the building alive except for the Incantalupo children.

The firemen who fought and extinguished the fire did a
cursory walk-through of the Incantalupo apartment and
concluded that the children had started the fire when they
were playing with matches. Unlike the fires in Angus Mc-
Nulty's kitchen and Janice Whitman's living room, this story
received a lot of media coverage. According to one long article headlined PROSECUTOR GOES AFTER NEGLIGENT MOM,
the district attorney initially planned to press charges against

Nora Incantalupo for child endangerment and negligent homicide in the deaths of Maria and Tomas. But as the months rolled by, except for a "Don't Play with Matches" campaign initiated by the local fire department, the DA's initiative lost momentum, and the whole thing went away.

The last incident documented in the blue scrapbook involved a fire in a fishing cabin a few hundred feet from Black Bear Creek. Loring Hawkins, a sixty-one-year-old poacher, trapper, trespasser, boozer, bully, and all-around transgressor, lived alone in the cabin and had done so ever since his common-law wife, Nelly Barber, had left him. According to the first of the two news clippings, Loring's cabin had no water and no electricity, and the plumbing consisted of an outhouse in the back.

The chief of the Black Bear Creek Volunteer Fire Department was quoted as saying that Loring Hawkins died because he had put a kerosene heater too close to a bag of dirty clothes he had been planning to take to the laundromat. The article also made a reference to the deceased's blood alcohol level, and to the coroner's conclusion that in all likelihood, Hawkins was dead drunk and had passed out before being overcome by fumes or flames.

The second clipping reported that he died without leaving a will and that the village of Black Bear was going to bulldoze what was left of his cabin in the interests of public safety.

That was the last entry in the blue scrapbook.

Sebastian and Billy put it aside and took up the thick green scrapbook. It contained every clipping from every newspaper that covered every fire in which a Tuttle child had died. Pasted at the beginning of each section were vivid and compelling photographs of Tuttle children taken when they were still alive: snapshots of babies wearing red elf-hats and surrounded by gift boxes at Christmas; candid photos of babies crawling, toddlers toddling, and little legs peddling on bright new tricycles; birthday shots of babies in party clothes; and posed pictures of older children with small, eager eyes— all oblivious to their fates.

The thick green scrapbook had been organized by the dates of the children's deaths.

The first newspaper entry described an electrical fire on May 9 in which June Cassidy Tuttle, age one and a half, had died. It was preceded by baby pictures, interspersed among which were sympathy cards.

> She's in God's hands now.
> Although His reasons are not always evident...
> Our hearts go out to you in your grief.
> Words can never express...

Over fifty cards for June had been pasted into that thick green scrapbook. Cards from Wilbur's boss, from the local Sertoma Society, from Girl Scout troops, from the mayor of the village, from the town supervisors, from the pastor of the Presbyterian church and the priest of the Catholic church. Even the nurses in the hospital who had helped to deliver June a year and a half earlier sent a card.

Of the two mass cards in the book, one was from Mrs. Cornelia Vesper, who had lived across the street from the Tuttles in Kipplebrook and who, eighteen years later, had given such an informative interview to the state police. Sympathy was expressed in pencil-scrawled letters written on dime-store stationery from Edith's sister Beatrice in California and her Aunt Georgia and Uncle Luke in Duluth. There also was a short letter from Lydia Pembrook, whom, according to a notation scrawled across the top, Edith had not seen since taking Miss Pembrook's home economics class in the tenth grade. On a page by itself was a mimeographed flyer inviting the people of Kipplebrook to a spaghetti supper for the Tuttles "who have been left homeless as a result of a fire."

At the very end of the section dedicated to June Cassidy Tuttle, a small lock of honey-brown hair was permanently held in place by a now yellowed piece of cellophane tape.

By far, the greatest portion of the scrapbook had been taken up by June, the first of Edith and Wilbur Tuttle's children to die in a fire. A single page contained baby pictures of June alive, but over twenty pages had been dedicated to the memorabilia of her death.

The rest of that fat, green book was divided more or less equally among the other Tuttle children. First came Sherwood Tuttle, followed by Rachel; the twins, Fiona and Rose; and finally Alisa.

It was the last two pages in the scrapbook that were the real heart stoppers, though, because under a handwritten caption dated Monday, May 1, were recent photographs of Gabriel and Minna Tuttle. Beneath each picture were three or four baby shots, and next to them were thick, healthy-looking locks of hair. The one beside Gabriel's photograph was short, springy, and the color of apricot jam. The one beside Minna's was long, brown, and looped in on itself like a figure eight.

Billy sighed and closed the scrapbook.

"Shit," he said.

Sebastian nodded. "Yep."

"Mamma Tuttle snipped off those pieces of hair before she killed them."

"Yep."

"But can we prove it?"

"Yep," Sebastian said again, and he pushed his chair away from the table. "She never went near their bodies at the fire scene, and they've been locked up at the morgue ever since, so we can prove that someone cut their hair before they died, and we can prove that someone pasted the hair in the scrapbook while they were still alive. We can also prove that somebody..."

"Mamma Tuttle."

"...knew they were going to die."

"And had planned to kill them," Billy added. "Which means that the deaths were premeditated. Don't forget that." He lined up the scrapbooks on the table so that they were side by side. Then he leaned forward and opened each to the first page. He continued to flip through the pages simultaneously, making notations as he proceeded. He compared a date or a fact from a press clipping pasted into the blue book to a date or a similar fire in the green scrapbook.

Twenty minutes later, Billy said, "On June 3 Angus McNulty is critically injured in a grease fire when he's frying doughnuts. On June 11, eight days later, Sherwood Tuttle dies in a fire caused by bacon grease igniting on Edith Tuttle's stove. Five and a half years go by. Nothing happens. Then on December 20 the Whitman house goes up in flames after their Christmas tree lights short circuit. Five days after that, there's a fire in Edith's living room and three of her children are burned to death. Cause of death? Defective wires on Christmas tree lights. About a year later, it's April 4, and a lousy mother leaves her two children alone on Saturday night. The kids find a box of matches, start playing with them, and die in a fire. Two days later Alisa Tuttle is dead. Cause of death? Playing with matches. Flash forward to less than three weeks ago, on April 14, when a mean old drunk dies in a fire in a fishing cabin because he set his bag of dirty laundry too close to a kerosene heater." Billy looked up and met his brother-in-law's eyes. "Two weeks later, Sebastian—just two weeks—Gabriel

and Minna Tuttle die when a kerosene heater in their bedroom is placed too close to combustible clothing."

He snapped the scrapbook shut.

"She's a copycat fire setter," he said.

Sebastian raised an eyebrow. "Why? What for? What's the
motive? If it isn't money, what is it?"

"Attention," Billy said firmly, and he jabbed a forefinger
at the cover of the fat green scrapbook. "First she kills them,
then she waits for the condolence cards to roll in. Edith Tuttle
is a glutton for attention, Sebastian. She's a sympathy junkie."
Billy stood and began to search the small, bleak motel room,
opening and closing the closets and bureau drawers. When
he was finished, he had twenty-three brand new copies of the
Sojourn Evening Sun in his hands.

"Gabe and Minna made the headlines," he said, thrusting
the stack of papers at his brother-in-law. "There's your motive, Sebastian. Read it and weep."

LATER ON, after making the blotter entries, vouchering the
scrapbooks and newspapers into evidence, and telling Sergeant Thunder what they had found, Sebastian Bly and Billy
Nightingale went home. Over coffee they told Annie everything, describing the sympathy cards and newspaper clippings in detail, and interrupting their narratives every few
minutes with off-the-cuff hypotheses and conclusions. When
they were finished, Annie got up and turned on all of the
lights in the kitchen and living room.

"To keep the wolves away," she explained.

When she sat down again, Billy asked her, "So what do
you think?"

"I think," Annie said grimly, "that this is a three-ring circus, and that Edith Tuttle is the Barnum and Bailey of death."

chapter 21

PEOPLE CONFESS to crimes for any number of reasons.

For a rare few, confession is a way of ridding themselves of terrible guilt. It's a catharsis followed by a lifelong commitment to make amends to those whom they have harmed. For others, a confession is just a final act of duplicity in a existence that is already committed to wrongdoing and lies. Rob a bank? Sure, why not. Kill the owner of a bodega? Seems like a good idea to me. Make a deal with the prosecutor to avoid a death sentence? Hell, yes. I'm guilty as sin.

Let's confess.

Then, there's a third type of person who confesses to a crime, and he or she may actually feel a small degree of guilt. But they feel it in a peek-a-boo manner that flits fitfully through their confused minds.

Now you feel it. Now you don't.

It was in this third group that Sebastian Bly and Billy Nightingale thought Edith Tuttle belonged.

"Not once," Sebastian said about Edith's confession, "did she express remorse about what she'd done. She cried. Oh, she was a regular Niagara Falls. She even carried on about the nursery rhymes she used to sing to her children. Rockabye baby, on the tree tops. She kept singing it over and over. Rockabye this and rockabye that. And she put emotion into it, too. A lot of grief. Fake grief. It was an act. The same as all her other acts. The only difference being that this time her audience wasn't going to throw her any church suppers."

WHEN THE STATE POLICE approached Edith Tuttle in her motel room, they waited until Wilbur was at work, reasoning that they would accomplish more if her principal cheerleader and support system wasn't around.

Then they invited her to accompany them back to headquarters.

They explained nothing.

They did not pressure her.

And they were ever so polite.

"Talk to us, Edith. Help us. Tell us what you know so that we can learn from your experience and prevent this from ever happening to another child."

They put her in a small interrogation room, deliberately made less threatening for the occasion by a vase of dried flowers and a plate of cookies. They offered her a cup of tea, advised her of her rights, and asked questions. And more questions. Evidence was elucidated. Each fire was dealt with in a nonthreatening manner by the state police investigator, Margot Bell, a motherly brunette ten pounds overweight, with too many teeth and the tenacity of a process server.

THERE IS AN ELECTRIC, exhilarating, roller coaster momentum that builds between an investigator and a suspect after a good interrogation has gotten under way. Each is acting at odds with the other. The detective is drawing out every last bit of pertinent information. The guilty party is giving away enough to maintain interest, but not enough to incriminate herself.

Both parties, for whatever reason, are equally anxious to keep the roller coaster hurtling, dipping, climbing, looping, or racing toward whatever lies at the end of the track.

A successful interrogation is a wild and heady ride. But it's only inside the minds and hearts of the adversaries who are sitting quietly at the same table, eyeball to eyeball, inhaling each other's breath. Internal turmoil is not evidenced by their outward behavior. The investigator patiently asks. The interviewee persistently evades answering. Until, at some unpredictable moment in time, miraculously and unreasonably, the suspect truthfully answers one question. She answers another one. Then another after that. And before you know it, she is in the full bloom of confession.

Why?

Nobody knows why.

But they *do* confess.

And Edith Tuttle did.

Without warning, her composure suddenly began to crumple. Weakened by Investigator Margot Bell's relentlessly gentle interrogation, the tent began to fall. And for a few hours Edith Tuttle was no longer the ringmaster of her own circus.

Guilt was not what broke Edith's spirit. And if it was pride, it was a weird sort of pride. And if it was innocence, it was a sullied innocence, for along with her confession to the acts that she had committed, she stubbornly refused to accept responsibility for the death of the first Tuttle child.

Margot Bell opened the green scrapbook to an article written eighteen years earlier.

"I didn't set no fires in Kipplebrook," Edith insisted. "That fire was electrical, just like the newspapers said."

Investigator Bell flipped to a different page. What about Sherwood Tuttle?

Yes, Edith said. She had killed Sherwood.

Did she sedate him first?

No. She hadn't started using Lullabide until the third fire. The one in Lucky Junction, where Rose and the twins died.

How had she caused Sherwood's death?

She held a folded towel up against his face until he stopped breathing.

Why?

Because she heard that dying in a fire is the most painful sort of death; she loved her children, and she didn't want them to suffer any pain. No matter what else anyone could say about her, Edith Tuttle swore, none of her children had suffered before they died.

You mean, before you caused their deaths.

Yes. Before I caused their deaths.

How was the fire initiated? What materials were used? Where was the child before the fire started? Where were the other children? What, exactly, had Edith done? When was the act committed? Where was Wilbur at the times of all of these fires? Did he play any part in setting them? Did Wilbur know that Edith had set them? Was Wilbur covering up for her?

No, no, and no.

Wilbur never did nothing.

Wilbur never knew nothing.

Wilbur loves me, and he loved his kids.

Edith answered each question, volunteering information that was dutifully recorded and later transcribed so that it could be used against her in a court of law. And when Investigator Bell went through the scrapbooks, placing the blue one opposite the green one, Edith eagerly and proudly agreed that they did match up and that the fires in the first book had indeed motivated the fires in the second book. Except—and she was adamant about this—for the first one.

"That fire in Kipplebrook was just like I said. I didn't have nothing to do with it, and I didn't do nothing to my poor little June."

It's very likely that this was true.

For in the blue scrapbook of strangers there was no comparable fire, which suggested that all of the subsequent fires and deaths had been inspired by that first, accidental conflagration. The one that had put Edith at the center of a sort of attention she had found intoxicating. Attention in which she could revel. Attention to which she had become addicted.

Inspector Bell pushed a cookie toward Edith Tuttle.

"Are you all right, Edith?"

"I'm a little dry from talking so much."

"Would you like another cup of tea? More cream? More sugar?"

Edith stared down at her hands.

"It won't do them no good."

"What, Edith? Who?"

"My kids. You said you wanted to talk to me so this wouldn't happen to no other children. But it won't help my children."

"You're right. Edith. It's too late for June."

"Not June. I never done nothing to June."

"Well, then it's true that what you're telling us now comes too late to help Sherwood, Rachel, Fiona, Rose, Alisa, Gabriel, and Minna. But if there's a heaven above, and most of us believe that there is, and if your children are up there, then maybe, just maybe, it will make eternity a little less hard on them to know that even if their mother did cause their deaths, she is very, very sorry that she did."

Edith stopped crying and nodded thoughtfully. Then, in a voice oddly devoid of emotion, she calmly and quietly related details of the seven homicides and four acts of arson that only the perpetrator could have known, each word of which was meticulously copied down.

Half an hour later, Edith was asked to read over the nine-page hand-written account of what she had told Investigator Bell. She held each sheet an arm's length away, as a farsighted person who has forgotten his eyeglasses holds a menu.

On page two, she changed "book of matches" to "box of matches."

On page four, she changed "her" to "them."

Then she signed her name.

DESPITE THE ACCUMULATION of evidence against her, the murder and arson charges against Edith Tuttle were never heard in a court of law. Edith's court-appointed attorney waited until her indictment to tell the judge that Edith had recanted her confession and that he was entering a plea of "not guilty" on all counts. Only after he had entered the plea did he find the time to read her confession and to evaluate the evidence against her. As a result of that evaluation, Edith's lawyer told Edith that the state's case against her was so strong, he thought they should try to make a deal.

"Do what you want," Edith said truculently. "It don't change the fact that I didn't do it."

"Didn't do what?"

"I didn't set fire to none of my houses, and I didn't kill none of my kids."

But by then her own lawyer not only didn't believe her, he was sure that a jury would disbelieve her, too.

So, serious negotiations got underway. Offers were made, withdrawn, reworded, and resubmitted. Charges were added and dropped. Postures were taken. Territories were marked off. And a deal was finally made. Edith Tuttle would plead guilty to two counts of murder in the second degree for the deaths of Gabriel and Minna Tuttle and guilty to one count of arson in the second degree for the fire that she set in Sojourn. In exchange, she would get a sentence not to exceed twenty-five years in prison. She would be sent to the Bedford Hills Maximum Security Correctional Facility, a women's prison in Westchester County, about an hour north of New York's Whitestone Bridge. Her last child, the forgotten daughter to whom she had never given a name, would be legally and permanently removed from her custody by the state.

And, according to comments made by Edith Tuttle's attorney after he had imbibed a bit beyond the dictates of discretion, she was damn lucky to get the deal he got her, because "any jury in its right mind would have found Edith guilty of eight counts of murder and relegated her to the last ring of hell."

BEFORE SHE WAS TRANSFERRED to Bedford Hills, Edith saw her husband one last time.

"Do you still love me?" she asked, her lips trembling and a tear balancing precariously on the tip of an orange eyelash.

Wilbur Tuttle had a big nose, drugstore eyeglasses, and a tired face. His thinning hair was combed over his skull like rubber bands pulled too tightly over the bottom of a glass bowl. He was thirty-seven years old, looked sixty, and his voice shook when he answered her question.

His answer consisted of only four words.

"You killed my kids," he said.

Then he turned his back on her and walked away.

Later Wilbur had a long talk with Sergeant Horace Thunder of the New York State Police. Then he spoke briefly to the people at Child Protective Services and met with Sebastian and Annie Bly. After that he signed the necessary papers to voluntarily and permanently terminate his parental rights to "Baby Tuttle," his only surviving child.

Annie said gently, "We're going to name her Meredith."

Wilbur nodded. He didn't smile. He didn't frown. He didn't ask to see his daughter one last time. He didn't even say that he wanted to kiss her good-bye.

"I think he didn't believe that he had the right to," Annie later suggested.

"He didn't," Sebastian said unsympathetically.

Six months later, a child who seemed to have been born thinking, calculating, evaluating, and making judgments, was issued a new birth certificate. On it, Annie and Sebastian were named as her parents.

The name for the little red-haired girl herself was registered as MEREDITH MARMALADE BLY.

book two

How dreadful knowledge of the truth can be
When there's no help in the truth.

—SOPHOCLES

chapter 22

ELEVEN YEARS had gone by since Sebastian and Annie met.

Each year and for each anniversary, they returned to the John Jay College of Criminal Justice to begin what they knew would be a fruitless trek in any of four directions to find that ephemeral restaurant where they'd had their first date. And each year, they discovered yet another distinctive, unforgettable restaurant—the location of which they promptly forgot.

Their house in Fawn Creek was about twelve hundred feet from Professor Sprenger Road. Dozens of Professor Sprenger crab apples grew on the Bly's property, in among sugar maple, weeping willow, white birch, and honey locust trees, all of which turned delicious shades of red, yellow, and gold in autumn, peaking on October 10 without fail.

It didn't take a lot of money to live comfortably in New York state, as long as you were at least three hours west of Manhattan. Gorgeous, fertile farmland populated by deer and punctuated by lush maples was so cheap that a twenty-five-acre plot with two creeks and fifteen hundred feet of road frontage could be had for less than eight hundred dollars an acre. A man working for the highway department or at a hardware store who had a wife working as a waitress or teacher could own a nice house, a few acres, and a couple of cars; and they could afford to do pretty much whatever they pleased, including going on trips to Los Angeles, London, or France.

In Rockland County, a white clapboard, three bedroom house with a porch, a stone fireplace, and a barn would sell for upward of a million and a half dollars. In Fawn Creek, a state trooper and his wife could pay for it outright in less than five years, even without the added income from mineral leases in Wyoming. The additional two hundred acres Sebastian and Annie bought from Sebastian's parents cost less than they had paid for the entire house, including two barns, the smaller of which was turned into a stable for twelve-year-old Meredith's horse, Clementine.

As horses go, Clementine made up in dumb loyalty for what she lacked in elegance. Annie said that she looked like a hairbrush with feet. Clementine was taffy colored, had mournful eyes and short, stubby legs. She had been, or so the farmer up the road had said, headed toward the glue factory when Meredith took up her cause, made an impassioned, Portia-like plea to her parents for the mare's life, and promised that she would personally do all of the work involved in the horse's care and maintenance for rest of her life, so help her God. Amen.

Shortly thereafter, Clementine became Meredith's "all time, number one, best friend in the whole, wide, world," along with her rabbit, George; her hamster, Daisy; and the family's sweet but ineffectual basset hound, Murdock.

Except for the rare occasions when Meredith was overwhelmed with extracurricular activities, she took great pride in doing what she had told her parents she would do. To

Merry, a commitment was like a bead on an abacus, one for each of the twenty-four hours of her day. Feed Clementine: move one bead from the right side of the abacus to the left. Clean the stall: move another bead. Take Clementine out for her morning stumble: move a third. Clean Daisy's hamster cage and give her fresh water: fourth and fifth beads. Drag Murdock on a walk and check his ears for burrs: two more beads. Give George the rabbit a carrot; clean his cage; do homework: more beads.

Meredith Marmalade Bly was an active child. She had places to go and things to do. There were gymnastics three times a week, piano lessons once a week, Girl Scouts every Saturday morning and, depending on the season, a great big "other" category that included swimming in Wilkins Creek, tennis on one of the four courts behind the grammar school, and ice skating on the high school football field, which was flooded every year after Thanksgiving.

Busy as Meredith was, there was more to her life than pets, sports, music, friends, and school, and the beads on her abacus extended beyond Fawn Creek, all the way to Manhattan.

The Metropolitan Museum of Art was six avenues west of the family's apartment on East Eighty-fourth Street. The Museum of Natural History was a short bus ride across Central Park, and the big snowflake outside Tiffany's at Christmas was less than a forty-minute walk. Meredith's other favorite places and things included the ladies room at Saks Fifth Avenue, the ice-like sculptures at Steuben Glass, the pastrami sandwiches at Katz's Delicatessen, the skaters at the ice rink in Rockefeller Center, and the lights, billboards, giant television screens and tawdry, flashy, preposterous people in Times Square.

Best of all, though, were the Broadway shows.

Particularly the musical revivals.

Annie and Sebastian had taken Meredith to see *The King and I, South Pacific, My Fair Lady, Annie Get Your Gun, Oklahoma, Kiss Me Kate, The Music Man,* and *Brigadoon,* and she had memorized the lyrics for every song from every one of them. At home in Fawn Creek, Merry's all-time favorite thing to do was to push the living-room furniture off to one side, put a tape of *Brigadoon* in the video player, and dance the role of the Scottish lass, Fiona.

Upstate, Meredith was allowed to roam the fields, swim in the creek, pedal her bicycle, or ride old Clementine anywhere that she wanted to. In Manhattan, she was not permitted to go anywhere by herself.

"Because, darling Daughter," Annie had cautioned. "Your judgment and instincts have never been honed to detect evil. You might consider someone a pervert if he smelled bad, staggered when he walked, and wore dirty clothes. But villainous fiends sometimes have perfectly captivating personalities and clean, bright white teeth." Annie leaned forward menacingly. "The better to *eat* you with, my girl!"

No bad guy could be just bad in Annie's world. Nor was good ever good enough unless it was magnified, amplified, and dramatized. And so everybody Annie and Meredith encountered was either a perfidious scoundrel or a spotless saint. They were blasphemous or magnificent. Ignominious or stupendous. Fantastic or foolish.

Life with the Blys was never dull.

What happened to any of them was shared by all of them. Sebastian told his wife and daughter about the traffic tickets he wrote, the domestic disputes he settled, the bad guys he arrested, and the good guys he helped. He related details about hotel robberies, drug busts, con artists, and arson. All were part of the vocabulary of Meredith's childhood, but none pierced the bubble of security with which her parents surrounded her. Bad things happened in the real world. Merry knew that was true. But bad things happened out there, beyond the great sea wall that Sebastian Bly had built to protect his family from the thundering waves of the worst that reality had to offer.

For the first few years after the adoption, Annie, Sebastian, and Billy kept a vigilant eye on Meredith to see if evidence of any insidious damage might crop up as a result of those terrible first months of her life. But other than her extraordinary agility and easygoing independence, both of which she seemed to have been born with, nothing did. Merry walked faster, leaped higher, and asked more questions than other children the same age, and she read everything within eye range, including the backs of cereal boxes and the warning labels on insecticides. But none of that was abnormal. Just unusual—as was her inclination to keep her own counsel and be alone.

It wasn't that Meredith went out of her way to avoid people. She just rarely sought them out. If her parents hadn't encouraged her to go to Girl Scouts, play tennis, and engage in after-school activities, she would have been happy doing her homework in the kitchen, reading a book, napping on the porch swing, or tossing a ball to Murdock, who would amble over and slobber on it, since he was too inherently inert to chase or retrieve anything.

Merry herself was both autonomous and resilient, characteristics that could have been derived from either the Nightingales or the Blys.

She was also consistently poised.

"Where did she get *that* from?" Annie once asked, staring in wonderment at her child. "I'm sure as hell not poised."

Meredith Bly walked like a princess, her shoulders elegantly erect and her head held high, as if she were balancing an invisible tea tray. As she matured, the features of her small-boned face remained delicate, her hair remained orange, and her eyes got even bigger. There was always a look of intense concentration in those deep brown eyes and, like the infant she had once been, she was still thinking.

Thinking, thinking, thinking.

Except when her Uncle Billy was around. Then and only then did Merry stop whatever she was doing and revert to being a child. She would tear across the room and throw herself into Billy's arms, clinging to him like a morning glory and kissing him half a dozen times before he could laughingly struggle out the words, "Down. Down, Marmalade. Down." Not meaning it and never succeeding anyway. Years ago, Billy Nightingale had unwrapped Meredith's clutching hand from around his finger, but he had never tried to disentangle his heart from hers.

And so for all intents and purposes and despite the tragedy of her early years, Meredith Marmalade Bly was an affectionate child and perfectly normal in all respects, except for what Annie considered to be her disconcerting poise.

It was the consistency of this poise, when Merry was younger, that troubled Annie.

"It isn't healthy for a seven year old to walk around all the time as if she's on her way to a coronation," she told Sebastian.

And she set out to teach Meredith how to laugh boisterously and loud.

Slapstick didn't do it. Neither did pratfalls or pies in the face. Bugs Bunny, Mickey Mouse, the Road Runner and Mister Magoo precipitated nary a grin. In fact, nothing made Meredith Bly laugh. At least, nothing made her laugh until Annie happened upon elephant jokes.

How can you tell if an elephant has been in the refrigerator?
From the footprints in the cottage cheese.

Why do elephants have wrinkled knees?
Because their panty hose are too loose.

What weighs two tons and wears a glass slipper?
Cinderelephant.

Occasionally, Annie would branch off into monster jokes.

What has wings, fangs, is black on the inside and clear on the outside?
A vampire in a plastic bag.

What's soft and mushy and found between a werewolf's teeth?
Slow runners.

Each orgy of terrible jokes would have mother and daughter falling on the floor and laughing until they were in tears.

Sebastian, too, developed an infallible technique for making Merry laugh. His involved sitting across from her at breakfast, waiting until she had taken a gulp of milk, and then wiggling his eyebrows, nose, and ears at the same time. The more she tried not to laugh, the harder it was, until she couldn't stand it any longer, and the laughter and the milk would come shooting out of her nose and mouth at the same time.

But the life of Merry's laughter was short, and when the joke was over, she would once again become remote, regal, poised, and relentlessly purposeful.

As a toddler, a child in nursery school, a kindergartener, a first grader, and a student in grammar school, Meredith Marmalade Bly had goals. The attainment of one goal in particular was profoundly important to her. She was eleven years old when she first communicated it to her mother.

"Mommy," Merry said somberly. "What's wisdom?"

Annie laid down her pencil, pushed aside the article she was writing on homemade pickles, and thought about the question for a few seconds. Then she took Merry by the hand to the dictionary, and flipped it open.

"Wisdom," Annie read aloud, "is the faculty of making the best use of knowledge, experience, and understanding. Good judgment. Sagacity. The quality of being wise."

Merry nodded. Then, looking far too young to be either wise or sagacious, she said, "Do you think that wisdom means doing the right thing?"

Annie stared at her child, walked over to the sofa, and sat down.

"I suppose that it does," she said cautiously.

Her daughter sat down primly beside her and folded her hands in her lap. "Do you know what I want to be when I grow up, Mommy?"

"No, darling. Tell me. What do you want to be?"

"I want to be wise."

LATER THAT NIGHT, after Annie had described this interchange to Sebastian, he sat up in bed, disturbed.

"What ever happened to little girls who want to grow up and become astronauts or movie stars?"

Annie sighed and stared at the ceiling.

"If only," she said.

Neither of them got very much sleep that night.

chapter 23

THERE IS MORE than one way to tell an adopted child how he or she became part of the family. There's the "Nicole has two mommies" approach, which can get a bit biological in describing the mommy in whose uterus Nicole grew. Traditionally this mommy is a wonderful person who chose or was forced by necessity to give Nicole up so that the other mommy could teach Nicole how to walk, eat with a fork, tie her shoes, not burp in public, write thank-you notes, get a job, and pay taxes.

The adoptive father with no uterus is usually irrelevant in this approach and gets short shrift.

There's the "other parents are stuck with the children they have, but we chose you, so you are even better and more loved" approach, which has much to recommend it, because any child in his right mind adores being complimented, and "you must be the best because we picked you" is a hell of a compliment. It also has the amicable virtue of including the father in the process.

There's the brutally honest approach: "Nicole, I'm your mommy, Rosemary, and this is your daddy, Bernard, but Brenda Sue over there, living in the trailer park next to the gravel pit, is also your mommy, and your daddy is Garth, a male exotic dancer, or at least Brenda Sue thinks so, or he might be Antonio the service attendant at the Hess Station on Route 17. And even though Brenda Sue loves you very much, we're going to be your parents because Brenda Sue can't afford to raise you. But Brenda Sue wants to be a part of our lives, so you're going to see her on alternate weekends, and you're going to send her Mother's Day cards, and . . . No, Nicole, I'm really your mommy, even though Brenda Sue is still your mother, but she's allowing us to adopt you and so she won't be your only mother anymore."

Then, of course, there's the old fashioned approach to adoption. That of keeping the details of the transaction a deep, dark secret until circumstances compel you to admit the truth. This approach has all the advantages of good theater, but doesn't seem to work in real life, generally resulting in re-criminations of the "Why didn't you tell me?" variety, which, if you read between the lines, usually translates to "How dare you provide me with gourmet food, exclusive suburban schools, and my own car to drive on my sixteenth birthday when I could have been sitting on my butt, analyzing the ins and outs of rejection, wondering who my real parents were, and feeling sorry for myself for the last twenty years."

Annie and Sebastian Bly chose none of these approaches.

Theirs, like the adoption, seemed to have evolved out of the personalities of the individuals involved.

"Darling," Annie said one morning to Meredith who, at the time, was only four years old. "What do you know about the Constitution of the United States of America?"

"Mommy, can I drink this?"

"No, Merry. That's glue. Give it to me. That's a good girl. The Constitution of the United States was an outgrowth of the Articles of Confederation."

"Where's Daddy?"

"Daddy is at work. After the Revolutionary War, our new nation established a government under these articles that lacked the authority it needed to make the states work together to solve national problems."

"Can I have a cookie?"

"*May* I have a cookie."

"May I have a cookie?"

"What's the magic word?"

"Please."

"Yes, darling, as soon as I explain this to you, you may have two cookies. The solution to the problem seemed to be to hold another convention to revise the Articles of Confederation. The purpose of this convention was to clearly define the powers of a national government that would protect the rights of the separate states and every individual living in them and that would create something more than just a loosely knit group of states."

"Where's Daddy?"

"I already told you where Daddy is."

"Can I give one of my cookies to Daddy?"

"Yes, you may, darling. When he comes back. Writing and ratifying the Constitution was a complicated process that succeeded only because the delegates eventually agreed to add a Bill of Rights. Don't bang your spoon against the table top, Merry. You're giving mommy a headache. After these twelve amendments were added, the Constitution of the United States was adopted, and for the past two hundred and some odd years, this has set the style, limits, opportunities, and parameters of our government."

"Where's Grandpa?"

"Grandpa is with Grandma in Wyoming. Now, listen, darling, because this is very, very important. The Constitution of the United States is the most wonderful document that has ever been written. It establishes justice, ensures domestic tranquility, provides for the common defense, promotes the general welfare, and secures the blessings of liberty for ourselves and our posterity. Here's a cookie, Merry."

"Thank you, Mommy."

"And this fabulous, truly awesome document was adopted by all thirteen of the original United States. Can you beat that? Where's your napkin, sweetie?"

"On the floor."

"Well, pick it up. Here. And let me wipe that goo off your hands. The point I'm trying to make, Merry, is that if the all-time most perfect document in the entire world was adopted, a document that ensures our liberty and guarantees our basic rights, and then if *you* were adopted, which, of course, you were, don't you see what a truly wonderful, incredible, and happy-making thing adoption must be?"

"Mommy, can I have a rabbit?"

"You mean, Mommy *may* I have a rabbit."

"Mommy, may I? May I . . . please?"

"Hell, yes. We adopted a constitution, and we adopted a little orange-haired girl. I don't see why we can't adopt a rabbit, too."

ONE BENEFIT OF this constitutional approach to the subject of adoption was that it brought "adopt" into Meredith's vocabulary at an early age, without it being connected to any emotionally charged or negative issues.

If there were any other benefits, including that of comprehensibility, neither Annie nor Sebastian was aware of them, their policy being to answer any questions that came along as allusively as possible.

"What do we do if she ever seriously wants to know where she came from?" Sebastian once asked after a third beer on a summer night.

"That's simple," Annie said. "We'll pack two bags, lock her in her bedroom so that she can't find or follow us, and move to a different state."

At one Thanksgiving gathering, a cousin of Annie's drew her aside and said, "Annie, our parents are getting on in years. We're older. They're older. You and I are going to have to face the fact that one of these days, they just won't be here."

To which Annie responded, "No, we don't," and walked out of the room.

Later that night, she said to Sebastian, "Denial is underrated."

And meant it.

DESPITE THEIR CAVALIER approach to the subject of adoption, Annie and Sebastian truly did realize that someday either reality or the curiosity of an adolescent girl was going to come whizzing at their heads like a stray bullet and that they would be confronted by questions they did not want to answer and issues they preferred not to face.

When that time finally did come, they were both prepared and unprepared for it.

Meredith was eleven years old.

The catalyst was Mrs. Candlestick's advanced reading class.

Joyce Candlestick was a dedicated teacher, an amateur genealogist and the great-, great-, great- (and a few more greats) granddaughter of one of the original Daughters of the American Revolution. Given both her interests and her lineage, it was not surprising that while discussing the book of the week, *The Little House on the Prairie,* she would rhapsodize for forty-five minutes about homesteading women who were the direct descendants of colonial housewives who had worn their bonnets at a rakish angle when they helped fight for America's independence—as Mrs. Candlestick's ancestors had done.

It was probably admirable that Joyce Candlestick, whose husband was a Korean War veteran with two purple hearts, would be proud of her connection to the past. But that she then chose to manifest her pride by chalking her family tree on the blackboard was bad timing for Meredith.

"Here, children, the tree branches off in five directions after my grandmother Evangeline married my grandfather Jeremiah."

Bad timing piled on top of more bad timing, because families, family history, family background, and heredity seemed to be the order of the day.

And week.

Joyce Candlestick was a tidy woman, impeccably outfitted for every class in brown, taupe, gray, or black suits, usually accessorized with brightly colored silk scarves and thick gold bracelets that dangled with charms commemorating events in the lives of each of her four children. She showed up in class every morning with modest makeup and her shoulder length hair sprayed to perfection. Unlike the other female teachers, most of whom wore slacks to class, she always wore skirts with one-inch black high heels.

Mrs. Candlestick had a pleasant face, a small chin, large

white teeth, and a warm smile. She truly loved children and would beam down at her students with sincere affection. She was a superb reading teacher, often combining the text of the books with facts about their authors, a technique that made both the books and their writers come to life.

"Laura Ingalls Wilder," she said that fateful day in late autumn, "actually lived through most of the experiences she described in her books."

The young Laura, Mrs. Candlestick explained, came from a tightly knit pioneer family. She had moved with them from one wilderness home to another, until she met Almanzo Wilder, the man she would marry in 1885. Almanzo, it turns out, also came from a long established lineage. Laura Ingalls Wilder wrote about both families in her book *These Happy Golden Years*.

By the time Mrs. Candlestick's advanced reading class had finally gotten around to discussing Laura Ingalls Wilder's daughter Rose, they were positively reeking with families. Heredity, roots, heritage, and tradition were bouncing off the walls and skittering along the baseboards of the classroom like manic marbles on the decks of the Nina, the Pinta, and the Santa Maria.

Such had been Meredith's day in class. It was both an eye opener and a revelation to a child who had always known that she was adopted, "like the Constitution," but who had never before considered the possibility of anything relevant to her existence having occurred prior to that adoption.

Meredith was a thinker.

She thought long and hard about pretty much everything, and she usually did her thinking alone. As she left Mrs. Candlestick's class, the thoughts filling her head were like dozens of hands waving frantically at a teacher, each clamoring for attention.

I want to know.
No I don't.
Where did I really come from?
I have the best parents in the world.
Who am I?
Uncle Billy always makes me laugh.
Where do I fit on my family tree?
Mommy and Daddy are my family tree.
No they're not. You're adopted.

If Meredith had been less sensitive . . . if she had loved her parents less and been less in love with her Uncle Billy . . . if she hadn't been so totally committed to doing good, "I promise to serve my country, to help people at all times, and to obey the Girl Scout Laws," or had been less of a thinker . . . she probably would have gone home that day and just blurted out, "Okay, already. So who am I? Really?"

Instead, she went to the library.

Where she encountered another bit of bad or good luck, depending on how you looked at it.

chapter 24

MISS SKITTER, the Fawn Creek librarian, was thin and brittle and looked exactly like a twig. Her bones came together at what looked like bud junctions, and her dresses alternately hung loosely or quivered gracefully around her linear frame like fluttering leaves on a tree. Since Annie Bly was on the library board, Sebastian had exchanged civilities with the librarian on more than one occasion, but he could never quite remember her name. Once he had called her Miss Knitter, and another time, he called her Miss Twitter. He usually thought of her as Miss Skittish, because she seemed like a child, apprehensive about some impending reprimand and always on the verge of running away.

Miss Skitter was terribly, terribly timid.

No one was sure of her age because there was an ink blot over that entry on her job application. It was fairly well known, though, that she had been the Fawn Creek librarian for over twelve years, starting when the library was still located in the small brick building behind the bakery and staying with it through the move to the annex that was added to the municipal building.

Officially, the Fawn Creek Memorial Library is open from 1 PM to 6 PM on Mondays, Tuesdays, Thursdays, and Fridays, and from 9 AM to 5 PM on Saturdays. Everyone in town knew that Miss Skitter came in early and worked late, so it wasn't unusual for a student writing an essay on the Peloponnesian War or an adult needing instructions on how to build a compost heap to tap on the window across from her desk at 8 PM and ask to be let inside. Nor was it unusual for Fawn Creek residents driving by at nine, ten, or even eleven o'clock at night to see the library's two front windows illuminated like a medieval manuscript, with the librarian moving back and forth between them like eyes skittering across a page.

Olivia Skitter lived half a block from the library in a white frame house with green shutters, a wide porch, and an intricately carved front door. Her grandfather had built the structure by hand in 1910, her parents had lived and died in it, and she had been installed in the little back bedroom on the second floor four days after she was born.

Every spring, plump gobs of purple wisteria hung from thick branches that clambered up to the house's second floor. In early summer, bold scarlet and white clematis with petals as big as tea cups clung to the porch trellises. By midsummer, the patch of earth in front of the house was overrun with burgundy peonies, pink and white stargazer lilies, purple gay feathers, coral foxglove, blue delphinium, and red roses. And as summer crept into fall, the hydrangea on either side of the driveway exploded into huge pompoms of pink, accompanied by vibrant color changes in the surrounding maples so dramatic that passersby would grind to a halt with their hearts caught in their throats.

Despite the lushness of the garden that surrounded her

house, nobody had ever seen Miss Skitter bury a bulb, plant a seed, or prune a bush. And how her garden got to be such an extravagance of vegetation was something of a puzzlement. Ida Herkimer, whose husband Lewis had been named Citizen of the Year five times and was a secret drinker, once whispered knowingly to the ladies in her sewing circle that in her experience, people with secret passions always found the time for them, no matter how inappropriate they might be.

After that, it was quietly assumed that the spinster librarian gardened in the dead of night.

Olivia Skitter had soft, silky hair the color of brown eggs. Her skin was pale and her bluish lips usually quavered tentatively before replying to a question or making a statement. She was a shy, dry, and brittle woman with an ageless face and eyes that always seemed to be pleading for permission to retreat. Her hands, though, were lovely. She had long, slim, elegant fingers with flawlessly manicured nails. Annie, who had actually seen Olivia Skitter snipping the dead buds from her rose bushes on several occasions, believed that the woman's hands, like her garden, revealed a secret sumptuousness in her soul.

Miss Skitter, however, seemed not to have been let in on the secret. She preferred to think of herself as one who, like Horatius at the bridge, was the guardian of a gate. It was her job to stand watch over the books in the Fawn Creek Lending Library, but instead of keeping the rioting hoards out, she granted access to the friendly people who lived in her small village and who sometimes had an urgent need to know.

ANNIE BLY liked Miss Skitter.

"I don't know why," she told Sebastian. "I positively loathe deferential people, and she's so deferential, I half expect her to kiss the hem of my skirt when I walk in. Except…"

Except that despite her shyness, the red blush of which added no charm to her colorless face, there was the distinct possibility that Miss Olivia Skitter actually enjoyed people, loved books, and felt genuine gratification when, with her encyclopedic knowledge of her subject matter and her keen sense of a reader's tastes, she was able to make the twain meet.

She had recommended a book on quilting to Martha Kennedy when poor Martha was sitting for hours in the library, not knowing what to do or where to go after her husband had died. Within a week, the no longer purposeless widow had joined a quilting circle, and soon Martha's quilts were being raffled off at the Fawn Creek Arts and Crafts Fair.

Miss Skitter also introduced Alan Bromwell to organic gardening, Lucille Kauffman to romance novels, and Khalid Balthazaar to Sir Arthur Conan Doyle.

"Perhaps you would like to read a Nancy Drew novel?" the Fawn Creek librarian had once suggested to Meredith Bly.

"I've already read all of them. Twice."

"Do you like to read mysteries?"

"I think they're stupendous, Miss Skitter. But I like to read everything. Don't you?"

"Oh, *yes,* Meredith," Olivia Skitter had responded breathlessly. And that thing inside her that was always poised to bolt like a startled fawn hesitated for a few seconds before she added, "I do *so* love books!"

Although in many ways, Annie Bly and the Fawn Creek librarian had the same message for Meredith, their methods of delivery were as different as those of Moses and the mailman.

"Stop what you're doing instantly and read this," Annie Bly would command, thrusting forth a novel as though the words had been typeset on two tablets by God himself. "You'll like it as much as I did."

And Annie would be right.

Miss Skitter's recommendations were delivered in a quieter and more cautionary manner, as if books were butterflies that had to be approached in silent awe, lest they hear you coming, lift off into the sky, and fly away.

Meredith felt that same reverent awe, not only for books, but about everything that she loved. Her parents; her Uncle Billy; her horse, Clementine; her rabbit, George; her hamster, Daisy; her dog, Murdock; the sunset over Wilkins Creek; the lilac bushes outside her bedroom window; the lavender growing under the evergreen tree. She felt that all of it was so precious, so perfect, so heart-rendingly lovely that if she even breathed too loudly it might shatter into a thousand pieces or dissolve like sugar cubes in a teapot—or like the books and butterflies, lift off into the sky and fly away.

It was this shared trepidation about approaching things they loved that drew young Meredith to Olivia Skitter, and it was why, despite the disparity in their ages, when Meredith had a problem too personal, too sensitive, and too terrible to discuss with her parents, she went to her librarian for help.

"Miss Skitter," she said the same Friday afternoon that Mrs. Candlestick had rhapsodized about ancestry, heritage, and family trees, "I would like to read some books about adoption."

Within five minutes, four books were stacked on the table in front of her. *How to Adopt a Baby, Adopting a Russian Infant, The Open Adoption Alternative* and *Should We Adopt a Special Needs Child?*

Meredith picked up each book. She read the title, perused the book flap, put it down, and went on to the next. When Miss Skitter saw her frowning, she offered cautiously, "The

Fawn Creek Library is part of the Four County Library System. If one of our other branches has a book that you think you'd like better, I can get it here for you tomorrow."

Meredith's intense brown eyes looked up hopefully. "Oh, could you, Miss Skitter? Could you please?"

SATURDAY MORNING found Meredith once again at the Fawn Creek Library. Piled high in front of her this time were books entitled *The Search for Who We Are, Unsealing Your Adoption Records, Finding your Birthright,* and *Tracking Down Our Biological Roots.* Instead of teaching the reader how to adopt, these books showed him how to pick at the fabric of adoption and unravel that which had been knit up by the efforts of ill-equipped mothers, childless couples, and the state.

As the eleven-year-old waded through chapter after chapter, her breath became shallow, her skin grew cold, and she became frightened. The sentences and ideas filling the books were so imbued with anger that they leaped off the page and clutched at her heart. Each book had been written by an adult who had once been put up for adoption, and all of the authors were mad. Mad at the world. Mad at the mothers who had given them up. Mad at the parents who had adopted them. Mad at the hospitals where they were born and where their records had been sealed. Mad at the government who had guaranteed their biological parents' privacy. Mad. Mad. Mad. Culminating in an implacable resolve to storm the Bastille of confidentiality and unlock records which would reveal the secret details of their birth.

Despite their undercurrent of rage, the books did, however, contain information. They were "How To" manuals on ways to obtain massive amounts of data by making a bewildering number of requests, using a variety of techniques, all of which were calculated to manipulate and overwhelm the bureaucrats to whom they were addressed. Among the forms suggested that an adoptee fill out and submit were: Request for Court Records, Request for Original Birth Certificate, Request for Amended Birth Certificate, Request for Hospital Records, Request for Basic Information from the State, Request for Waiver of Confidentiality, Request for Adoption Petition, Request for Adoption Decrees, and Request for Relinquishment Papers.

Meredith dropped her head into her folded arms on the table and sighed.

This, the librarian concluded, was unacceptable. It was obvious to her that the books the child was reading were either too complex or too unrelenting and that with every turn of the page she was becoming more disillusioned and defeated. Meredith needed concepts easy to grasp. And accumulating such easy-access information had been the purpose of Olivia Skitter's life. It was why, for the past twelve years, she had been coming into the library early in the morning and leaving late at night. It was why, she believed, she had been born.

In her own mind, Miss Skitter referred to the work she was doing as "The Project," because it had started as a simple project for stockpiling ephemeral, interesting, or amusing knowledge that, according to library policy, she could retain in no other way. It began with just a few three-cut manila folders stuck in the drawer of an old metal cabinet at the back of the library, where Miss Skitter ate her yogurt, three figs, and an apple for lunch.

The library's board of trustees had dictated that the magazines that the library subscribed to be maintained for general circulation for a period not to exceed six months; after that the librarian could dispose of them in any way she saw fit. Excluded from this rule were back issues of *National Geographic,* which were kept forever.

Before Miss Skitter was assigned to the job, old copies of *Good Housekeeping, The Rifleman, Redbook, U.S. News and World Report, Time, Popular Mechanics, People, Science Digest* and *Psychology Today* were left in a carton outside the ladies room, under a sign that said TAKE ME. After Miss Skitter began The Project, the carton disappeared, and the magazines were either donated to local old people's homes or trashed, depending on how many of them were left.

Miss Skitter tore out articles on using deer repellants, cleaning oriental carpets, purchasing a handgun, making herbal remedies for arthritis, and setting up a home office. She saved articles on alcoholism, agoraphobia, serial killers, the uses of sunflower seeds, and classical ballet, with extensive folders dedicated exclusively to British prima ballerinas. She had a particular affinity toward dead celebrities and never missed the obituaries of movie stars, opera singers, authors, and Nobel Prize winners. She had clipped out numerous articles on the negative effects of dumping the mentally ill into the general population and had equally large files on the pros and cons of the death penalty, solar energy, Hong Kong under the Red Chinese, the history of the Baseball Hall of Fame, and Dutch Elm Disease. Crafts occupied a not insignificant place in Miss Skitter's spinster heart, and one entire file drawer was dedicated to making Halloween, Christmas, and Valentine's Day decorations.

In deference to the local population, Miss Skitter had salvaged articles on hunting quail, crocheting afghans, and preserving jams, jellies, and tomatoes. She had cut out recipes for making a tantalizing assortment of pies, including apple, blueberry, pecan, and pumpkin. There were articles on digging wells, installing a septic system, and getting rid of gypsy moths, ant hills, bee hives, wasp nests, hedgehogs, and moles. Of local interest, Miss Skitter had kept every article written in every newspaper that recorded the fight against Albany when, under Mario Cuomo, the state attempted to locate a radioactive nuclear waste dump in Chenango County.

Also included in her file cabinets, two of which were situated on either side of the library's front windows—which explained why she was so often seen darting back and forth between them at night—were articles on volcanic eruptions, tidal waves, mud slides, icebergs, divorce, suicide, matricide, filicide, child abuse, prison reform, mood-altering chemicals, drug rehabilitation, sexual dysfunction, abortion, the Ku Klux Klan, counterfeit money, immigration, bilingual education, digital photography, the history of glass-making, and . . . adoption.

About a year before Meredith first displayed an interest in the subject, adoption was all the media rage. In women's magazines and national periodicals, as well as on radio and television, a fierce debate was generated on whether adoption records should remain sealed, as they had been for over fifty years, or if they should be opened to anyone who claimed to have a verifiable interest in their contents. The debate became even more heated when television's most popular talk-show host, who claimed to have been adopted herself, started to sponsor reunions between adults who had been put up for adoption as children and the women who fifteen, twenty, thirty, or forty years before had given those children away.

One organization, not a government agency and thus able to bypass the bureaucratic entanglements that had so intimidated Meredith in the books she had read, was surprisingly successful in locating parents and children. Its name was Point de Reunion, it had been founded by a Frenchman and because of the talk-show reunions that it had staged, coverage on the agency was profuse.

These were the articles that Miss Skitter had saved and given to Meredith.

These were the articles Meredith devoured. Articles about the way Point de Reunion worked, the simplicity of its application process, the lack of fees, and the ease with which an adoptee got results. According to the words on the pages—and words don't lie, do they?—all an adoptee on the prowl for her biological progenitor had to do was write a letter giving his or her sex, birth date, the name and location of the hospital where she were born, the name of her adoptive family, where they were living when the adoption occurred, where the applicant is living now, and so on. Presumably, the parent at the other end of the microscope, the one who had given up the child and was also on the hunt, could do the same, but with the opposite set of information. She would write when and where she had given birth, the name of the hospital, the name of the agency to which the child had been relinquished, and so on.

The letters would be received at Point de Reunion, all of the facts would be fed into a gigantic data bank, a search would be instituted, and quite often, a BINGO would occur. Sometimes within hours. Sometimes within weeks. Sometimes over a period of years, depending on when the adoptee sent her letter, when her biological parent did the same, how much verifiable data was included in each one, and if a sufficient number of those facts were present to make a match.

Included in the articles that Meredith read were bits and pieces quoted from letters written by grateful applicants to the organization that had served them so well.

Dear Point de Reunion,
    All of my life, I have been longing to find my roots
and learn who I really am. When I registered with you, I
had little hope of ever finding...

Dear Point de Reunion,
    After searching unsuccessfully for my own mother
for over twelve years, I contacted your agency and...

Dear Point de Reunion,
    Imagine my joy when after only six days, a match
was made...

Dear Point de Reunion,
    Finally I know where I got my eyes, my curly hair,
and even the freckles I'd always hated but now love,
because in them I see my real mother's face...

Dear Point de Reunion,
    My mother was searching for me too. Now that I
know where I came from, I finally know who I am...

Not stated in the articles Meredith read, perhaps because
none of their authors had envisioned them being read by
an eleven-year-old child, was that if an applicant was under
eighteen years of age, the whole process broke down. Yes,
the letters would be kept on file. And yes, the parent would
be permitted to register, to receive the Point de Reunion
newsletter, and go to the Point de Reunion meetings. But
that was it. Until the child reached maturity, no matches
would be made.

Meredith, however, did not know that. She borrowed a
sheet of paper, an envelope, and a stamp from Miss Skitter,
wrote to Point de Reunion, and dropped the letter in the mail
slot in the center hall, between the library annex and the

Fawn Creek municipal building. Before she left the library that afternoon, she asked the librarian, "May I take this article home with me? Just for a day or two? Please?"

"Take it and keep it, Meredith," Miss Skitter nodded, pointing to a jumble of magazines that she had not gone through yet. "There's more where that came from."

And that was why on Sunday morning, when Annie Bly was in her daughter's bedroom putting away a stack of freshly laundered T-shirts, she saw pages torn from a magazine on top of her daughter's bureau. The article was lying face-up, audacious and unfolded, between the moonfaced clock Meredith's Wyoming grandparents had given her for her eighth birthday and a snow globe her Florida grandparents gave her for Christmas. It was lying exactly where she knew that her mother or her father couldn't fail to see it.

The title of the article was "Finding Your Real Parents: No More Hide and Seek."

chapter 25

"WELL, MERRY, it's like this," Annie began with the enthusiasm of one who was about to stick a wet finger into an electrical socket, "we can...can..." But with each consecutive syllable her voice lost more impetus, "We can look...at... the...problem...from...the...perspective of..." until, with apparently nothing left to say, she drifted to the stove, picked up the kettle, filled it with cold water, brought it back to the stove, and turned on the gas.

"Anyone for hot chocolate?" she finally asked.

"I'll have a cup," Sebastian volunteered in a miserable monotone.

"Me, too. Thank you," Meredith barely whispered.

Nobody was smiling. Nobody added any words to the halo of gloom hovering over the table. Annie fussed with the chocolate tin. Sebastian buttoned and unbuttoned the top button of his shirt. Meredith sat in her chair as stiff as the bristles of a broom.

It was Sunday afternoon.

Two hours had passed since Annie had read the article that had been left, both innocently and confrontationally, in her daughter's bedroom. First she read it quickly to herself. Then she woke up her husband, sat on the edge of the bed, and read it to him while he rubbed the sleep out of his eyes. Sebastian had been up all night tracking a bank robber who had killed a teller, a guard and a state trooper, and he hadn't gotten to bed until eight o'clock Sunday morning. He had gotten only three hours of sleep when he felt his shoulders being shaken, and he heard an urgent whisper prodding him back to consciousness. "I'm so sorry, sweetheart," Annie said softly, kissing his forehead, his eyes, and his nose while continuing to jostle his shoulders, "but we have this little, tiny crisis that's about to destroy our daughter's life, and you have to wake up."

Half an hour later, mother, father, and child were seated at the kitchen table, drinking hot chocolate and listening to Merry describe her encounter with *The Little House on the Prairie* and Mrs. Candlestick's hideous outcropping of ancestors and family trees. With a please-forgive-me look in her eyes, Merry explained that she had gone to the library to research adoption, and she ended by reciting the words that she had unconsciously memorized from the letters to Point de Reunion she had read, "I need to know where I came from before I can know who I really am."

Annie pushed aside her hot chocolate mug, pushed her chair away from the table, crossed one silk pajama-clad leg over the other, and said, "You see, darling, it's like this."

And she began to talk about threads.

"We human beings are all different. We look different, we have different abilities, different senses of humor, different personalities, hopes, and aspirations. Some humans, like me, are inherently charming and simply can't help stopping traffic with our *je ne sais quoi.* Some, like your father, are plain and simple heroes, even though they themselves are completely oblivious to that fact. Some, like you, are brave and innocent children, hungry for knowledge and blissfully unafraid of what you might find out. Then, there are the others. The geniuses, bores, crooks, madmen, hypochondriacs, crusaders, explorers, innovators, leeches, ruminators, and rapscallions. And all of us, Merry, all were imbued with certain characteristics intrinsic to our being. These might include our intelligence, agility, eyesight, skin color, liver size, hair texture, bone density, and temperament—attributes with which we are born. They, my child, are the threads."

Annie leaned forward and cupped Merry's face in her hand. She waited for her daughter to lift her head, to nod, to make eye contact or to indicate somehow that a brain was still functioning under that luminous tangle of bright orange hair. But Meredith would not look up. Her eyes moved to the kitchen table, to the chocolate congealing at the top of her cup, to her shoes. Anywhere but to her mother's eyes.

Annie dropped her hand to her lap and recrossed her legs.

Sebastian looked at her, an uneasy question in his eyes. "Threads, Annie? Threads?"

But she ignored him and continued. "The raw material from which thread is made can come from plants and animals—like flax, wool, angora, mohair, cashmere, or cotton. Or the thread can be man-made from nylon, rayon, Dacron, polyester, or spandex." Annie flipped up the bottom hem of her pajama top, pulled at a loose thread, yanked it out, and held it up. "Depending on how these strands are combined, braided, twisted, coiled, crimped, or curled, they are transformed into single yarns, ply yarns, cord yarns, novelty yarns, or textured yarns. In turn, these yarns become the fabrics with which we are familiar, such as burlap, damask, felt, chiffon, taffeta, satin, and lace."

Annie reached for her daughter's hand, opened it, and placed the single strand of thread on Meredith's palm. Instead of closing her hand around it, the child tipped her palm and watched it drop to the floor.

"Merry, look at me." Annie said, her voice a maternal imperative. "Stop fighting for a second and look into my eyes. What I'm telling you is a principle for living. It's axiomatic and necessary to your survival. I'm saying that after the warping, the wefting, the weaving, and the braiding, after *life* happens to us, what we become is a million light years away from the raw material out of which we were made.

"Think, Merry, of a cotton field in ... Oh, hell. I don't know. Sebastian, where does cotton grow?"

"Mississippi."

"Okay. You're a scruffy wad of cotton on some sharecropper's farm in Mississippi. A few feet away from you is another scruffy wad. That second unlucky wad is shipped to Oklahoma where it's made into coarse thread, woven into rough yarn, and turned into a cheap bath towel for a girl's reformatory in Tulsa. You, on the other hand, are shipped to a fancy schmancy textile mill in upstate New York, where you're made into a smooth, lightly twisted yarn which is then woven into a luxurious, satiny fabric. That fabric is shipped to a couture designer in Manhattan, where you are cut, hemmed, trimmed, and basted so that by the time you're finished, you can be worn by Prudence Pouty Lips to the Academy Awards.

"Meanwhile, the clump of cotton that grew up next to you, who in its natural state was neither a better nor a worse clump of cotton that you were, is wiping bugs off windshields at the exit from the Williamsburg Bridge.

"What I'm trying to say, Merry, is that your genetic heritage, your gene pool, your whatever you want to call it, is only so much raw material, and it has no more to do with what you will eventually become than do all of those puffs of cotton on that sharecropper's farm in Mississippi.

"Your basic biology—your eyes, nose, skin, hair and maybe even bits and pieces of your disposition—make up the thread. But unlike a wad of cotton or a hank of mohair, we can make choices. We are people. We are human beings. We grow, develop, and take control. We make our own yarn, weave our own fabrics, and become the stylists, publicists, and designers of our own destinies. We are so much more than just the specific thread of DNA from which our souls evolved on the day that we were born."

Annie reached for her daughter's hands. At that moment, Merry's hair was unruly, her head was bent, and she was emanating an aura of obstinacy, none of which suggested satin, luxury, or something that one would wear to the Academy Awards.

Merry looked like a lump.

A lump of marmalade.

"Darling," Annie said softly.

No response.

"Will you please look at me?"

Meredith lifted her head. She did not, however, lift her eyes.

"Say something, Merry."

She mumbled something.

"Louder. Your father and I didn't hear."

The child finally raised her head. "Mommy." Her huge brown eyes were tearful and unfathomably sad. "Daddy." She turned those same soulful eyes to her father. "I *have* to know where I came from. I *have* to know who I really am."

Annie took a deep breath. "Merry, didn't you listen to a single word I said?"

But instead of answering, Meredith Bly thrust her hands across the kitchen table and, as though groping for a lifeline through a sea of pain, she implored, "Please."

chapter 26

THE SPRING BEFORE Meredith Bly's eleventh birthday, an epidemic of adolescent suicides swept the country. Alert parents shivered when they contemplated the tragedy of these young people's lost lives and shivered again when they looked at their own vulnerable children.

A fourteen-year-old boy and a twelve-year-old girl hanged themselves in the attic of the boy's parents' home. The note they left behind said that nobody had understood their love, and since they couldn't stand the agony of separation, they had chosen to die together rather than to live apart.

A fifteen-year-old boy stole his grandfather's car during the Christmas break. Going straight on a stretch of road that led to the local beach, he crashed the car at 120 miles an hour into the base of a brick lighthouse and died instantly. He had skipped three grades in grammar school, gotten As in every class in high school, and entered Yale on an early-admittance scholarship. He had been an honor student, the assistant editor of the school newspaper, the vice chairman of the yearbook committee, and the star of the varsity tennis team. The note he left behind for his parents said only, "I'm sorry that I let you down."

A thirteen-year-old girl, two fourteen-year-old girls, and a sixteen-year-old boy killed themselves at sunrise on the first day of spring. Their bodies were found in the gazebo behind their school's soccer field. They had ingested a combination of barbiturates which they had read about in a book called *Silent Ascent.* The book was written by a self-styled messiah, and its thesis was that suicide is a means of attaining a deeper connection with reality and a higher state of consciousness. The boy, who previously had belonged to a witch's coven and before that had been arrested for painting swastikas on graves in Jewish cemeteries, had stolen the drugs from his uncle's pharmacy.

A seventeen-year-old boy whose father was a deputy sheriff invited a sixteen-year-old girl to the high school prom. After she turned him down, he stole his father's gun, pedaled his bicycle to the girl's house, climbed the tree outside her bedroom, and called out her name. When she came to the window, he jammed the barrel of the revolver against his forehead and pulled the trigger.

Children everywhere in the United States, mostly from middle-class to upper-middle-class backgrounds, were killing themselves at an alarming rate. Frantic school boards and cautious principals were hiring trained psychologists to teach parents and teachers how to recognized warning signs. Articles and books were being written. Interviews with experts were being sought and granted. Dead children were turning into social icons, and it was feared that suicide, already epidemic, was also becoming contagious. *Stay alive and you are punished if you fail algebra or get drunk and throw up on the rug. Kill yourself and you are the recipient of unrelenting sympathy, uncritical celebrity, and spotlight-grabbing grief.*

"For the sensitive girl or boy," wrote one very sad and very sincere pediatrician in an article for a small South Dakota medical journal, "childhood is a constant assault of imperatives, might-have-beens, and missed opportunities. An incident as trivial as an unzipped fly about which he is teased can create in a boy a foreboding about his future as great as the announcement of the beginning of World War III. A flunked test, a disparaging remark from a teacher, a dress purchased in the wrong style or worn on the wrong occasion, are disasters of titanic proportions to teens and preteens. All can create grievous mortifications that break small hearts, pierce thin skins, and loom in the adolescent mind like ravenous monsters eager to devour fragile egos as if they were sugar-coated Christmas treats."

IT WAS SUNDAY AFTERNOON. Annie had finished her solemn dissertation on thread, yarn, cotton, silk, genetics, heredity, and DNA. She was tired of touting the wild and wooly benefits of self-determination and certain that she had failed to talk her daughter out of the quest to attach twigs, leaves, and branches to her own godforsaken family tree. She, her husband, and her child were still seated at the kitchen table. Meredith was staring down at her hands. Sebastian was staring up at the ceiling, and Annie was staring at the two of them. Suddenly she took a deep breath, rose to her feet, and said, "To hell with this. Let's go to the movies."

Sebastian nodded and stood up. "I'm game." He touched Merry's shoulder. "Sweetie, get your coat."

Merry sat as still as a stone.

"Darling girl-child," Annie said and took a step forward. She kneeled and studied her daughter's face. Meredith was scowling, her brows, eyes, and nose scrunched together like a tightly pulled cord on a laundry bag. Annie's eyes narrowed, her voice lowered, and she scowled right back. "Coat," she said relentlessly. "Now."

Meredith finally looked up.

"But I don't *want* to go."

Annie turned to Sebastian. Sebastian turned to Annie. Their eyes met. They exchanged a silent signal. Then both parents looked down at their daughter and at the same time said, "Tough."

chapter **27**

A WEEK LATER Annie packed Meredith's tennis shoes, sun screen, and bathing suits, and sent her to visit Sebastian's parents—who Meredith had suddenly decided weren't her grandparents anymore because a graft from another plant does not legitimately constitute a branch of a family tree.

"Well boo hoo," Annie said. "You're going anyway."

In the car on the way back from the airport, she and Sebastian mapped out the rest of their strategy for dealing with what they referred to as "Identity Crisis 101." Step one, which had taken nothing more than a quick phone call to Florida, was to send Merry to Orlando for a long weekend of meals eaten on paper napkins and giddy rides in rotating tea cups. Step two involved drawing Uncle Billy into the proceedings, so that they could more expeditiously take advantage of the time they had bought in step one.

Instead of driving back to Fawn Creek, Annie and Sebastian settled into their Manhattan apartment and called Billy Nightingale on the phone.

"Come down to my place," Billy said. "Bring a bottle of wine, I'll order a pizza, and we'll get this show on the road."

IN THE DECADE SINCE finding Merry under the stairs at the ugly house, Billy Nightingale's face had thinned out and his jaw had become as square as that of a comic-strip hero. He had an easy smile, an easy laugh, hair the silvery blond of corn tassels, and eyes as blue as a mountain lake reflecting a Wyoming sky on a perfect spring day. He had occupied the same garden apartment on East Eighty-fourth Street, a floor below Annie and Sebastian, for most of the ten years that he had lived in New York.

Billy was thirty-four years old, unmarried, and had been a supervising fire marshal for just under one year.

As a supervisor, it was his job to turn the neophytes assigned to his squad from firefighters into fire marshals, a task for which there were no guidelines, since most supervisors just partnered new marshals with veterans and hoped that something in the way of knowledge and experience would migrate from one side of the squad car to the other.

This haphazard approach did not appeal to Billy. He trained and drilled his men as if they were pivotal members in an antiterrorist team. He taught them what to look for at a fire scene; he set up hypothetical scenarios with vanity fire setters, revenge fire setters, and paid arsonists; he taught his squad how to follow a suspect, what to do if they caught one, how to identify a pyromaniac, how to investigate a business fraud fire, how to interrogate a perpetrator, and how to interview a witness. He brought his men to the firing range and taught them target and combat shooting. He imparted to them everything he knew about discovering the origin and cause of a fire and never let them forget that bad guys are dangerous because they do bad things.

He loved being a fire marshal, and he loved keeping it simple.

His men respected his know-how, his standards, and his sense of humor. He was funny. He was kind. He was cynical; he distrusted politicians, bureaucrats, bosses, cops, and FBI agents. He was a romantic; he opened doors for all women, even the ugly ones. He knew the lyrics to every song written by George and Ira Gershwin and sang numbers from Comden and Green musicals in the shower. He rarely dated. He had embarked on a few love affairs over the years, but only one had lasted more than three months.

Billy Nightingale had never said "I love you" to a woman and long ago had concluded that he probably never would.

"I figure there's only so much luck in life," he told his sister. "Lucky at work or lucky at love. I got lucky at work."

"Silly Billy," Annie responded. "You're a Nightingale. We larger-than-life types always fall madly in love. Be patient. You'll meet the right woman someday, and if you're a good boy, I'm sure that she'll be almost as magnificent as *moi*."

THE NIGHT THEY DECIDED to deal with Merry's identity crisis, Billy was sitting on the floor of his living room with his back to a dwindling blaze in the fireplace. He had a piece of pizza in one hand; his other hand was resting casually on his knee. Sebastian was sitting in an armchair opposite him. Annie, also on the floor, was in almost the exact same position as Billy, with her back resting against Sebastian's knees.

Brother and sister. Husband and wife. Two parents. One

uncle. All loved each other and all loved the little orange-haired girl that they had rescued. All believed that unless they could quickly build a bridge across it or turn her in an opposite direction, the road ahead for Merry was paved with razor wire and serpent's teeth.

"Hypothesis," Annie said, sipping wine. "I am eleven years old, and I want to know everything about my sperm and egg donors. I want to know what they look like. How they met. Who they turned out to be. Does that make sense to either of you?"

"No," Billy reached over to refill his sister's glass. "If I had parents like you and thought it would upset the applecart, I wouldn't even ask which solar system I came from."

"But Merry isn't you, and she isn't me. She's not the least little bit like either of us, Billy. We're brash; she's reserved. We're tactless; she's intuitive, sweet, and kind. There's something fragile and fine about her."

"Don't forget mule-headed. She's obstinate, too."

"Okay, obstinate. But that isn't the point." Annie pushed aside the pizza box and placed her wineglass on the coffee table. "The point is that Merry is a sensitive eleven-year-old girl who has just decided that she must, emphasis on *must*, know who her biological parents are, which brings me to the question of why she's so . . . so . . ."

"Obsessed?" Billy suggested.

". . . with this whole heredity and roots thing. Why such passion? Why such desperation if all of this 'from whence we came' stuff doesn't matter anyway?" Annie craned her head to look up at her husband. "We're agreed on that, aren't we? That if a beautiful princess saunters out of a nauseating swamp, it isn't the swamp that matters. It's the princess. Right?"

"Right," Sebastian said.

"Wrong," Billy tossed the uneaten crust of his pizza back

into the box. "It shouldn't matter, and the world would be a happier place if it didn't matter. But it does."

"To whom?"

"To her."

"But why?" Annie lamented. "Why? Why? Why?"

Billy shifted so that he was sitting face-to-face with his sister. "Remember when we were kids, and we had to walk a balance beam in gym class?"

"No."

"Well, I do. And the secret to walking one is that you have to believe you can do it. It's that simple. As soon as you start to doubt yourself, you fall off."

"So?"

"So that's the way it is with Merry. Where she came from matters to her because she thinks that it matters. Since she doesn't believe in herself, she's falling off the balance beam. And she'll keep on falling until she believes that she isn't falling anymore."

Sebastian snorted and pointed an accusing finger at his brother-in-law. "What makes you such an expert on eleven-year-old girls?"

"I'm not. But I know Merry."

"I'm her father. I live with her. I know her, too."

"I saw her first. I found her under the stairs in that crawl space. That counts for something."

"But I adopted her."

"Yeah. Yeah. Right. Right." Annie held up her hand like a crossing guard. "You're both Sir Galahad, and each of you saved her from a different fire-breathing dragon. Congratulations and big deal. What else, Billy?"

"Nothing else. If you're walking a tightrope, and you think you're going to fall, you will fall. If you have to take a math test, and you're sure you're going to dump it, it doesn't matter if you were up all night studying, you are going to dump that test. The same thing applies to life. If you've made up your mind that your fate is locked into your biology and that all you are is the Manifest Destiny of your DNA, then you will be."

Annie tapped her fingers impatiently against her knee-cap. "And your point is?"

"That it's all about suggestibility. The same thing that makes first-year medical students think they've got whichever diseases they're studying. Chapter one deals with cancer; they think they have tumors growing on their lungs. Chapter two describes muscular dystrophy; they start tripping and dropping things. Just like Marmalade. If, in chapter one of the 'Who Am I?' course she's taking, she finds out that her biological mother was a nuclear physicist, Merry will believe she's destined to become a nuclear physicist or a biochemist. If it suggests her mother was in the arts, she'll be convinced that when she grows up, she's going to be a painter or a honky-tonk piano player in a bar."

Annie leaned toward Billy, an anxious expression on her face.

"And if her mother committed suicide?"

"From that moment on, Merry would be terrified that someday she is going to stick her head in an oven and turn on the gas."

"What if our hypothetical eleven-year-old found out that mommy was an arsonist and murderess and that daddy, at best, was an oblivious and coconspiratorial jerk? What would happen to a sensitive, sweet, loving child who is also head-strong, impressionable, and wired way, way too tight? How would she respond if she found out about her real family tree?"

"She would think she was the fruit of a poisoned tree," Billy said somberly.

"And knowing Merry," Sebastian added, "she would also believe that the poison was inside her and that somehow it was all her fault."

Nobody spoke for a long moment. Sebastian reached down and took his wife's hand.

"Damn, damn, damn," Annie muttered.

Billy dug back into the pizza box and pulled out a discarded piece of crust. He chewed on it meditatively for a few seconds. "I just thought of something."

Annie leaned forward eagerly.

"How about if," he tossed the crust into the fireplace. "Instead of letting events unfold as a logical progression of the disaster Marmalade has just set in motion, we engage in some sleight of hand, so the poor kid won't have to go to sleep every night wondering if someday she's going to grow up to kill her own kids?"

"What do you mean?" Sebastian asked darkly.

"I mean that when reality isn't all that it's cut out to be, and your family tree turns out to have homicidal roots, it might be advisable to switch trees."

"I know where you're going with this," Annie grinned. "And I like it, Billy. I like it."

Sebastian, however, held up a wary hand.

"Well, I don't. I don't like lying to Merry. What if she found out?"

"Found out what?"

"Who her real mother is?"

"I'm her real mother."

"I mean her biological mother."

"You mean Edith Tuttle?"

"Yep."

"Exactly when do you think Merry would find this out? When she's eighteen? When she's twenty-one? When she's sixty?"

"Hell, Annie," Sebastian shrugged. "I don't know."

"Neither do I. But I do know that if it takes a lie to get Merry past the brain-addling, self-confidence eroding, and suicide-inducing morass of adolescence, I want to take a chance. If the lie sticks, then hallelujah to us. If she finds out that we're liars anytime before she's knitting booties for her great-grandchildren, then she can curse us, hate us, disown us, call us abductors, kidnappers, body snatchers, and thieves, but it won't matter, because we'll have bought her time."

"Time for what?"

"Time to grow up. Time to have the childhood that, if we don't do what my brilliant brother suggests, Merry is already too close to losing."

Sebastian crossed his arms over his chest.

"I don't think happiness can be bought with a lie," he said glumly.

"Well, darling. Since nothing but grief can come from the truth, not only do I vote for lying, I vote for a lie with long enough legs to do high kicks at Rockefeller Center." Annie held out her wine glass. "So fill 'er up boys. It's going to be a long night and we've got a lot of work to do."

chapter 28

BY 11 PM, two empty and one half-filled Chianti bottles stood on the coffee table amid a clutter of empty plates and wine glasses. Annie sat on the floor, her legs folded Indian style, a legal pad on her lap and a pencil in her hand. She read aloud from her notes.

"This is what we've decided so far. One, Merry's mother was twenty years old when Merry was born."

"You decided that," Billy said. "I think she should be eighteen."

"Why?"

"Younger is more tragic. Boys Merry's age love gore; girls her age love tragedy."

Annie tapped the eraser of her pencil against the pad. "You're right. Romeo and Juliet. Cyrano de Bergerac and Roxanne. Healthcliff and Cathy. Popeye and Olive Oyl. They were all eighteen."

"Popeye was thirty-eight, going on forty," Sebastian said ponderously. It took very little wine to make him ponderous.

"Scratch Popeye," Annie nodded. "Scratch math, and thank you for your contribution. Merry's mother will be eighteen. How old shall we make dear old dad?"

"Eighteen," Billy said again.

"Why?"

"Why not?"

"I'm sold. Sebastian?"

He patted Annie on the head. "I'll let you know if anything strikes me wrong."

"Bless you for entering into the spirit of the thing, Sebastian, even though you disapprove."

"I disapprove of income taxes, too. But I still pay them by April seventeenth."

"Fifteenth, but who's counting." Annie took his hand off her head, kissed it, repositioned it on his knee, and turned to Billy. "What's next?"

"A profession. A vocation. A job."

"Right. Right. Right." Annie's eyes shined excitedly. "They should do something brilliant. Something exemplary. Something patriotic and sublime. But what?" She stared blindly at the ceiling. "What did Merry's mother do? What was Merry's father's occupation?"

Billy held up his hand. "Shush. It's coming to me. It's coming . . ." He leaned forward and snapped his fingers. "I've got it!"

"Got what?"

"How we're going about this."

"How *are* we going about it?"

"Wrong."

"Why?"

"Because we shouldn't be talking about Merry's parents now, we should be focusing on Merry. Once we figure out what we want her to be when she grows up, we can work backward and concoct a mother and father. So, what do we want Merry to be?"

"Happy," Annie said.

"Happy," Sebastian said.

"What makes her happy?"

"You do, Billy. She adores you."

"Smart girl. What else? Word association game. Off the top of your head. I say, 'Merry' and you say . . ."

"Clementine. Her horse."

"Would she want to be an equestrian when she grows up?"

"She hates horse shows."

"A veterinarian?"

"No."

"A stable boy?"

"Billy!"

"Forget horses. What else does she like?"

"Swimming."

"Laps? Relay races? Competition? Olympics?"

"Somersaults, handstands, and diving for pretty rocks in the creek."

"Keep it coming," Billy made a beckoning gesture with his hands. "I say, 'hot'; you say, 'cold'. I say, 'blue'; you say 'sky'. I say, 'potato'; you say 'potaaato'. Merry likes to . . ."

"Pick wild flowers," Annie said.

"Catch butterflies and let them go," Sebastian added.

"She likes to climb trees."

"Wax the car."

"Read, read, read. Merry loves books. Hey, Billy, that's an idea. We could make Merry's mother a writer. A poet. A wounded, tremulous, talented and misunderstood poet who . . .

"Nope," Sebastian said.

"Why 'nope'?"

"Think about it a second, Annie. Merry is a soul-searcher."

"Right."

"And she's solitary."

"Yes. True. A very independent child. If we didn't force her to have friends, she would probably just sit around all day watching the hanging crystals in her bedroom make rainbows against the wall."

"That's my point. Do you think it's smart to encourage an introspective kid to spend a lot of hours by herself, writing poetry, and..."

Annie looked speculatively at her husband. "You are so smart. And you are so right. Scratch poet. Scratch writer. What next?"

A pensive silence ensued.

Sebastian said, "Merry likes the theater."

"Right," Annie nodded. "She loves musical comedies, and she loves to sing.

"She could be a singer."

"No, Billy. She has a terrible voice."

"Croaks like a frog," Sebastian agreed.

More silence. Longer this time. Then Billy said, "Doesn't Merry take trampoline lessons or something?"

"Twice a week. And it's gymnastics, not trampoline. Her teacher said that if she had competitive instincts, which she doesn't, she could be world class."

"No killer instincts?" Billy stood up.

"Merry shows us her letter tiles when we're playing scrabble, and when she and her friends are running a race, she waits for them to catch up."

"But her gymnastics teacher thinks she's good?"

"Merry is the best student he's ever had on floor work."

"What's floor work?"

"Tumbling. Leaping. Cartwheels. Handstands. Doing impossible things gracefully."

"To music?"

"Yes, indeedy," Annie said. "Merry rolls up the carpets, pushes aside all the furniture, and makes the living room into a stage. She plays album after album from Broadway shows and gets so lost in the movements she's making that it takes our breath away."

"In other words, and for the sake of this conversation, what you're telling me is that Merry likes to dance."

"Not 'likes.' Loves. The only time she ever lives up to her name and really is merry, as in merriment, is when she's dancing."

"Does she take dancing lessons?"

"Nooooo," Annie said slowly. Then she turned to Sebastian. "Idiots! Of course she should be taking dance lessons. What were we thinking? Or not thinking is more to the point."

"Does Merry have the discipline to become a dancer?" Billy continued. "I'm not talking about the rest of her life here. Just the next few years."

"I've seen Merry not in the mood to read, not in the mood to swim, ride Clementine, or play tennis," Sebastian said firmly. "But when the music is playing, I've never seen her not in the mood to dance."

"She's passionate about the ballet," Annie added. "I once asked her what she wanted to be when she grows up, and she answered 'Aurora.'"

"Who's Aurora?"

"The princess is Tchaikovsky's *Sleeping Beauty*."

"Aurora, huh?" Billy took the legal pad off his sister's lap and the pencil out of her hand. He wrote in big letters across the top of the page:

MERRY'S MOTHER WAS A BALLERINA.

Annie looked down at the pad.

"Should we make her father a dancer, too?"

"Hell, no," Sebastian blustered. "No kid of mine is going to have a father who prances around on stage like a fairy in tights."

Billy gave Sebastian an encouraging thumbs up. "No tights." Billy agreed. "No prancing."

"But it's so romantic!"

"Romantic is a regular guy with pants on who can plaster a wall and change a spark plug."

"And spit," Billy said, scratching an armpit to make sure that Annie got the point. "Why don't we make him a cab driver?"

"A cab driver," Annie sniffed disdainfully.

"Yeah. A cab driver who's really a playwright. He wants to write the great America drama. Maybe, someday, one of his plays will be turned into a ballet, and what's her name will dance in it."

"What *is* her name?"

"We'll figure that out later."

"Are the ballerina and the cabbie married, or do we want them to be star-crossed lovers?"

"Married," Sebastian said firmly. "Merry's stars are crossed enough without adding to the mess. Her parents stood in front of a judge and got that piece of paper. This is nonnegotiable."

"Okay. Okay."

Billy stared into the fireplace, as though seeking inspiration from the flames. Then, abruptly, he turned his head and announced, "She's Russian."

"What?"

"She's a Russian ballerina. The year is nineteen eighty-something; the USSR is stockpiling nuclear weapons, and the wall between East and West Berlin hasn't come down yet. But every once in a while, both sides of the Cold War pretend that some sort of artsy-fartsy cooperation is possible, and our people go to Moscow, and the Soviets send a few circuses and symphonies here."

"I saw the Bolshoi Ballet dance *The Stone Flower* when I was a kid," Annie said dreamily. "It was gorgeous."

"The Bolshoi Ballet," Billy considered. "I like it. It sounds legitimate."

"It *is* legitimate."

"Good." Billy leaned against the fireplace mantle. "Because I'm all out of brilliant ideas." He smiled at his sister. "From now on, it's up to you."

"Challenge accepted," Annie bowed her head. "Do either of you mind if I make Merry's mother very, very young when she comes to the United States?"

"How young?"

"Barely seventeen. Talented enough to become a prima ballerina, but not yet. We want her to be young, gifted, and anonymous. If anybody has heard of her, it would complicate the story. She dances in the corps."

"What's a corps?"

"The corps de ballet. They're the foot soldiers of a dance company. Like a chorus line."

"Got it. Keep going."

"Okay. So, according to Billy, the Cold War has thawed and the Bolshoi is in New York City on a cultural exchange, which gives Merry's mother a perfect opportunity to defect. She hates the USSR. Hates its creative restrictions. Hates being spied on. Hates communism and has always wanted to come to America."

"Hoorah for Hollywood," Billy sang.

Annie ignored him, held out her wine glass, pointed to it, and tapped Sebastian's knee. He reached for the bottle of Chianti.

"Good husband," she said affectionately. "What else do you and Billy want to know about our little ballerina?"

"Does she speak English?"

"An endearing, adorable, lame duck sort of English."

"How does she meet Merry's father?"

"The entire Bolshoi Ballet Company was invited to a party."

"Where?"

"At the United Nations."

"I didn't know they threw parties."

"They do that night. And at the party, her ballet mistress..."

"What's a ballet mistress?"

"Part teacher, part trainer, and part spy for the Soviet secret police. Her name is Galina Oblenskaya, and on the night of the party at the U.N., she gets drunk and passes out on a chair next to the Vodka punch, if there is such a thing."

"Then what?"

"Then Merry's mother—we have to find a name for her—sneaks out of the party and defects to the United States."

"How?"

Annie got up, walked to the living room window overlooking Eighty-fourth Street and stared down at the traffic. She tapped a finger against her chin. "I'm thinking," she said, looking and sounding very much like her brother at that moment. When she turned back to the room a few seconds later, her eyes were bright with excitement. "She hails a cab and tells the cab driver to take her to the American Embassy."

"There is no American Embassy in America."

"Well," Annie scoffed. "Merry's mother doesn't know that."

"Does she have any money?"

"No. But she doesn't need any."

"How come?"

"Because the cab driver takes one look at her anguished, elfin face and falls madly in love."

"What's the cabbie's name?"

Annie tapped her jaw again. "It has to be a real American-sounding name, because this guy is going to become Merry's father." She turned a questioning glance toward her husband and brother.

At exactly the same instant, both men said, "Joe."

"Joe. Joe what?"

"Joe Smith," Billy said.

"Joe Jones," Sebastian suggested.

"Neither." Annie said smugly. "His name is Joe Brown."

chapter 29

THE YEARS BILLY SPENT fighting and investigating fires in Brooklyn had given him a working knowledge of where Russian immigrants dined, shopped, partied, courted, married, and lived. And where, when they were done eating, shopping, partying, dating, and marrying, they were buried after they died.

Annie, Sebastian, and Billy were in Sebastian's car, and Sebastian was driving.

"Turn right onto Ocean Parkway," Billy said from the back seat. "Right again before you get to the mausoleum. Okay. Go past the gate. Now pass the administration building. Slowly. Slowly. Good. Turn left here."

"Here" was the Washington Cemetery, located in the Borough Park section of Brooklyn. Bordered on one side by Ocean Parkway, on the other by Nineteenth Avenue, and bisected by McDonald Avenue, its entrance is across the street from the elevated subway on Bay Parkway.

That Sunday morning had begun with brunch at the St. Petersburg Diner in Brighton Beach, after which Billy took

Annie and Sebastian to the Black Sea Book Shop. This was a long, narrow, second-floor store where all of the customers were Russian, all of the books were written in the language of their youth, and all of the transactions were conducted behind a black curtain with change being made from a cigar box. Annie browsed through a shelf of old maps and worked herself around a table filled with over-priced CDs, before she sought out a sales clerk and, in a voice that could be heard at the back of the store, explained that she was writing a book about a young Russian ballerina and needed help on the logistics of the girl's living arrangements. Of particular interest, she said, was where the girl should get an apartment after she had defected to the United States.

A short, stocky woman eyed Annie speculatively for a few seconds after she emerged from behind a shelf filled with Dostoevsky novels. "Have your little refugee live on Ocean Parkway," she said in a deep, whisky voice with a heavy Russian accent. She had fiercely intelligent black eyes, wore a full-length mink coat, and had thick eyebrows that looked like woolly bears marching in single file across her forehead. "That is where most of us went."

Annie smiled down at the Russian. At less than five feet tall, the woman looked like a well turned-out troll.

"Where specifically on Ocean Parkway? I'm not from around here. I need an address."

"I lived at 363 Ocean Parkway. It had good windows. Nice parquet floors. Go look at it. You will see that I am right. Yes. Your little refugee should live there."

HALF AN HOUR LATER, Annie, Billy, and Sebastian were sitting on a bench on Ocean Parkway, manufacturing the background of an imaginary dancer who, over a decade earlier, had met and loved a playwright/taxi driver named Joe, lived with him for a short, happy time, and then died.

Two service roads run along either side of Ocean Parkway; between them are sidewalks with well-tended lawns and lush, leafy trees. Women push baby carriages up and down the walkways, while young couples stroll and old people sit on park benches to watch the world go by. Ocean Parkway itself is a wide esplanade reminiscent of the Champs-Elysées in Paris.

"It looks like a pointillist painting by Seurat," Annie said softly.

"Why are you whispering?"

"I'm afraid if I talk too loudly, I'll wake it up, and it will disappear."

"It *is* nice," Sebastian said.

Annie turned to her brother. "How could an obscure exiled Russian ballerina afford to live here? She's not famous. Just..."

"A chorus girl."

"She's a dancer in the corps." Annie arched an eyebrow. "*Not* a chorus girl."

Billy ignored his sister. "She can't afford it, but Joe Brown can."

"On an eighteen-year-old cab driver's salary?"

"Joe's Uncle Erwin," Billy explained patiently, "owned his own cab. He lived here for forty years with his wife, Sybil, who was a beautician. When Uncle Erwin and Aunt Sibyl died of botulism on a cruise, they left the medallion and the cab to young Joe. He moved into their rent-controlled apartment."

Annie stared admiringly at her brother. "You are getting really good at this."

"Yeah. Scary, isn't it?"

Sebastian jutted his head toward the building. "This is where Joe took the ballerina after she defected?"

"Uh huh."

"Was she happy here, Billy?" Annie asked. "I mean in America. With Joe?"

"I don't know. You tell me."

For a few seconds, Annie sat quietly, staring at the anonymous apartment building. Then she said, "All right. I will tell you." And she began to unravel the complicated past of a beautiful ballerina and the cab driver who loved her.

Here is their story.

Once upon a time, a still-unnamed girl, barely a young woman, defected to the United States. Although her defection would ordinarily have made headlines, it was relegated to page nowhere because Viktor Nikolayevsky, known as much for his incredible leaps as for his striking good looks and bizarre personality, sought political asylum on that very same day.

Within a week of Victor's defection, his aesthetic face and perfect body had appeared nude in a two-page spread in the magazine section of the *New York Times*. Another photographer caught him in a leap reminiscent of nothing that anyone had ever seen before, and that picture made the cover of *Time* magazine. Dozens of articles written about Victor Nikolayevsky during the first two months of his stay in New York conveyed his disdain for communism, his hatred of capitalism, and his belief that he had the God-given right to manipulate people for the greater aggrandisement of his ego and the promotion of his exceptional talent. He was wined, dined, fawned over, and feted; and his celebrity drew all of those people who otherwise would have harassed and hounded Joe Brown's obscure ballerina, leaving her, with the help of her faithful cab driver, pretty much to her own devices.

She found a teacher, Natalia Lenochka, and every day, without fail, she practiced, practiced, and practiced in "Madam Lenny's" dance studio above a bagel shop on Brighton Beach

Avenue. She did her battements, developpés, pirouettes, pliés, and fouettés. She worked daily at the barre in front of a mirror, evaluating herself against a standard to which Russians believed that only they were privy. Adagios, arabesques, entrechats, and when she was partnered in class with Alexis Ergorova, yet another Russian émigré, one exquisite pas de deux after another.

The dancers ate dance, talked dance, slept dance, and wept dance, which was why Joe Brown, who had always loved the theater, told them that he thought they should form their own dance company. It would be small, he suggested, and an agent Joe knew who also handled country western singers, jazz bands, and ventriloquists could represent them.

"Albany, Buffalo, Utica, Cassandra, Plattsburgh, Watertown, Binghamton, and Oneonta," the agent promised. "Monticello and Saratoga Springs during the racing season. And next year, if all goes well, maybe I can get you bookings in Connecticut, New Jersey, and Pennsylvania, too."

A modest start.

Joe Brown leased his cab to his cousin and retired from the taxi business so that he could manage the troupe. Joe was also the dance company's stage manager, sound man, lighting director, publicity agent, prop man, and set designer.

Natalia Lenochka, who had once toured with Alexandra Danilova in the Ballet Russe de Monte Carlo, remembered most of the choreography for all of the great roles that she had danced and what she didn't remember, she made up. Madam Lenny became the company's drill sergeant and muse, with five female and five male dancers under her artistic control, all of whom had romantic-sounding Russian names. Even Peggy Porter, born in Cleveland, Ohio, and about as Russian-looking as a Dallas cheerleader, had become became Vera Orlova by the time the stage bills were handed out.

Joe Brown bought a used airport shuttle bus, painted it peacock blue, filled it with props, audio equipment, costumes, and scenery and stenciled the words BALLET DE TERPSICHORE over the side door. He and his ballerina drove in the van. The rest of his shabby, happy, talented troupe traveled by train and bus from town to town, their performances always sold out, their reviews always good, and their success gratifying. But expenses were high. There was food to pay for, ads to purchase in the local newspapers, gas, insurance, train and bus fares, dry cleaning, and hotel bills. The dancers slept two in a room. Boys with boys and girls with girls, except for Madam Lenny, who slept alone, and Joe Brown who, being married, shared a room with the prima ballerina, his wife.

Salaries were negligible but, as Joe proudly exclaimed, "Nobody goes hungry, and if laughter were dollars, we'd all be billionaires."

Everyone, when he or she is very, very young and if she is very, very lucky, has one season in her life like the summer of the Ballet de Terpsichore, a summer where each evening an art deco moon is perfectly positioned in the sky. It's not too high, not too low, not too bright, not too dim, and it has been put there especially for you. You have a lover. Of course. He is handsome, and you are beautiful. Neither of you is capable of uttering a single sentence unless it is sparkling with wit and charm. At night, when you are ready to go to sleep, the racket of crickets outside your window is like the happy clatter of castanets.

A talent scout from the American Ballet Theater attended a Friday night performance. He murmured encouraging words to the dancers, made impossible promises, and left them on a pink cloud of unrealistic expectations. Even Madam Lenochka was affected by the magic of the season. It was murmured that she had rediscovered an old lover, once a famous violinist, now a retired music teacher; that every night Madam's bed remained unslept in; and that during the full run of the troupe's engagement in Saratoga Springs, the steely glint of determination in Madam's eye was replaced by an ineffably soft and dreamy look of sweet saturation.

It was a summer of great talent, great aspirations, near poverty, irrepressible laughter, youth, and joy.

That first season Ballet de Terpsichore ended on October 15. Merry was born at the beginning of the second season, on the first day of May.

The ballet troupe began year two of its existence with an expanded repertoire that featured scenes from rarely performed ballets, including *Pillar of Fire, The Lady of Camellias,* and *Selina.* This last contained a scene in which Selina wears a simple gold locket that is coveted by her evil stepfather, Lord Ravensgarth. During the course of the ballet, desperate struggles and a dramatic plunge over a waterfall ensue, but all ends happily with Lord Ravensgarth vanquished, and the locket still around Selina's neck.

Later, this locket becomes relevant to Annie Bly and Billy Nightingale's confabulation.

As to the Ballet de Terpsichore itself, other than its exhausting and exhilarating schedule, the troupe was also responsible for the care and sustenance of a red-headed infant, one whom Madam Lenny proclaimed would some day "become a great ballerina, like Danilova, like Pavlova, like Markova, like me!"

Merry had been ensconced in Suite 28 on the second floor of the Warwick Hotel when tragedy permanently ended the tour of the Ballet de Terpsichore. It was the month of October. At three minutes after seven that Saturday night, sirens started to sing their bone-chilling song not far from the hotel. They were loudest on Route 12, near the Chenango River, where Clarence Thrumm, an eighty-year-old retired machinist, had been caught in a flash flood. The moonless sky, the whipping frenzy of rain, and the black night just about blinded him, and in a sudden panic, he slammed on his brakes, turned the key, and stopped his car right where he was, in the middle of the road. Too frightened to think, he didn't realize that when he had turned off the ignition, he turned off his head and taillights, too.

The coroner's report indicated that Clarence Thrumm died immediately upon impact. The impact was from a peacock blue van that, not seeing him, had rammed into Clarence from behind.

"What about the others?" Sebastian asked as Annie approached the end of her tale.

"They weren't in the van. They all lived. But without Joe Brown and its prima ballerina, the Ballet de Terpsichore ceased to exist. Madam Lenochka went back to teaching pirouettes and developpés in Brighton Beach. Alexis Ergorova continued to dance with regional companies for a few more years. Then he disappeared. The others drifted this way and that, and went on to other things."

"What if Merry tries to trace Madam Lenochka?"

"Good point. Maybe Madam Lenny should abandon Bright Beach altogether and leave no forwarding address."

"Not a bad idea."

"Where were Joe Brown and Merry's mother buried?"

"Nobody knows where Joe is."

"Why not?"

"One of life's unanswerable questions. But his wife is buried in Brooklyn, right here in Washington Cemetery."

"Then maybe we ought to find her gravestone, because it's about time we gave our little ballerina a name."

chapter 30

FOR THOSE ACCUSTOMED TO artfully landscaped cemeteries graced with opulent foliage and dignified by the gentle dilapidation of markers dating back to the American Revolutionary War, Washington Cemetery comes as something of a shock. Instead of slim, elegant, time-weathered slates, the headstones in Brooklyn are cumbersome, squat, and dumpy. Many are over a foot thick, and some are in excess of six feet tall. Most are black, brown, or dark gray, and all are jammed together with nothing to separate them but a sliver of air and a patch of scraggly grass.

If, in the vast acreage of Washington Cemetery, there had ever been more than ten or twenty lonely pines, they have long since been sacrificed to the need for more room for more dead. Looking in any direction but up, all that is visible are densely packed gravestones intersected by occasional cramped pathways, producing an impression, not of a city of the dead, but of a tenement of the dead.

After Sebastian parked his car on the shoulder of one of the cemetery's gravelly lanes, he, Billy, and Annie picked their way along slim sidewalks, under archways, past mausoleums, and through small rusty gates that seemed to have been designed for the admittance of hobbits instead of full-sized human beings. Cast iron benches, now old and rusty, had been placed here and there among intimate clusters of graves—silent resting places where friends could sit for a while and visit. Coffee klatches without the coffee, for one-sided conversations where words, like lost loved ones, drift silently away.

The three intruders moved slowly and cautiously through the cramped, self-contained world, where not a scrap of paper was driven by the wind and not a stone or a rock was out of place. As they walked, they read inscription after inscription on stone after stone. They absorbed the desolation of each death and the depth of each loss, and soon their perspective began to change. Instead of perceiving the cemetery as a dead man's slum, they began to see it simply as a bleak place. A lonely place. A place where strong sentiment from the living reached out to venerate those who were, as so many of the gravestones proclaimed, "gone but not forgotten."

Gone but not forgotten.

Four words repeated over and over again on thousands and thousands of graves.

Annie stopped. "Where's Billy?"

She looked to her right; she looked to her left.

"Over here," he called from fifty feet away. "I found the Russian graves."

Annie and Sebastian followed his voice, weaving in and around a maze of plots until they arrived at a subsection of the cemetery where all of the inscription on the gravestones were in Cyrillic lettering and where each marker was imprinted with the facsimile of a face, as perfectly defined as a studio portrait.

Billy stared down at one of them. Peter Rostropovitch, as

robust and happy in death as a suitor about to go out on a first date, smiled back up at him.

"This is weird," Billy said.

Annie touched the surface of the stone. It was smooth. Flawless.

"How did they do this?"

Sebastian's fingers traced the same path as hers over the stone. "Beats me. But I agree with Billy. It is weird."

All of the Russian graves had the same high-gloss, handsomely polished headstones, and unlike the somber memorials in the rest of the cemetery, all bore the images of those who were buried beneath.

"Yelena Grushchina. 1960 to 1995." Annie read aloud. Tulips bracketed either side of Yelena's intelligent and humorous face.

"How about her for Merry's mother?" Sebastian asked.

"No. She was thirty-five when she died. Pretty, but way too old and way too sexy. We're looking for a ballerina here. Not a Rockette."

They wandered past Chertakovskayas, Bidarskys, Rudasheevskayas, Olskys, and Moyas. They zigzagged between grave beds, seeking—they weren't quite sure what. Serene faces stared back at them, frozen in time, space, and memory. Men wearing suits and ties and looking as though they had just been polished and pressed for a christening or a bar mitzvah. Women perfectly coiffed and crisply rigid like matrons emerging from a beauty parlor ready to be mothers of the bride.

For hours, they wandered through the fields of stone, ignoring fatigue and frustration until Sebastian, swatting at a bee that had been dive-buzzing him for the past twenty-five minutes, slumped against the side of a mausoleum and said, "I quit."

Annie squeezed his arm reassuringly, but walked right

past him. She continued to serpentine around the graves, not stopping until she had reached a trio of headstones arranged neatly, one, two, three, in a row. Other than the Russian names on them, they bore no resemblance to the eastern European markers the trio had already inspected. They were not shinny, they did not have images of the dead embedded in the stone, each bore a sepia photograph in an oval frame at the top of the marker, and the inscriptions were in English.

"Guys," Annie called out. "Come here."

The first stone they examined belonged to Yakov Blekher. BORN 1920. DIED 2000. REST IN PEACE.

The second they inspected identified the resting place of Riza Libman. BORN 1928. DIED 1995. GONE BUT NOT FORGOTTEN.

The third, however, was different. Inside a oval frame not unlike that of an Edwardian cameo, was the photograph of an elfin woman whose fair hair was pulled severely back the way a dancer wears her hair. Her forehead was high; her skin was pale; and there was a sweet, sad expression in her large, soulful eyes. Her lips were slightly parted, as if on the verge of forming a word she would never say, and there were small pearl and diamond earrings dangling from each of her dainty ear lobes.

Billy moved to one side of Annie. Sebastian moved to the other.

They stood that way for about five minutes, staring in silence at a single word engraved on a diagonal in large calligraphy across the sandy pink marble headstone.

It was a name.

YELIZAVETA

"We found her," Billy said.

———

ON THEIR WAY to pick up Merry at the airport on Monday morning, Annie and Sebastian made three stops. The first was at the school of the New York City Ballet, where Sebastian double parked his car on Columbus Avenue so that Annie, clutching a fistful of tens, could take the escalator outside Alice Tully Hall to the courtyard entrance to the Rose Building. Twenty-five minutes later, Annie came out, triumphantly dangling two pink satin ballet slippers by their ribbons.

"Size five," Annie said, slipping into the passenger seat. "Perfectly consistent with Yelizaveta being too short to have danced for Balanchine."

Sebastian shook his head in amazement. "What did you do? Mug a ballerina?"

"No. I sneaked into the school locker room, eavesdropped on a few conversations, and bought them off a skinny brunette who was complaining about not being able to break them in right." Annie pulled the car door shut. "When I offered her seventy bucks, she grabbed the money and ran."

THEIR SECOND STOP was at Antonio's Artifacts and Antiques on Second Avenue, where Annie found exactly what she was looking for in a jumble of estate jewelry at the back of the store. She returned to the car after ten minutes and handed Sebastian a black velvet box, the nap of which had been worn off along the edges.

"Go on," Annie said. "Open it."

Inside was a small gold heart dangling from a thin gold chain. The chain was tucked behind a velvet insert, and the heart was engraved with delicate forget-me-nots.

Sebastian held the necklace up toward the light and turned the heart this way and that.

"Where's the clasp, Annie?"

"No clasp," Annie said. "It doesn't open. I can deal with a hypothetical mother who's a thousand times nicer, wiser, and more beautiful than I am, but no way in hell can I deal with Merry mooning over her picture whenever I ask her to do the dishes. The locket is real gold, though, and it looks legitimate enough to convince her that Yelizaveta wore it every time she danced the role of Selina in the ballet."

THEIR LAST STOP was the Gordon Glass Shoe Store on Ninety-seventh Street, still run by the Glass family, with the original, fully-functioning Gordon Glass, now age ninety-nine, manning the cash register and greeting customers as they walked inside.

Annie went through the door. When she came out ten minutes later, she was carrying a shoe box easily as old as she was. She blew dust off the top of the box and positioned the pink satin ballet slippers and the worn black velvet jewelry box inside. She closed the lid. She opened the lid. She looked inside and shook her head. "It doesn't look right." She slipped out of the car again and went back into the store. A minute later, Annie returned with several large sheets of tissue paper. She tucked them neatly into the bottom of the box. Then she nestled the ballet slippers in the paper, placed the jewelry box inside one of the shoes, wrapped them in the rest of the tissue, and closed the shoe box.

Again she removed the lid and looked inside.

This time she turned to her husband and smiled.

"Perfect," she said.

book three

The fire which seems extinguished often slumbers
beneath the ashes.

—PIERRE CORNEILLE

chapter 31

NEW YORK STATE LAW mandates that an inmate serving an in-
determinate sentence, such as five to fifteen years or ten to
thirty years, "may earn good time towards the maximum
term not to exceed one third of the maximum term imposed
by the court."

Translated into English, which even parole officers sometimes find difficult to do, this means that a prisoner who is
not eligible for parole because of the nature of her crime,
such as murder, will only have to serve two thirds of her
prison sentence if she never, never misbehaves.

On the day that an inmate enters into the prison system,
she is advised of her conditional release date. "The establish-
ment of this conditional release date assumes the granting of
all available good time. However, poor judgment in prison . . .
could result in the withholding of good time and the revision
of the established conditional release date."

"Poor judgment in prison" is generally referred to as
"misbehavior." Categories of misbehavior include assault and
fighting, sex offenses, threats, bribery and extortion, riot,

disturbances and demonstrations, unauthorized assembly or activity, escape, impersonation, contraband and smuggling, destruction and theft of property, making and/or using an explosive device, setting a fire, gambling, self-mutilating, and refusal to obey a direct order.

Edith Tuttle always obeyed orders, direct or implied, and she never, never misbehaved.

When she had arrived at prison sixteen years earlier, she looked twenty years older than her real age of thirty-eight. By the time she left at age fifty-four, she didn't even look forty. Given that set of circumstances, it was impossible to conclude anything other than that behind barbed wire, Edith Tuttle had thrived.

Some inmates lose weight after they are incarcerated. Some do not. Edith lost fifteen pounds. She never lost her double-chinned, flush, and fleshy look, though, and her torso remained a shapeless slope. She continued to wear her hair very much as she had worn it on the outside, drooping into a lank and unstylish blunt cut that ended about two inches below her ears. Stray strands of silver intermingled with the red, and instead of the overall effect being pumpkin orange, it was now more suggestive of a bloodless autumn maple leaf.

All in all, Edith had adapted perfectly to prison life, and if the Bedford Hills Correctional Facility could ever be said to have had a model prisoner, it was without a doubt Edith Tuttle.

However, Edith was different from other inmates who seemed to have adjusted to prison life. Foremost among the differences was that she never claimed her life had been miraculously transformed by religion. She was not a born again Christian. She did not suddenly drop down on her knees, thump a bible, and claim to have found the Lord. She did not convert to Islam, and she did not see the image of Jesus on the underside of a loaf of bread. Nor did she take computer courses, seek out attorneys to file appeals, or spon-taneously develop an appetite for the Great Books of the Western World. Edith did not, in fact, read anything at all ex-cept for knitting and sewing patterns and torn-out recipes from magazines for easy-to-make party treats.

Since disputes with other inmates would be construed as "misbehavior," Edith also assiduously avoided confronta-tions. Religion being a particularly hot issue, she neither snubbed nor encouraged any True Believers, and when ap-proached, as she often was, by inmates or guards with a "Let's Go to Bible-Study" gleam in their eyes, Edith would respond, "I don't know nothing about no religions, but for two days I've been watching that button on your shirt hanging by a thread. I'm handy with a needle. Why don't you come on over, and I'll fix it for you?"

Edith, it turned out, was good at doing quite a few things and had evolved from a semi-idiot on the outside, apparently incapable of setting a thermostat or driving a car, to a walk-ing repair shop and comfort station. Inmates were permitted to wear their own tops along with regulation green skirts, jumpers, or pants, so this came in handy. If the hem on your pink blouse was loose, Edith was always there with her needle and thread to do a quick stitch.

If you were running late, but your bed had to be made, Edith would make it for you.

If your back hurt, she would take out your trash.

If your boyfriend or your father or your son was coming for a visit, Edith, who had graduated from the prison's school of commercial cosmetology, would do your hair and your nails. And since she had learned calligraphy in an arts and crafts workshop, if you needed a professional-looking grad-uation card, birth announcement, or Best Mother of the Year award, Edith could make one of those for you, too.

"Mom, my daughter's coming to see me on her birthday. Can you make one of them wreaths you make out of potato vines for me to give her?"

"That soap your sister sends from California sure smells good, Mom. Can you chip off a chunk for me?"

"Hey, Mom, I ran out of Camels, and I'm dying for a smoke. Got an extra cigarette?"

"You weren't going to eat those peanuts by yourself, were you, Mom? Got a few left over for me?"

NOBODY, NOT EVEN EDITH, could put a date on when people started to call her "Mom," but by the time she had moved from the general prison population into Friske Cottage, everybody did. Even the social workers, the administrators, and the guards.

Friske Cottage dates back to 1901, when community activists created Bedford Hills as the then New York State Reformatory for Women. Believing that women who had broken the law could resume a normal role in society if they were treated with dignity, these turn-of-the-century idealists insisted that instead of putting the women in bleak, dehumanizing penitentiary cells, the female prisoners should be housed in cottages. To provide each prisoner with a homelike setting, each cottage was surrounded by a flower garden and beyond that was farmland. There were no guard towers and electrified fences back then.

From those gentler and more optimistic times, Friske is the only cottage that still remains, and in terms of livability, it far exceeds in personal comfort, privacy, and extra privileges anywhere else in the penitentiary, including the coveted Honor Floor.

During her last five years in prison, Edith Tuttle had her own room in Friske Cottage, as well as the enviable option of opening and shutting the door to her room at will. She was permitted to hang her own pictures on the wall, she had her own television set, and if she wanted to, she could even keep plants on her window sills. Along with the other twenty-six inmates in Friske Cottage, Edith also had access to a washer, a dryer, a vacuum cleaner, and a sewing machine. This last enabled her to become an expert at stitching bed coverings and curtains from fabric donated to the prison, her specialty being a multi-ruffled bedspread that she had made for just about everyone in the cottage.

Edith mended her housemates' clothing.

She made Crispy Crunchies out of marshmallows and Rice Krispies for inmates' birthdays.

She ironed the complicated necklines of their pleated blouses.

She knitted scarves for their children.

When asked, she would even show them how to prepare a patch of soil or how to plant a bulb in a garden. Not, however, in her garden.

Her garden, which was really the public garden at Friske Cottage, existed on a "look but don't touch" basis. No one was permitted to pick a single one of her flowers. Not a daffodil or a tulip. Not an iris, a delphinium, or a poppy. Or, as she said to the other women at Friske, "I don't want nobody meddling with my flowers."

Nobody did.

Edith's aptitude for gardening had come late in life. Even though she was brought up in a farming community, she hadn't known which end of a bulb was up when she first arrived at Bedford Hills. "Them things have ends?" she said when confronted with a dormant tulip. "I thought they was like grass, and they didn't have to know which way was up until they was already planted."

During her second year at Bedford Hills, Edith Tuttle took a class in horticulture. According to a booklet she had been given when she arrived at the facility, the class would provide her with instruction in "horticulture, floriculture, landscaping, design coordination, and planning." As early as her first day in class, she took to growing things the way she had taken to having babies. Soil seemed more fertile where Edith had touched it. Plants seemed happier, lusher, greener, and more alive.

"See them seeds over there," she would explain to those who lacked her gift. "A little water. A little soil. Spread it over the top like I done. Gentle. And then don't do nothing else. They don't need much attention. Put 'em in the sun and leave 'em be. Nature knows how to do the rest."

The man at the prison who taught Edith everything she knew about plants was Alfred dos Santos. Alfred had gotten a degree in social work at Columbia University while working at his parents' nursery in Brooklyn. After six months with Alfred, there was nothing Edith couldn't grow, and he considered her his protégé. Aside from teaching horticulture at Bedford Hills, Alfred taught the women in his classes how to make bouquets and how to create flower arrangements for weddings, bar mitzvahs, and funerals. His goal was to provide his graduates with useful vocational training so that when they were released from prison, they would be able to get jobs working for florists at above minimum wage.

"I'm telling you, Mom," he had said countless times to his favorite student, "you're the best. Just let me know a few weeks before you're released, and I'll find you a job on the outside. Guaranteed."

The outside.

It was something dreamed of, fantasized about, ached after, and pined for. It was something for which one could make plans, but only tentatively, vaguely, and without confidence, because reality behind the electrified fences in the world of Bedford Hills was no more predictable than the next mistake an inmate might make or the next misbehavior of which she might be accused.

None of which, in the least, had affected Edith Tuttle's "good time," because to the last second of the last minute of the last day of her incarceration, Edith Tuttle did not misbehave.

chapter 32

UNLIKE OTHER BALLERINAS, Arabella McKenzie was neither cool nor aloof. She was not an ice princess.

She did not shimmer with poise.

She sent firey crackles of celestial energy across a stage. She was electrified; she smoldered.

Each iris of her startling aquamarine eyes was rimmed in black, as though outlined by a felt pen. Her thick eyelashes clung together like the points of stars. Her ivory skin had a dusky tint. Her hair was black. Like raven feathers. Like cap-sized bottles of ink.

In the world of contemporary ballet where lean giantesses ruled, Arabella McKenzie was small enough to make a short man look tall.

She was a pocket Venus. A pint-sized Pavlova.

She had danced to great acclaim in London, Paris, Rome, St. Petersburg, and Tel Aviv. She had never had a bad review, she was not plagued with the laundry list of injuries that afflicted so many of her colleagues, and she was still madly in love with the ballet. And yet, shortly after the greatest performance of her career, Arabella stepped off the red carpet that had been unrolled for her and without even the hint of an explanation, suddenly walked away.

How could she said gossip columnists. *Why would she* fellow dancers, musicians, and balletomanes wondered aloud.

After all he had *given* to her.

After all he had *done* for her.

The media questioned. The telephone wires hummed.

The "he" in question was a choreographer. Not just any choreographer, but the choreographer considered to be the greatest practitioner of his profession who had ever lived. Greater than Frederick Ashton. Greater than Fokine. Greater than even Cecchetti. He had discovered Arabella McKenzie when she was barely sixteen, and had promptly fallen in love with her; this was not unusual for him, since he had fallen in love with, married, and divorced five of his previous protégés.

"I will make you the prima ballerina absoluta of the world," the choreographer promised Arabella as casually as another man might say, "I will pick you up for dinner at eight."

"I will mold you, transform you, transfigure you, and turn you into the embodiment of my principles until all that is left of Arabella McKenzie is a confluence of bones that responds to my will." And his will, he was certain, was *the* will.

"Arabella is more than a goddess," he had proclaimed often and loudly to journalists, ex-wives, enemies, and friends. "She is music leaping from toe to toe; she is a soul fluttering in the wind. She is dance itself. Just as I am dance. For I am she and she is me."

Under the choreographer's tutelage, Arabella McKenzie had danced the Black Queen in *Checkmate*, Lizzie Borden in *The Fall River Legend*, Beauty in *Beauty and the Beast*, and Euridice in *Orpheus*. She had danced *Cinderella*, *Giselle*, *The Firebird*, and *Coppelia*. She was celebrated, toasted, idolized, imitated, and adored. What she was not, however—and it was a big however—was consulted. Never during all of their years of collaboration had she been asked what parts *she* might want to dance.

Not once.

At the end of their seventh year together, the choreographer, whom the ballet world also believed to be her lover, decided to make George du Maurier's novel *Trilby* into a ballet. The book's plot revolves around Svengali, a cruel but brilliant pianist with a mysterious power over women that manifests itself through his music. When women are under its spell, they will do anything for him. Give him money. Give him love. Kill themselves.

Enter Trilby, the free-spirited, uneducated, but kindly artists' model who is in love with the British painter, Little Billy. Svengali takes one look at Trilby and decides that he must have her. Overhearing her complain of a pain in her eyes, he offers to cure her. Instead, Svengali hypnotizes her. From that moment on, Trilby belongs to him. In her natural state, Trilby's voice is a horrible croak but under hypnosis, it becomes sublime, and even people who can't distinguish one note from another weep with pleasure when they hear her sing. Trilby, Svengali realizes, is going to be his ticket to the top. He grooms her, coddles her, and trains her, keeping her always at his side. Then he dazzles the world with her repertoire, her beauty, and her brilliance, mesmerizing audiences everywhere, as she herself is mesmerized by Svengali's inexorable power.

The rest of the story concerns Little Billy, Trilby's true love, his efforts to free her from Svengali and the tragic events that follow.

For the opening night performance only, the choreographer cast himself in the role of Trilby's evil but ardent suitor.

To better adapt the storyline for a ballet, instead of Svengali being a pianist, as he is in the novel, he becomes a dance instructor, and instead of Trilby having perfect vocal chords, she develops an exquisite mastery of movement and dance.

Arabella, it was said, merged with the part she was playing so completely that she literally *became* Trilby. When Trilby was falling in love with Little Billy, Arabella danced with enticing coquetry; when Svengali was controlling her, she drifted somnambulistically or twirled and whirled with spell-binding velocity across the stage; when Trilby was trying to break away from her master's influence, the effort Arabella made was heart-breakingly poignant; and after the curtain finally came down on a pale and depleted Trilby, dying in the arms of Little Billy, Arabella was honored with an unprecedented one hundred and fifteen curtain calls. For the first ten, the man who had been her personal Svengali joined Arabella to thunderous applause upon the stage.

"*Trilby* will break your heart," said the *New York Post* in its review the following morning.

"*Trilby* is brilliant," blazoned the *New York Times*.

"*Trilby* is ballet as it has never been danced before and may never be danced again," raved the *Daily News*.

"*Trilby* is dance," proclaimed *Time* magazine in an article that accompanied her picture on the cover. "And Arabella McKenzie is *Trilby*!"

ON THE MORNING after *Trilby*'s premier, two things happened that had never happened before. The first was a marriage proposal. "Arabella," said the choreographer gracefully assuming the lover's position on bended knee. "You are my muse and my divine inspiration. Will you marry me?"

The second was her response.

"No."

It was the only time that she had ever said no to him.

After politely waiting a few seconds for him to get up, which he seemed reluctant to do, she added, "And when the run of *Trilby* is over, I quit."

"Quit!" the choreographer leaped to his feet. "You *can't* quit. Nobody but you can dance Trilby. I created her for you. You *are* Trilby."

Arabella turned on him, her jet hair an angry swirl and her aquamarine eyes flashing. "That's exactly why I'm quitting. Because I am not Trilby, and I just figured it out."

ARABELLA SOLD HER Manhattan apartment, took out her life savings, and opened the McKenzie School of Ballet on the second floor of a recently defunct ribbon factory in Norwich, New York. At the same time, she founded the Lyric Ballet Company, in which she was both prima ballerina and chore-ographer. The company was subsidized in part by the pro-ceeds from her school and in part by ticket sales during the four months when the company was on tour. After only two years, the McKenzie School was attracting students from as far away as Syracuse and Albany, and the dance company had become so successful that it was self-sustaining, self-supporting, and was able to add another month to its season.

The year that Arabella turned twenty-six, a shy and skinny girl applied at one of the auditions the school held twice a year. The girl had brown eyes, alabaster skin, a mil-lion freckles, and curly orange hair. Her moves were quick-silver, her stage presence was illusive and fairylike, and she listened to every word Arabella McKenzie said with a pas-sionate intensity that reminded the ballet dancer of herself when she, like Meredith Bly, was only eleven years old.

chapter 33

THERE IS A LOOK to a ballerina, and there is a style.

There is an entire universe of accoutrements, and there is a language.

The language is French.

The look is elegant, practical, and austere. The ballet dancer wears a leotard, usually pink or black, and tights, usually black, pink, or white. On her feet, she wears ballet slippers until she is eleven or twelve. After her bones have set, she can wear toe or pointe shoes. The pointe shoes have long, satin ribbons that are pulled across the instep and then wound around the ankle, with the ends tucked in and neatly hidden.

The hair of a ballet dancer must always be neat. Ideally, it is long enough to pull away from the face, which emphasizes clean bone structure and healthy skin. The hair is contained in a bun at the back of the head. Often, the bun is adorned with a pretty, satin-covered, elasticized ribbon.

When confined to these minimal embellishments, even homely girls look lovely. And the look is unmistakable.

The essence of a dancer is that of a compact, trim, efficient organism devoid of excess and frippery, taught to perform with optimum grace and efficiency. Even if her face is plain, a ballerina's spirit is always luminous.

Ballet dancers stand with their heads held high and their slim and muscular shoulders thrust back, as though defiantly facing a firing squad. When at "parade rest," their feet unconsciously assume the third position, with the heel of the right foot in front of the hollow of the left. When they move their upper bodies, they do so elegantly, aware of the curve of their arms and the positions of their palms, their fingers, their wrists.

Young ballerinas in training are always expected to be courteous, ladylike, and feminine. They do not wear nose rings, their bodies are neither pierced nor covered with tattoos, and they never slump about in torn T-shirts or dirty blue jeans. Ballet, being an art that was created by royalty, demands of its practitioners that they live up to its royal origins.

Elegance, grace, and femininity however, break down completely when it comes to the contents of a dancer's ballet bag. This bag, for a professional, is akin to a soldier's knapsack and survival kit. Typically, it might contain an assortment of leotards, tights, and leg warmers, along with a pair of soft ballet slippers, at least one pair of pointe shoes, and a small box of needles and heavy-duty thread to sew long strips of satin ribbon and elastic into the folds of the shoes. The bag might hold an upholstery hammer to thwack the cleating of new shoes in order to break them in properly, extra thread and needles to darn the ends of the pointe shoes so that they would last longer, surgical tape, and lamb's wool or thin silicone pouches for insulating toes against blisters and pain.

Dancers also have idiosyncratic items in their bags indicative of their personal approach to dance. One former principal of the New York City Ballet carried two bicycle tires, which she used to spin around her forearms as an exercise to develop her upper body, as well as a can of Fabulon Floor Wax to harden her toe shoes. Since so many dancers smoke to curb their appetites, some bags include cigarettes and matches; some are filled with eye shadows, eye liners, mascara, blush, assorted lipsticks, and pancake makeup; others are weighted down with bottles of water or cans of fruit juice.

During Meredith Bly's first year at the McKenzie School of Ballet, her bag held the usual assortment of tights, leotards, and ballet slippers, as well as a small diary in which, for about three weeks, she religiously wrote letters to her dead mother, Yelizaveta. At the bottom of her bag were battered copies of Nancy Drew mysteries and a framed picture of her Uncle Billy taken at a fire scene, with a fireman's helmet on his head, a cigar in his mouth, and a far off look in his eyes. Annie also made Merry bring along an apple, an orange, or a box of raisins for energy, which Merry never ate until she was in the car on her way home from class.

Cherished items that Merry did not carry around in her bag included Yelizaveta's pointe shoes and the small gold locket her parents told her Yelizaveta wore when she had danced the role of Selina. Both were presented to Merry in an old shoe box the day she returned from Florida. Merry draped the shoes over a mirror in her bedroom so that she could look at them every night before she went to sleep, and she wore the locket around her neck and never took it off.

Merry attended four classes a week during her second year at the McKenzie School of Ballet, including technique, stretch, performance, and pointe. Along with her leotard, tights, and ballet slippers, her bag contained leg warmers and a sweater. The most important additions, however, were her pink pointe shoes, tufts of lamb's wool for her toes, band aids for blisters and abrasions, and an ice pack for sore muscles when and if they occurred. Also in the bag were hair knots, bobby pins, and novels such as *Daddy Long Legs, Little Women,* or *Anne of Green Gables.* Along with the fiction, Merry toted biographies of Anna Pavlova, Maria Tallchief, Margot Fonteyn, or Alegra Kent.

By the time she was twelve years old, Merry was starting to look very much the way she would continue to look for the rest of her life. She was small boned, long limbed, and five foot, seven inches tall. Her mouth was wide, she had a wistful, tentative smile, and creamy white skin, from which her freckles had already begun to fade. Her tiny ears were beautifully sculpted, and her enormous, dark brown eyes were surrounded by long, golden red eyelashes.

Merry's eyes caught the light no matter where she was standing in a room. And her copper hair was a wild and uncontainable sun-magnet so inappropriate to her delicate and well-shaped head that Annie had once whispered to Sebastian in the dead of night, "She's still a baby, but her hair just walked into a nightclub and ordered scotch on the rocks."

From the back, Meredith Bly looked like the adult dancer she would one day become. From the front, she looked like a sweetly serious and completely naïve twelve-year-old girl.

AT AGE THIRTEEN, Merry was taking five ballet classes a week, including modern, variations, character, partnering, and pointe. When she wasn't too busy with homework, she assisted Arabella with beginner classes, sometimes helping her teacher rehearse the younger children.

As Merry grew up she altered the contents of her ballet bag very little, only exchanging Uncle Billy's large photograph for a small one and replacing the novels she had been reading with tomes that had ponderous titles like *Technical Manual and Dictionary of Classical Ballet* and *Basic Principles of Classic Ballet*. Also, instead of pink ballet slippers like all the other girls wore, the pointe shoes in her bag were red.

Arabella McKenzie noticed Merry's new footwear in class and immediately telephoned Annie.

"Last week," Annie said, "she saw Moira Shearer in *The Red Shoes* on TV. She bought the video and has been watching the movie nonstop ever since."

Remembering her own response to the same film at the same age, Arabella laughed. "Of course," she said. "That explains everything."

WHEN MERRY TURNED FOURTEEN, both her ballet bag and her brain had begun to reflect a commitment toward professionalism.

"When I grow up," she announced to her parents, "I will be a prima ballerina, like Margot Fonteyn."

In fact, her real hero was Arabella McKenzie, but she was too shy to admit it.

"You must study dance all summer," her teacher had said decisively a few days after the winter break.

"But I always study dance in the summer, Miss McKenzie."

"I know. But this summer, you won't be studying with me. You will... don't interrupt. Listen. A good teacher is like a good parent. First she teaches her child how to walk, and then she teaches her how to walk away. Do you understand what I'm saying, Meredith?"

"Oh, no, Miss McKenzie. I don't want to understand what you're saying, and please, please stop saying it. You're breaking my heart."

"Don't be silly," Arabella continued, heedless of Merry's pleas. "This spring you are going to audition for the New York State Summer Program for the Arts. You have natural dramatic instincts and more technical skill than I've ever seen in a student your age. Up until now, you've been too encouraged, too supported, and too protected. You haven't been exposed to choreographers who will hate you and jealous classmates nowhere near as capable as you are, who are going to get preferential treatment because they're some other teacher's pet. It's part of the toughening up process, Meredith, and if you're going to succeed as a professional, we're going to have to start to cut the cord."

Merry looked up hopefully. "Start?"

"That's right. Start. Once you've been seen in Saratoga, talent scouts from other institutions are going to offer you full scholarships to attend their schools of ballet."

"They will?"

"And you're going to turn them down."

"I am?"

"Yes, you are. You're going to continue at the McKenzie School for another year. When you are sixteen, you will join my company for one season, and dance professionally in the corps."

"Oh, Miss McKenzie," Meredith started to cry.

"Of course, you don't have to do any of this if you don't want to."

"Don't want to! Oh...Oh...I'm so happy, I think I'm going to die."

"Don't die yet. After your season with me, I want to talk to your parents about transferring to the Professional Children's School for your junior and senior years of high school, because if you're serious about a career as a dancer..."

"Oh. I am!"

"Then you should move to Manhattan to continue your study of ballet."

chapter 34

WHEN ANNIE BLY decided to move back to New York City, she put on a very red, very sexy summer dress with very red sling-back high heels, and she popped in on her old boss unannounced. Her cheekbones were more defined, her crimson lipstick was a shade subtler, and her overall look was sleeker and more sophisticated than it had been. But she still wore her hair in that same spiky pixy, and there was still way too much mischief in her eyes.

Annie whispered to Noel Abbot the Third's secretary, "Don't announce me, Ginny. I want to surprise him." Then she flung open the art dealer's door and stood for a moment.

Noel Abbot the Third looked up.

"A . . . An . . . Annie," he eventually managed to utter. He sank helplessly back against the cushions of his chair and stared. And stared. And stared. Then, his eyes still pinpoints of disbelief, he said, "Darling. Swear to me there isn't a painting of you in your attic that's put on fifty pounds and is wearing a pink, terrycloth bathrobe."

Annie laughed, perched on the corner of his desk, and said, "Honey, I'm home."

Noel Abbot the Third rehired his former assistant on the spot.

IT HAD TAKEN Sebastian longer than Annie to arrange his transfer, because the New York State police have only one troop in all of the five boroughs of New York City. Operating out of the Jacob Javits Convention Center, Troop NYC includes a drug task force, a criminal squad, and a uniformed detail. After filling out the required paperwork at his new headquarters in the Bronx, Sebastian Bly reported to the Javits Center for work. For the next two years of his daughter's education, it was there that he intended to stay.

SEBASTIAN'S TRANSFER came through three months before Merry enrolled as a junior in the Professional Children's School in Manhattan, a structured environment that had been created specifically to provide talented children with "a rigorous academic program, combined with appropriate flexibility to enable our students to pursue their dreams in the arts."

Where Merry would pursue that dream was another story.

During her last year at the McKenzie School, Arabella dragged Meredith to every troupe performing and ballet school teaching in New York City, including institutions affiliated with the American Ballet Theater, the Dance Theater of Harlem, the New York Theatre Ballet, and dozens of others. Despite their overall skill and competence, however, none possessed the demon flash of brilliance that Arabella believed her student needed.

At least, none did until the Manhattan Delacourte Ballet Theater came to town.

The Delacourte's summer repertoire consisted of story ballets based on two poems by Robert Browning and one by Alfred, Lord Tennyson. The choreographer of all three ballets was Armand Delacourte, the dance company's founder and artistic director.

Friday night's performance, the first that Merry and Arabella had attended, was based on Robert Browning's poem "Youth and Art," and told the story of an impoverished young opera singer and the equally young and poor sculptor who lived across the courtyard from her tenement window. It was a bittersweet tale of missed opportunities, success achieved, love unfulfilled, and paths not taken.

My Last Duchess, based on another Robert Browning poem, was the Saturday night performance. It was a truly frightening ballet about a naïve and unsuspecting duchess, doomed by her innocence and her beauty. The dancer who portrayed her had a demanding role in which she needed to come to life out of the frame of a painting, attract love, inspire jealousy, and then die, returning once more within the static portrait frame.

Sunday's matinee was *Enoch Arden,* a wonderfully original story that has been retold and reinvented so many times that few people realize Tennyson actually wrote it. Enoch Arden is lost at sea. His wife, thinking him dead, remarries. She and her new husband prosper. Many years later, Enoch Arden returns to where his wife has been living. He gazes at her through the window. Despite his urgent longing for a reconciliation, what he sees holds him back, for inside are his wife and her children, comfortable, secure, and happy. Determined not to destroy her new life, Enoch Arden turns his back on the window and walks away.

For two of the ballets, Armand Delacourte consulted a magician whose area of expertise was grand illusion. This enabled the Duchess, when she emerged from the picture frame, to come to life with startling realism, and in *Enoch Arden,* allowed the returned sailor's substantive wife to stay behind and play with her children, while her shadow-self drifted through the window and joined Enoch in a pas de deux fantasy of the life that they might have lived. The effects of these illusions were dramatic and eye-catching and left both Merry and her teacher weak with joy.

"That," Arabella McKenzie later announced to anyone who would listen, "is ballet theater. And Armand Delacourte is the man who put theater back into ballet."

AFTER THE PERFORMANCE, Arabella went backstage to introduce herself to Delacourte.

"For the great Arabella McKenzie," he said, "no introduction is necessary."

He kissed her hand.

She praised his ballet.

He praised her dancing.

She cut to the chase.

"I have a student," she said.

"Tell me about him."

"It's not a him. Her name is Meredith Bly. She'll be sixteen years old this summer, and I want her to audition for your school."

"Do you vouch for her talent?"

"Yes. Absolutely."

"Will she one day be as good as you are?"

"Possibly. But I can't take her there. We've gone as far together as we can go. You could take her the rest of the way."

"Classes start on September the eighth. Forget the audition. Send her to me."

chapter 35

ALMOST ALL CHILDREN who study ballet love it.

Perhaps, because the life of the young ballerina exemplifies the rewards of self-discipline. For her, the means and the end are the same thing. Using herself as a tool, she must create, through learned and imitated movement, the beauty of dance.

She feels it. She does it. She *is* it.

She is the implement, she is the raw material, and she is the finished product.

Ballerinas are said to be utterly self-absorbed. Given the requirements of their art, this should come as no surprise.

All young ballet dancers are intense. Some are obsessed. Dance is everything to them. It is how they define themselves; it is what they want to do; it is what they want to be; it is who they are.

Their lives revolve around their classes.

If a teacher fails to appreciate the elevation of their grand jeté, they are devastated.

When a teacher nods approval at the line of their pointe tendue, they are elated.

Their evaluations of themselves hinge totally on how they are perceived as physical entities. Failing to execute ten perfect fouettes is not the equivalent of receiving a failing grade on a term paper in college. It is receiving a failing grade on themselves. On their essence. Each failure is a twelve-foot icicle driven into their hearts.

Their successes are equally personal. Their happiness is excruciating because the beauty to which they have so desperately aspired has finally been incorporated into their very being.

Most young dancers are socially inept.

All they can talk about is dance.

The only people they know are other dancers.

Most young dancers have experienced the gratification of mastering difficult steps, combinations, and positions, but they have never experienced the joy.

They are working too hard. Joy doesn't have a chance to get a foothold.

They are so possessive of the skills they have already acquired and so fearful about the technical challenges they have not yet met that they're afraid to take a breath. They can smile on a stage if the part they are playing requires a smile, but they cannot smile in their hearts. They don't remember how.

Joy is not taught between the first and fifth positions in contemporary schools of classical ballet. It is neither discussed nor deemed necessary. It is assumed that technical expertise is its own reward.

But it isn't.

And Armand Delacourte had figured that out.

IT TOOK THE FACULTY at the Delacourte School of Ballet twenty months to unclench Merry's psychic fist and remind her that the reason she had decided to become a dancer was that she loved to dance.

"*I* couldn't do it," Arabella McKenzie explained over lunch to Annie Bly. "But Armand did. I saw it happen in front of me. Merry was trying to execute a chug step. She was hopping around on one foot with the other up in the air, like a tin soldier who had mistaken one of his legs for a bayonet. When she was in that impossible position, she was supposed to spin around quickly and gracefully. The harder Merry tried, the stiffer her body became, and the stiffer it became, the more she lost her balance. Then Armand walked into the studio. He told her that the chug step is a real crowd pleaser, that can-can dancers do it all the time, and that it's supposed to be a lot of fun. He said she should straighten her shoulders, tuck in her behind, and relax her lower back. As Armand was talking, Merry rearranged her body to follow his instructions, and within minutes, instead of wobbling around like a top losing its momentum, she was spinning like a pro. And as she spun, Annie, she had the most irresistible smile on her face."

ONE NIGHT, shortly before Merry's eighteenth birthday, during one of those mother-daughter moments when the mother is hoping that the daughter will at least try to stay awake, Annie was perched at the end of Merry's bed.

"Darling," she said. "I haven't got it in me to be great. I don't know if I lack the drive, the talent, or the creative spark, but I know that what I lack, you have. In spades. You're going to be one hell of a great ballerina someday, sweetheart. But I want you to do something for me first."

Merry affectionately patted her mother's hand. "What do you want me to do?"

"I want you to promise me that you won't let talent and ambition interfere with having a fabulous time."

Merry cocked her head to one side.

"I don't understand."

"Fabulous time. It's a simple concept. It means enjoying yourself without the veins in your forehead popping out because you're so tense. Let me put it to you this way. Remember when you were a little girl and I let you buy those red toe shoes?"

Meredith laughed. "The other girls were so jealous. None of *their* mothers would let them wear red shoes. They thought I was lucky to have you."

"You were lucky, darling. You still are. But putting my virtues aside for the moment, I want to tell you what my dream for you is. Are you listening?"

"Yes. I am."

"All right. My dream is that you'll be able to put on those magical red slippers, wear them with all of the love and passion that you're capable of, and dance your little heart out. But also that you'll know when it's time to take them off."

Merry's large brown eyes narrowed suspiciously at her mother. "But...but to succeed as a dancer, one must be totally committed."

"Committed, yes. Compulsive, no. Do you understand?"

"I'm not sure."

"Okay. Remember Joan of Arc?"

"Of course. We read about her last semester in history class. She led the armies of France against the British."

"That's right, Merry. So, let me put it to you this way. It's all right with me and your father if you want to put on your ballet slippers to drive the English out of France. But please, please, darling, for all of our sakes, cease and desist before you get burned at the stake."

chapter 36

EDITH TUTTLE WAS already enrolled in a pre-release work-shop when her sister Beatrice forwarded a letter from Hemet, California. Before Edith read it, she had planned to take a train to Manhattan, check in with her parole officer, and re-quest a travel pass to go to Hemet, where the State of Cali-fornia had approved her serving out her parole.

Then she got the letter.

It was enclosed in a white, number ten envelope. Beatrice had clipped a note to the outside of the envelope: *Edith, Dear. This has been following me from here to kingdom come. Hope it isn't important. See you in a few weeks.*

Twelve months prior to Edith's conditional release date, Beatrice Dzubak, for reasons that would interest no one but herself, divorced her husband, resumed her maiden name of Hedge, and moved to Hemet.

Initially, the white envelope was addressed to Edith Tuttle c/o Beatrice Dzubak at her Elsinor, California, address. A series of forwarding addresses, cross-outs, and stamp-pad imprints subsequently brought the envelope to the right building, but the wrong apartment. Over the last cross out, somebody had written, TRY HEDGE—APARTMENT 2–D, and Beatrice had finally received it.

The return address in the upper left corner of the envelope indicated that the letter was sent from an organization called Point de Reunion.

> Dear Mrs. Tuttle:
>
> By law, we were restricted from disclosing the information provided to us by your daughter until she had attained her majority. However, we have kept your letter and her letter in our Pending File, and we are happy to inform you that her eighteenth birthday was last week, on May 1.
>
> Although we have no way of knowing if the addresses she gave us seven years ago are still valid, that information is herewith attached.
>
> We wish you the best of luck in effecting a reconciliation with your child, and we are gratified to have been instrumental in helping you to achieve this end.

Two addresses were typed on a sheet of paper stapled to the letter from Point de Reunion. One was in Fawn Creek, New York. The other was on East Eighty-fourth Street in Manhattan. Underneath both addresses, somebody at Point de Reunion had handwritten:

> *Your daughter's name is Meredith Bly.*
> *Good luck! I'm sure that she'll be thrilled to see you!*

chapter 37

DURING THE SCHOOL YEAR, Merry's day started at 6 AM. Her academic classes consisted of precalculus, nineteenth-century literature, biology, and constitutional law. Her ballet classes, which she took between academics, were in technique, variations, advanced pointe, and pas de deux. Both schools were over by 5 PM, but her day wasn't over until she had taken Murdock for a walk, helped her mother to make dinner, and finished her homework.

In contrast, Merry's summer schedule was a breeze. Her parents got up at 7 AM, Sebastian to go to his eight-to-four shift at the Javits Center and Annie to walk to work at the Paris Noel Abbot Galleries on Madison Avenue. Merry got out of bed at eight, dressed, drank a glass of orange juice, hooked Murdock to a leash, and then dragged him downstairs for his walk.

Their ritual at the bottom of the stairwell was always the same. Merry would pull the inside foyer door to their apartment shut behind her while Murdock pulled impatiently on his leash. She would push open the outside door, follow

Murdock down the stoop steps to the wrought-iron fence surrounding their property, and drape Murdock's leash around the fence post. Then she would run back up the steps, push open the outside door to the foyer, and lock the inside door to the apartment. This generally took more than a minute, because the key usually got stuck in the lock.

After that, she would scurry down the front steps, unloop Murdock's leash, and take him for a walk.

During those leisurely summer mornings, Merry did not have to get to the Delacourte School until 10 AM. She had been picked by Armand Delacourte to represent the school at a benefit to be given at the Manhattan City Center, and she would be dancing her debut performance as a soloist to the eighteenth variation from *Rhapsody on a Theme of Paganini* by Rachmaninoff.

From 10 AM to 11 AM, Merry rehearsed with her teacher, Sylvia Braggin. From 11 AM to 4 PM, she took classes in technique, pointe, pas de deux, repertoire, character, and variations.

By 6 PM, she was home for the day.

chapter 38

THE GATEWAY IS a halfway house located at Pleasant Avenue and 116th Street. It is on the dividing line between Spanish Harlem and East Harlem and within easy walking distance of Manhattan's Upper East Side.

Arrangements had been made for Edith Tuttle to move to the Gateway after her release from the Bedford Hills Correctional Facility. Particular attention was paid to her age, since she was twice as old as most of the other parolees; her sincerity, exemplified by the letter she wrote to the Executive Director pleading for the opportunity to become a useful member of society; and her horticultural skills.

During the final prerelease phase of her imprisonment, Edith was given a social security card, a copy of her birth certificate, and her divorce decree. She was briefed on budgeting her money and time; she was taught how to conduct herself during a job interview; and she was warned about the temptations and challenges that she would encounter when living on the outside.

The day of her release, she gave a list of instruction on the care and feeding of her plants to her housemates at Friske Cottage, and she said good-bye. Then Edith went to see her horticulture teacher.

"Once you're settled in at the halfway house," Alfred dos Santos said, "call Nestor at the Apollo Nurseries on Second Avenue. He's a personal friend of mine, Mom. He'll be expecting your call, and he'll give you a job."

It was early morning when Edith Tuttle finally walked out of the gates of the maximum security correctional facility for the first and last time. She was given a ride to the Bedford Hills train station, a ticket to Grand Central Station, and two bus tokens. The first got her to her parole officer on West Fortieth Street; the second got her to the halfway house.

By early afternoon, she found herself sitting across from the executive director of the Gateway in a small, comfortable, plant-filled room. "Although we were expecting you, Edith," Althea Davis said, shuffling through loose printouts in a folder on her desk, "for some reason, we haven't received your release papers yet."

Edith pushed herself heavily out of the chair. "I'm real sorry to hear that, Mrs. Davis," she shook her head sadly. "'Cause when me and the social worker decided where I should go, this sure looked like the right place to me."

"It *is* the right place. Oh, for heavens sake, Edith. Sit down. It doesn't take a miracle for parole to screw up paperwork. You aren't going anywhere. You're staying right here with me."

During Edith Tuttle's first week at the Gateway, she spent most of her time learning what was what, who was who, and what would be expected of her. The "her" at the halfway house, however, was barely recognizable as the same "mom" who couldn't do enough for her housemates at Bedford Hills. For one thing, she never offered to help her new roommates with their chores; for another, when they complained about boyfriends, children, parents, husbands, or jobs, her responses were rarely supportive and usually inappropriate. Once, when Edith said, "That's too bad" after being told a story with a happy ending, her roommate looked at her skeptically and said, "Honey, I think you and I is tuned to opposite channels."

Another change in the normally sedentary Edith was that she started to take walks. Every day and in any weather.

"Where does she go?" one of the social workers asked.

"She always heads east on 116th Street toward First or Second Avenue. After that, she disappears."

"Isn't she the one who's supposed to be such a hot-shot gardener?"

"Uh huh. She's got a job interview next week at that nursery, whatever it's called, over on Second Avenue."

"Apollo Nurseries. Between Ninety-second and Ninety-third. Nice place. I brought a Christmas wreath there for my front door. Maybe she goes there."

"To look at plants?"

"Can you think of anything better for her to do?"

EDITH TUTTLE WAS not looking at plants. Nor did she always go to the same place. On one of her outings, she went to a storefront medical clinic on Lexington Avenue and complained to a sympathetic doctor that she couldn't sleep at night and was suffering from anxiety. An hour later she walked out the door with a week's supply of sleeping pills in her purse.

On another outing, she went to a pet supply store on Second Avenue. She wandered around inside the store for a while, staring at goldfish, and glaring at puppies before she bought a box of dog treats and left.

All of her other excursions were to the same location. She would get on a bus at the corner of Second Avenue and 116th Street, take it to Eighty-fourth Street, get out, turn east, and walk two blocks to an apartment building separated by an alleyway from the corner delicatessen on York Avenue.

That was her hiding place.

Every morning, the superintendent of the building lugged huge, black garbage bags from the compactor room in the basement to the narrow alleyway outside the cellar door. Twice a week, he hauled the garbage bags up eight steps from the alleyway to the sidewalk and dragged them across the sidewalk to the curb for pick-up by the sanitation department.

Otherwise, nobody ever went there.

It was from this dim passageway that Edith Tuttle could observe without being observed; it was from there that she scrutinized the brownstone apartment building across the street.

chapter 39

ANNIE BLY STOOD for a moment in the doorway to her daughter's room, staring in stunned silence because, framed by the room's blue walls, her sleeping teenager looked like a breathtaking work of art.

Merry's flame colored hair was a glorious mass of tangles and curls, her long, light lashes cast delicate shadows on pale cheeks, her blue silk nightgown was a sea of sapphire that startlingly offset her white skin, and her lips were slightly parted, as though she were tasting something delicious deep inside a dream.

Annie walked across a small stretch of carpet, turned the rods, and opened the Venetian blinds. Bright, white shafts of sunlight streamed through the slats and fell on Meredith's face. Her eyes were closed.

"Wake up infant," Annie said and sat down on the edge of the bed.

Merry sighed softly, stretched like a cat, and opened her eyes.

"Hi," she murmured sleepily. "What day is it?"

"Friday."

"Are you sure?"

"Positive."

"Today's my last rehearsal."

"That's what I wanted to talk to you about. Scrunch over and make room for me."

Fully dressed in a tailored green suit with matching high heels, Annie stretched out next to Meredith on the bed. "I have a confession to make," she said. "I've done something dreadful. Or rather, I *am* dreadful because I haven't done something. Either way, I've committed a thirty-lashes-with-a-wet-noodle offense."

Merry smiled through another soft stretch. "I'm braced for the worst. Confess."

"All right, darling. Your idiot mother forgot to pick up the tickets for your performance tomorrow night."

"No. You didn't."

"Then why aren't the tickets in my purse?"

"Because the box office is holding them and has been holding them ever since you gave me Daddy's credit card and told me to buy the tickets a month ago."

"That's good."

"And every twenty-four hours since then, you have been telling me that you forgot to buy them. It's a recurring theme in our relationship."

"Do you think that I'm a little bit nervous about your debut?"

"Just a little."

"And you are one thousand million percent certain that you purchased four tickets?"

"One for you, one for Daddy, one for Uncle Billy, and one for Miss McKenzie. That's four."

"Funny, isn't it, that in all these years, I never introduced her to him. I can't imagine why it never dawned on me before."

"Never introduced who?"

"Your Uncle Billy to Arabella. I wonder if they'll like each other. Fireworks or ho hum? What do you think?"

Instead of answering, the young dancer turned her head toward the window and stared off dreamily, her brown eyes reflecting gold speckles in the sunlight.

"What are you thinking, darling? Are visions of sugar plum fairies dancing in your head?"

Merry rolled her eyes slowly over to Annie and smiled.

"You're happy. Aren't you?"

"I'm ecstatic."

"Because of tomorrow night?"

"Because of everything. The eighteenth variation from *A Rhapsody on a Theme of Paganini* is my all-time favorite piece of music, and Mr. Delacourte choosing me to dance to it is like getting Christmas for Christmas. My costume is as wispy and fluttery as a dream, and when I'm wearing it, I feel like a feather in the wind. So light and airy, I could float away. And..." Merry sighed again and smiled again, a gentle, far off, ethereal smile.

"And what? There's some other special happiness you're feeling today, isn't there?"

Merry sat up in bed, wrapped her arms around her legs, and hugged her knees.

"What is it, darling?"

"I just know," she answered softly, reverently, "that if my mother could see me today, she would be so proud."

Annie sat up, too. She leaned over and kissed her daughter on the forehead. "I *am* proud of you, sweetheart. I'm so proud, I could..." Then Annie saw a sudden look of horror and a flicker of terrible guilt in Merry's eyes. Almost as quickly, Merry recomposed her face, but it was too late.

"I see," Annie nodded. "When you said 'Your mother,' you didn't mean me. You meant Yelizaveta."

"No," Meredith shook her head. "No, I didn't."

"Merry," Annie insisted. "Look at me."

There were tears in the young dancer's eyes. "I hadn't meant to say that. I'm so sorry. I love you. I...I...I would never, never want to hurt you."

"Merry!" Annie said sternly. "A second ago, you were so happy, you were ready to burst. Now, you're so miserable, you're ready to cry. Darling child, you did *not* hurt me, and you are *not* going to be sad. Sad is off limits this weekend, in this household, and in this room. Are you listening?"

Merry shook her head.

Annie reached over, placed one hand over each of Merry's ears, and forced her daughter's head to nod.

Merry laughed.

"That's better," Annie stood up. "Now, do you want me to walk Murdock this morning, or does the prima ballerina want to do it herself? I don't mind, and it would give you an extra few minutes in bed."

Merry swung her feet to the floor. "I'll do it."

"Okeedokey. And when you get to school, remember to buy four tickets for tomorrow night's performance."

Merry stifled a groan of exasperation.

"Only teasing," Annie said. "I know that we already had this discussion."

"We've had it fifteen times!"

Annie crossed her eyes and made a popping noise with her mouth. "Just trying to interject a little levity into the proceedings."

chapter **40**

BY NINE O'CLOCK that same morning, Merry's parents had already left for work, and she was alone in the house with their dog.

"Okay, Murdock," she commanded. "Up on your feet!"

She knelt to hook Murdock's leash to his collar, but the basset hound didn't move. He didn't blink or bark.

Merry stood up again. "Murdock. Pay attention."

Murdock looked up.

"You're going to have to be more responsive."

He looked away.

Merry dragged him, unresisting, all the way across the dining room. When she dropped the leash for a second to open the door to the hall, he turned and shuffled into the kitchen, not stopping until he had arrived at the cabinet that contained his dog food. Then he lifted his head and stared at it wistfully.

"No way, José." Merry wagged a scolding finger. "I'm not putting a morsel in your bowl until after your walk. Consider this a motivational lecture. Come on, slowpoke. Move!"

Merry dragged Murdock back into the dining room. After getting snagged on a few area rugs, he resigned himself to the futility of further resistance and padded along behind her into the living room. She pushed open the door to the staircase and, one step at a time, pulled him down the stairs. When she got to the bottom step, she unlocked the door to the lobby and quickly moved to one side, because the instant the door was opened, Murdock shot into the foyer.

"What *is* it with you?" Meredith gazed down at her dog. "One minute, you're like a bag of wet laundry, and the next, you're Super Dog."

Murdock pawed frantically at the door to the world outside.

"Be patient. These things take time. First I have to take the key out of my back pocket. Then I have to lock this door behind me. Then I . . ." Murdock began to thud his head against the outside door.

"For heaven's sake, animal, can't you just wait?"

Thud. Thud. Thud.

"Okay. All right. You win. I lose. As usual."

She pushed the lobby door open, and Murdock scrambled down the steps as fast as his clumsy basset hound feet would carry him. Kerplop. Kerplop Kerplop. He continued his graceless descent. As soon as he got to the sidewalk, he stopped and looked up, as if to say, "There. That wasn't so bad. Was it?"

Merry looped Murdock's leash around the iron fence post at the foot of the stoop. "You are completely impossible," she scowled. "You add a new dimension to the concept of uselessness. You are slow, stubborn, inattentive, disobedient, and . . ." Murdock stared at his mistress. The expression in his big, dopey eyes was one of hopeless adoration.

"You big goof," she added affectionately, noticing that one of his long, floppy ears was caught like a tablecloth under his right paw. Merry lifted his leg, released his ear, bent down, and kissed him on the head. Murdock proceeded to lick every part of her face that was available.

"I love you, too." Merry laughed and kissed him again on the top of his scruffy, ugly old head. Then she ran back up the stoop and through the foyer to lock the door at the foot of the stairs to their apartment. As usual, her key got stuck in the lock. She pulled up on the doorknob with her left hand, wiggled the key with her right, and tried to ease it out. A little over a minute later, it was free.

She started down the steps.

It was a beautiful morning. A slow, poke-along-with-Murdock sort of a morning. Merry felt jaunty, joyful, and self-confident. A leisurely walk with her dog, followed by a quick subway ride to school. Then an invigorating rehearsal of a dance she adored to music she loved with the absolutely positively best and most wonderful teacher in the world.

Yes, indeed. It was going to be a glorious day.

"MURDOCK!" MERRY SCREAMED from the bottom step of the stoop, looking to her right and left along the sidewalk. "Murdock! Murdock...where *are* you?"

In all the years that the Blys had owned him, Murdock had never wandered away, and his only acts of subversion had been confined to foyers and hallways, where he would exhibit uncharacteristic eagerness to get outside. Otherwise, his favorite activity was pretending to be a rock or a rug.

"Murdock!" Merry shouted frantically as she walked in fits and starts, searching up the north side of Eighty-fourth Street and down the south side. "Murdock. Murdock. Murdock. Please...please come home. You're breaking my heart!"

Merry stopped in every courtyard of every townhouse

and at every apartment building on the street. She called out to residents, "Have you seen my dog?" and eagerly described him as a goopy, friendly, slow-moving hound, so gentle you could tie his ears into a bow, and so complacent he would rather sit and watch a squirrel scamper off than chase it, even if the squirrel was no more than a foot away. Merry questioned doormen, sales clerks, bank tellers, pretzel vendors, cab drivers, policemen, bag ladies, the kids at the newspaper distribution center on First Avenue, and all of the countermen who worked at the delicatessen diagonally across the street from her house.

She told everyone that she lived "in that brown brick building over there. If you see my dog or if you know of anyone who has seen him, please have them bring him back to me. His name is Murdock. He's a basset hound, and I promise that my parents will give them a nice reward."

Sylvia Braggin, Merry's teacher at the Delacourte School of Ballet, waited until 11 AM before calling her student at home. She let the telephone ring twenty times before her annoyance turned into concern. "But," Sylvia cautioned herself, "Meredith is an adult, and she may have a reasonable explanation for being late. So I won't call her mother. Yet."

Two and a half hours after Murdock disappeared, Merry collapsed in tears on the bottom step of her stoop and cried without restraint. She was too caught up in grief and too tired from her hopeless search to realize that she hadn't called her parents and that she had forgotten to call her school. She sobbed with her hands hiding her face and her eyes blinded by tears, completely unaware that between the tears, she was staring at two fat ankles stuffed into two scuffed brown walking shoes.

The feet shuffled listlessly.

Merry wiped her eyes with the back of her hand and

raised her head. She saw a portly figure wearing loose poly-ester pants and a shapeless brown pullover.

"Hey," the woman said. She had sandy beige eyes, silver-streaked orange hair, and a round face that was flushed as though from uncharacteristic exertion. "I found your dog."

Merry leaped to her feet.

"You found Murdock?"

She grabbed the stranger's hands.

"Is he all right? Is he here? Is he safe? Where is he?"

She swiveled her head from side to side, scouring the street with her eyes.

The woman jutted her chin toward a brownstone less than sixty feet away. "I tied her to a railing over there."

Merry released the stranger's hands, tore up the street, and located her dog behind a forsythia bush and a gate post. She untied the leash and hoisted Murdock into her arms. "My big, sweet, darling fatso," she cried, hugging and kissing him as she carried him back to the stoop in front of her house.

The shabbily dressed stranger had not budged from where Merry had left her.

"You dear kind lady," Merry said. "Where did you find him?"

The woman pointed a thick finger. "Over there. By the dry cleaner's."

"On York Avenue? Oh, my God. I never thought to look there."

"She was headed out..."

"He. Murdock's a boy."

"He..." The woman corrected herself with a strange and slyly self-congratulatory smile. "He was walking into traffic. I didn't want nothing bad to happen to him, so I grabbed him by the leash."

Murdock's leash was, indeed, still attached.

"Thank you," Merry sang out, deliriously happy. "Thank you, thank you, thank you. You are an angel. You're heaven sent. You're a dear, dear, wonderful human being, and you are my friend for life. Don't be offended by this, but I know my parents will want to reward you for finding Murdock, and they'll..."

"Parents?" the stranger interrupted, the flesh suddenly tightening around her jowly mouth.

"Yes. They're absolute darlings. They aren't home now, but if you give me your name and address, I can..."

"I don't want no reward," the woman snapped. Then, seeming to hear the harshness of her own voice, her tone abruptly changed, and she became down-home friendly. "I'm just real glad to do something nice for another human being."

"Well, you have. For a human and a dog. Murdock and I are so grateful." And before the other woman could stop her, Merry impulsively leaned forward and kissed her on the cheek.

The women took an abrupt step backward. Once again her face became flushed. So flushed, it was more purple than pink.

Merry noticed. Horror-struck. "I've embarrassed you," she said. "First you save my dog. Then you refuse to accept a reward. And *then* I embarrass you. I am so sorry. May I please say thank you in some way that won't cause you discomfort? Isn't there something I can do to show you my appreciation?"

The woman continued to stand motionless. Merry wondered if she hadn't turned to stone like a creature in a fairytale. Then an odd light of eagerness illuminated the stranger's otherwise expressionless beige eyes, she lifted up a fat hand to pat down an errant strand of red hair, and she said, "Now that you mention it, I wouldn't say no to a nice, hot cup of tea."

chapter 41

"I'm sorry," Merry said when they reached the top of the stairs. "I just realized that I never introduced myself. My name is Meredith Bly."

For a long few seconds, Murdock's rescuer stared at her hostess, unblinking and unresponsive. She said nothing and she did nothing. Then Merry reached behind herself to close the door, and the woman stepped forward.

"Edith," she said. "My name is Edith Tuttle."

"Hello, Edith." Merry responded cheerfully, Murdock still in her arms. "Wait here for a second, please. I have to get my dog settled, and I'll be right back."

Edith waited. She did not look at the paintings on the walls; she did not look at the books on the shelves; she did not wonder about the slim horizontal bar affixed to the mirrors that covered an entire wall; and she did not notice that there was an upright piano less than six feet away. She remained totally inert. A few minute later, Merry returned to the doorway and said, "Now, Edith, let's see about that cup of tea."

———

THE BLY RESIDENCE consisted of the top two floors of a four-story townhouse, access to which was gained through a door in the lobby on the second floor. A private staircase behind that door led to another door at the top of the stairs. This door, which was never locked, opened into a comfortable living room decorated with two huge sofas, an uncomfortable Edwardian love seat, and three plush reading chairs. Highly polished parquet floors were covered with vivid oriental carpets, and pre-Raphaelite and Victorian paintings, all borrowed from Annie's art gallery, hung on thick plaster walls. A few small tables boasting colorful potted plants were scattered here and there beside the chairs, and plump, colorful cushions lined the window seat under two large casement windows overlooking Eighty-fourth Street.

The mirrored wall and ballet barre that Edith Tuttle had shown no interest in were directly across from the entrance door. The piano was flush up against the wall, perpendicular to the mirrors, and between the piano and where Edith was standing were two French doors.

"We'll be more comfortable in here," Merry said, leading her guest through the French doors. "You can keep me company while I make tea."

"In here" was a combination dining room, television room, and study that maximized, as all small apartments do, the uses of a limited amount of space. The Blys called it their dining room. Aside from a round oak table and four matching chairs, the room contained a television set, a corduroy sofa, a low slung coffee table, and a small lady's desk covered by a scattering of pens, pencils, and unpaid bills.

Merry paused outside a miniscule powder room just inside the French doors.

"Would you like to freshen up?"

Edith didn't answer. She shuffled past the powder room and peered through the doorway to the kitchen. Then she smiled that same, slyly strange smile.

There was nothing particularly remarkable about the Bly's kitchen. Like all Manhattan kitchens, it contained an assortment of cabinets, a refrigerator, a sink, a microwave oven, and a stove squeezed into a space too cramped to fit even a tiny table and two chairs. Edith studied the oven, situated under a double hung window looking out on the backyard. She stared at the ruffled cotton curtains covering the window frame, and she seemed fascinated by a plastic bracket that held a large roll of paper towels underneath a cabinet to the right of the stove.

Merry tapped her on the shoulder, pointed, and led Edith into the dining room. She deposited her on the corduroy sofa. Edith perched rigidly on the edge of a cushion with her large, plastic purse anchored to her lap.

"I won't be a minute," Merry said.

She spun around and entered the kitchen to make her guest that "nice, hot cup of tea."

IN FACT, IT TOOK Merry more than a minute. First she had to put water into the kettle and set it on the stove to boil. Then she had to take out her mother's Royal Doulton teapot and cups, rinse off the dust, carefully dry them, and arrange everything on a tray with saucers, sugar cubes, and lemon wedges. After that, she realized that tea alone was not a sufficient reward for the person who had recovered her beloved pet, and she raided the cabinets for animal crackers, sandwich cookies, and breakfast treats, placing them in concentric circles over a paper doily on a large cake plate. Finally, several minutes after she had left the dining room, she carried in the tray, placed it on the coffee table in front of Edith Tuttle, and sat down beside her guest.

Merry poured tea into Edith's cup. She poured tea into her own cup. She picked up a plate of lemon wedges and held it out toward Edith.

"I don't want to give you no trouble," the older woman said. "But I like milk better in my tea."

Merry leaped to her feet.

"No trouble at all!"

She disappeared back into the kitchen.

THE REFRIGERATOR DOOR opened and closed.

Edith removed a small white envelope from her purse.

Earlier that morning, she had taken her prescription Zolpidem Tartrate tablets, crushed them to a fine powder, and put them into that envelope.

She poured the envelope's contents into her daughter's cup.

The door to a kitchen cabinet opened.

The powder dissolved instantly.

China clinked against china.

Edith jammed the empty envelope back into her purse.

A cabinet door closed; the refrigerator door opened and closed again.

She dropped her purse to the floor and picked up an animal cracker.

Cream pitcher in hand, Merry paused for a moment in the doorway between the kitchen and the dining room and beamed affectionately at her guest. "You saved Murdock's life, and I will never, never, never forget you."

She returned to where she had been sitting beside Edith and placed the china creamer on the table. Then she picked up a tiny pair of tongs, added four sugar cubes to her cup, swirled around a spoon, and quickly drank down her whole cup of tea.

"You sure do like it sweet," Edith commented mechanically, her eyes never leaving Merry's cup.

"I sure do. And it's a good thing that I have a fast metabolism, or I'd be as big as a barn. It's important that my body be slim, since I'm a dancer. I have to be strong, of course, and in excellent condition, but if I ever got fat, there'd be hell to pay. That's why I'm so lucky, because I eat like a horse."

Merry glanced down and noticed that Edith hadn't touched her tea.

"Don't you like it?"

The older woman raised her cup and took a distracted sip.

"Is it all right?" Merry asked eagerly.

"Yeah. It's real yummy."

"Would you like a cookie or..." Merry held out a breakfast treat. "Maybe one of...of..." She yawned. "Excuse me. I don't know where that came from." She yawned again. "I'm so sorry. It's not the company, I assure you. It's...what was I saying?"

Edith stared at her.

"Oh, I know. I was talking about food." Merry popped a cookie into her mouth. "I could eat hundreds of these." She yawned again. "And I'd never gain an ounce. I'm so lucky, I..." She slumped back against the sofa. "I can't imagine *why* I'm so tired."

Again, Edith lifted her cup to her lips. She stared at Merry. She sipped. She lowered her cup. "You're just like your father," she said, her voice flat and her beige eyes as blank as a bucket of sand. "He could eat a loaf of bread and a gallon of ice cream, and he'd never put on no weight, either."

Merry blinked heavily, struggling to stay awake. "What . . . what did you say about my father? That he . . . Oh, no. You're . . . you're . . ." She yawned. "I can hardly keep my eyes open, but you . . . you're all wrong. Daddy is . . . he's . . ." Another yawn. "Daddy's always . . . worried about his . . . his . . . weight."

Edith placed her cup on the table and leaned her head so close to Merry's that the young woman winced from the sour taste of Edith's breath. "Listen up, girl. I'm talking about your real father here. My husband. Wilbur Tuttle. There wasn't nothing he couldn't eat, and he was still as thin as a rail. Like you. Me? I was never no beauty. All you and me got in common is . . ." Edith extended her right hand and laid her pudgy fingers against Merry's flaming orange hair. Then she touched those same fat fingers to her own lank, drab, hair, that had once been the exact same shade of red.

Merry struggled against the effects of the drug. "Who . . . who are you? Why . . . why . . ."

She fell asleep.

AS EDITH BEGAN to tidy up the coffee table, she hummed *Rock-a-bye Baby* softly, gathering up the cups, saucers, lemon wedges, cookie plates, creamer, and tea pot, and putting them on the serving tray. She carried the tray into the kitchen, opening and closing cupboard doors until she had figured out where everything belonged. Then she carefully washed and dried the china and put it away.

"In the tree top."

Edith returned all of the uneaten cookies, breakfast treats, and animal crackers to their appropriate boxes; she continued to search through the kitchen cabinets until she found a bottle of cooking oil.

"When the wind blows."

She opened the bottom drawer of the stove and pulled out a frying pan.

"The cradle will rock."

She poured all of the cooking oil into the frying pan and turned the burner on high.

"When the bough breaks."

She backed away from the stove and folded her arms across her chest.

"The cradle will fall."

And that smile—that horrible, sly, self-satisfied, gentle smile appeared like the rigid creases in a bronzed baby shoe.

Edith stared at the frying pan, willing it to burst into flames.

Slowly at first, a soufflé of white flames appeared, no higher than the sides of the pan. Then individual bolts of fire shot upward, each bigger, higher, and wider than the last. The flames sprouted, stretched, and rose, becoming a dancing fountain of yellow and white.

"And down will come baby."

The fire reached toward the ceiling and spread to the curtains above the stove. There were flames above the windows, flames eating into the cabinets, flames consuming strips of wallpaper like sulfuric acid eating skin. And Edith Tuttle watched it all. Chuckling and humming complacently. Too absorbed to hear the jangling noises of somebody struggling with the door lock at the foot of the stairs. Too self-satisfied to hear that same somebody bounding up the steps three at a time. Too excited by the speed of the conflagration to hear, feel, or notice Annie Bly, until Annie had stormed into the dining room and was standing at the door to the kitchen, paralyzed with horror and appalled by what she saw.

Annie stared at the flaming stove, at the flaming curtains,

and at the roll of paper towels that suddenly exploded into flames. She shifted her eyes to the dumpy, middle-aged intruder who despite the passage of years, was instantly recognizable as the woman she had once been.

Edith glared at Annie Bly. Edith did not know who she was, and she had never seen her before. She did not know that it was Annie's apartment they were standing in or that it was Annie's kitchen she had set on fire. But she knew enough to be afraid. She stepped back from the inferno she had created and edged her body along the countertop, her hand slowly creeping along its surface as she inched away.

Annie watched the woman. Wondered about the woman. Watched the flames. Wondered about the flames. And then thought... *Merry!*

Where's Merry?

Annie turned. She glanced at the dining room table, the lady's desk, the television, the sofa.

The sofa!

There she was. Slumped against a pillow. Alive? Dead? No time to find out. Annie took a deep breath, turned again, and reentered the kitchen. Her eyes smarted from the smoke, heat, and fire. Her lungs raged against the foul air. But her mind was clear. Focused. Sharp.

She took another step.

An amalgamation of fear and delight glinted in Edith Tuttle's eyes. Edith's shapeless bulk was backed up against the counter, and her fingers were blindly groping along the countertop for something that she could use as a weapon. Searching, groping, and finally finding a cylinder—a marble rolling pin—narrow, heavy, firm. Quick as a snake, Edith lifted it high and slammed it hard and fast into the side of Annie Bly's head.

She dropped the rolling pin and grinned, waiting for Annie to fall.

Blood streamed out of Annie's head, but she did not fall down.

And she didn't stop coming. Arms extended and fingers splayed, Annie slammed her palms into Edith Tuttle's chest. She pushed. She pushed again. And again.

Edith dodged to the right.

Annie blocked her.

She dodged to the left.

Annie blocked her again. Then, her eyes narrowing and her adrenaline surging, Annie clenched her hands, slammed two fists into Edith Tuttle's chest, and gave one, last, great, inexorable heave.

Edith toppled into the ravenous maw of the fire.

A ceiling tile hissed.

It fell at Annie's feet.

A cabinet shelf ignited.

Annie turned, dived through the kitchen door, and slammed it shut behind her. She grabbed the nearest chair and wedged it under the doorknob. If she heard the sound of someone pounding against the door, she ignored it. If she heard screams, threats, and imprecations from somewhere inside the kitchen, she tuned them out as she struggled to breathe. She drew two deep drafts of air into her lungs, blinked rapidly to clear her sight, and rushed to her daughter on the sofa.

Alive? Dead? Alive? Dead? The words chased each other around in her brain as she pressed her fingers against the girl's carotid artery.

Alive.

"Merry," she shouted. "Can you hear me? Wake up!"

Merry shifted on the sofa, but did not open her eyes.

Annie shook her.

"This is an emergency, child. You simply must move."

Merry didn't budge.

Annie leaned down. She wrapped her daughter's arms and legs around her neck in a fireman's carry, as she had seen her brother do dozens of times, and she stood up.

Miraculously, the unconscious girl came up with her.

Annie staggered into the living room and snapped, "Murdock. Come. Now." And the three of them slowly, laboriously, descended the steep, narrow flight of stairs. Before they got to the bottom step, the lobby door swung open.

Sebastian Bly took a step forward.

Billy Nightingale lunged in after him.

Annie's husband's face was gaunt with fear.

Her brother's eyes were fierce with anger.

She stood in front of them, immobile and devoid of emotion. Sebastian lifted Merry off his wife's shoulders. Billy reached down and scooped Murdock into his arms.

Annie's knees buckled. She hacked, coughed, and spit up soot for about sixty seconds. She wiped her mouth, raised her head, and said, "By the way, I just killed Edith Tuttle."

Then she collapsed, a motionless huddle at their feet.

chapter 42

"YEARS AGO, BILLY, even before we arrested her, you called Edith Tuttle something," Sebastian said from his chair beside Annie's hospital bed. "It had to do with opposites."

"Oxymoron," Annie Bly suggested, her voice still hoarse from the fire. "Cold passion. Cruel kindness. Sweet misery."

"Nope," Sebastian lifted his wife's hand. "And don't talk." He kissed her hand on the palm, the knuckles, the wrist.

"Truly, darling," Annie said kindly. "I'm not dying and, unlike some people who shall remain nameless, I'm not dead. I just have a sore throat, a little, itty, bitty concussion that hurts like hell, and a broken nail." Annie raised her free hand and wiggled a finger. "Damn that bitch. So give me my hand back and explain what an oxymoron has to do with dumb, dead Edith."

Sebastian maintained possession of her hand and kissed each finger tip. "Nothing. And that wasn't the word."

Billy, like Sebastian, was wearing rumpled clothes and had a day's growth of beard. "Idiot savant," he said. He was leaning against the window ledge. "I told you that Edith was an idiot savant of arson. A moron with a streak of genius when it came to setting fires and killing kids."

"Idiot savant," Sebastian repeated thoughtfully.

Annie leaned forward in the bed. "I'm at a loss here, guys." Her face was pale and fatigue had drawn charcoal shadows under her eyes. "My frame of reference starts and ends in my kitchen. How did Edith find us? Why did she set that fire? And why on earth did Merry let her in?" Annie turned first to her husband. Then to her brother.

"Enlighten me."

"Okay," Billy said. "Sebastian can slobber over you while I talk. Where should I start?"

"At the beginning. Which was...when?"

"Years ago, when Marmalade was going through all that family tree business."

"Eleven," Annie cringed at the memory. "Merry was eleven years old."

Billy pushed away from the window ledge and walked to the end of Annie's bed. "That was when daytime television was giving a lot of press to those organizations that staged reunions between adopted children and the people who gave them up. Mother and daughter. Father and son. Sister and sister. Lovey dovey, sob story stuff. Marmalade found out about one of them. The outfit was called Point de Reunion. She wrote without telling us and asked them to find out who her real parents were."

"We tried so hard to prevent that from happening," Annie said morosely.

"Edith Tuttle must have written to Point de Reunion, too." Billy paced at the end of the bed. "We found a letter from them in her purse."

"Ouch!" Annie's hand shot to her forehead.

Sebastian lurched forward. "What?"

"Psychic pain." Annie said. "My brother just gave my headache a headache."

Billy reached down and squeezed his sister's big toe. "Buck up, kiddo."

"I'm bucked. Keep talking."

"Okay. I'm guessing that after we invented Yelizaveta, Merry forgot all about Point de Reunion. But by then it was too late. Edith had sent her letter from prison, using her sister's return address in California, and Marmalade had already mailed her letter from Fawn Creek."

Annie shuttered. "Billy, you're giving me the creeps."

"I mean to." He sat on the edge of her bed. "Flash forward seven years. Merry has come of age, and it's legal for Point de Reunion to process the letters. They go into the hopper. One, a confused appeal from an eleven-year-old girl. Two, a devious inquiry from a homicidal maniac. Bingo. A match is made. Next thing you know, Point de Reunion is sending Merry's letter to Edith's sister, and Edith's sister is forwarding it to the wacko lady at Bedford Hills, including, of course, your names and addresses in both Manhattan and in Fawn Creek."

Sebastian punched his fist into the palm of his hand and began to mutter a string of invectives loud enough to be heard by his wife and brother-in-law, but not by the patient in the next bed.

"Down, sweetheart." Annie grabbed his hands and held them still.

She turned back to Billy.

"I get it that fate and Point de Reunion were cheerfully conspiring to murder me and Merry. What I don't understand is how that Tuttle creature was able to waltz out of prison and, right off the bat, stalk us on the upper East Side. How did she get so close? Where did she stay? Where did she get the money?"

"Before Edith left Bedford Hills, she had already made arrangements to go to a halfway house called the Gateway in Spanish Harlem. She picked it because it's only about thirty blocks from us. The executive director told me that if she'd known Edith was a fire setter, she never would have let her in."

"Well, bully for her."

"But Edith's release papers got lost, so she didn't know. More bad luck for us. Bad luck or sheer cunning."

"Cunning," Sebastian said.

"Cunning," Billy nodded. "Edith was sly, cunning, and well prepared. She set herself up in an alley across the street from our house, and for the past few weeks, she's been spying on us. I checked it out, and she made herself a pretty comfortable nest."

"I think I'm going to throw up," Annie said.

"Seriously?"

"No. Go on."

"She found a crate somewhere and hid behind it. She kept a notebook, a ball point pen, and some dog biscuits in the crate, and used it as her command center. In her own crude way, she conducted a pretty sophisticated surveillance."

"Why the dog biscuits?"

"To lure Murdock."

"Poor Murdock."

"He had a rug, dog toys, and a water bowl. Save your sympathy, Annie. Murdock was treated like a king."

"What kind of dog toys?"

"A rubber fireman and a rubber state trooper. Chew toys to sharpen his teeth."

"Tell me that you're kidding."

"The trooper didn't look much like Sebastian, but the fireman looked a hell of a lot like me."

"What was in the notebook?"

"Dates. Times. Stuff."

"What dates? What times? What stuff?"

"Who walked Murdock. When you walked him. When you and Sebastian left in the morning. When you got back. When Marmalade left."

"Ooooooh. I could kill that woman!"

Billy and Sebastian looked at each other. Annie intercepted the glance and gave a short, bitter laugh.

"Don't worry. I'm not delusional. I know that I already did."

Sebastian stood, stared down at his wife, and said with uncharacteristic firmness, "Edith Tuttle used deceptive means to enter our apartment, and she died in a fire of her own making. The fire was incendiary, and the intent was homicide. Those are indisputable facts. What goes around comes around. That's indisputable, too. It was the fire that killed Edith, Annie. Not you."

"Yeah. Right. I just wedged a chair under the door, so that the fire wouldn't make any mistakes."

Sebastian turned to his brother-in-law. "I didn't see any chair wedged under any door when I got upstairs, Billy. Did you?"

"Hell, no. And I didn't pull any chair out from under any door either. Did you?"

"Hell, no."

Both men stared at Annie with innocent, wide-eyed looks on their faces.

Annie's face crinkled adoringly. She turned to Billy.

"Tell me the rest."

"We pieced the rest together from what Merry told us after she woke up."

"Was she woozy?"

"Not for long. She was here last night, worrying about

you, hovering over you, and driving us crazy, so Sebastian sent her home. She came back this morning, but we chased her out."

"Why did you do that?"

"So she could go to rehearsal."

"Which rehearsal?"

"The one she missed when Edith stole Murdock."

"Poor Merry," Annie said, a lone tear sliding down her cheek.

"No 'poor Merry,'" Sebastian thumbed away the tear. "Our girl is just fine."

"Is she traumatized by this two mothers thing?"

"Three, if you include Yelizaveta."

"Oh. My head!" Annie moaned.

"Just joking. No. She isn't the least bit traumatized."

"But she almost died."

"No, Annie. *She* took a nap. *You* almost died."

"What did that Tuttle creature give her?"

"A mild sedative. We found the rest of the pills in her purse."

"How did she get Merry to take them?"

"She put them in her tea."

"So that's how it happened. She put sleeping pills in Merry's... wait a second. Why did our beautiful, intelligent, street-smart daughter invite that horrible woman into our sanctum sanctorum?"

Sebastian described Murdock's kidnapping, Merry's frantic search, their daughter's despair when she thought her dog was gone forever, and her tremendous relief when an apparently kind woman appeared, claiming to have found Murdock.

"I can't see a savvy kid like Merry bringing a total stranger into our house. But a good Samaritan who's just returned your dog—I can see why she did that."

"When Merry didn't show up for her ten o'clock rehearsal, her ballet instructor called our house. She called every fifteen minutes for an hour and a half. At 11:30, she called Annie at work."

"And scared the hell out of me," Annie said. "Merry would never miss a dance class. Never. So I phoned home. When I got no answer, I called the two of you and headed out the door."

Billy took up the story.

"By then, Edith had already drugged Merry's tea. She washed the dishes, put the food away, and set the scene to look as if Merry had been alone all morning. That's how it would have seemed. A careless teenager who put cooking oil on a stove, set the burner on high, forgot about it, and fell asleep."

Billy stopped and shook his head.

"You know, I never got over the way Edith killed her other kids. I don't talk about it, but I still see their faces. Faces, names, and those pathetic little bits of hair. I think about them, too. The pages keep turning in my mind like Edith's damn scrapbook. First, I see little June, the youngest. Dead at just one and a half years old. Then comes Sherwood. Edith killed Sherwood when he was two. Rachel and Fiona, the twins, died when they were five. Rose and Alisa, when they were four. But it's Gabriel and Minna that haunt me most. Gabe was eleven and Minna was nine. Those are the ones we didn't save, so I take it personally." Billy took a deep breath, and then blew it out as though he were expelling toxic air. "She killed them all, and nobody stopped her."

"Edith didn't kill Merry," Annie said emphatically.

"She was so clever. So cunning. So much the . . ."

"Idiot savant?" Sebastian asked.

"Yeah. Idiot savant. And she almost got away with it. The fire marshals would have examined the physical evidence.

They would have attributed the cause of the fire to 'cooking carelessness,' and nobody would have known that Edith Tuttle had come, killed, and gone." Billy looked at his sister. "If it hadn't been for you, Annie, Merry would have died the way all of the other Tuttle children died. Alone and unavenged."

He reached over, clasped his sister's hand, and repeated with vehement pride, "If it hadn't been for you."

chapter 43

AT ONE O'CLOCK that same afternoon, Merry Marmalade Bly rapped her knuckles against the door to her mother's hospital room and tiptoed inside.

"Hi, Daddy," she said. "Hi, Uncle Billy." She hugged them both firecely, whispered to each, "I love you," and sat at the foot of Annie's bed.

Annie slowly opened her eyes. She looked at Merry. Then she turned to her husband and brother. "Why don't you guys track down my doctor and tell him that I'm leaving here in exactly one hour, with or without my discharge papers."

Sebastian leaned down and kissed Annie on the forehead.

"I know," she said. "I love you, too. Now, go. *Go.*"

The two men left the room.

Annie silently studied her daughter. Merry was staring at her hands. She hadn't moved or said a word since sitting down.

Annie broke the silence.

"You know," she said, her voice matter of fact, conversational. "The advantage of having a brain concussion is that when you have to tell your daughter that you've been fibbing to her nonstop since the day the fairies left her on your doorstep, you can be *non compos mentis*, and you don't have to take the flack."

Merry looked up. She bit her lip.

"I love you, Mom," she said.

"Mom," Annie repeated pensively. "You haven't called me 'Mom' in...let me think..."

"Seven years. I stopped calling you anything after you and Daddy invented Yelizaveta."

"Credit where credit is due, darling. Me, Daddy, *and* your Uncle Billy."

"I really do love you."

"Good judgment on your part."

"And even though I never admitted it to myself, not even for a second, I've always known that Yelizaveta wasn't real. I always knew that she was made up."

Annie cocked her head to one side.

"Now you're getting my attention. I'm awed by what you're telling me. And, of course, I don't believe a word of it."

Merry slid up from the foot of the bed, kicked off her shoes, swiveled her legs, and said, "Make room for me."

Annie stared. Stunned.

"Excuse me, young woman, but what have you done with my daughter? And who is this imposter that they've sent in her place?"

But Annie did shift over.

"Do you want me to tell you a story, Mom?"

"I don't know. Do I?"

"Yes. You do. It's about an eleven-year-old girl."

"Oh. That story. I already know it."

"You only know the first draft."

"Which was...?"

"About a ridiculously vulnerable eleven year old, and what she thought she didn't have. It wasn't a very good story."

"Ah ha!" Annie nodded with owlish inscrutability. "The 'I didn't have roots, heritage, and warm fuzzy DNA' story."

"That's the one."

Merry rolled over to face Annie. She propped her elbow under her head. "The revised version is much better. It's about two immensely wise parents who knew that no matter how much their ridiculously vulnerable daughter begged, wheedled, cajoled, and pleaded, she would never have survived her childhood if they had told her that her roots, heritage, and much-revered DNA inextricably linked her to a mother who had murdered her eight brothers and sisters, and a father who had let her do it."

"Mom," Merry choked, tears streamed from her eyes, "Daddy told me everything. I even know that she tried to kill me."

"Actually," Annie said coolly. "She tried to kill you twice. Once, when you were a baby, before the fairies brought you to us. And once seventeen years later. But who's counting. Your mother may have lacked certain maternal instincts, but nobody could fault her for a lack of persistence."

Meredith sat up abruptly.

"Edith Tuttle was *not* my mother," she said hotly. "You are."

Annie did not respond.

"I know I'm dense, but I did finally figure that out."

Still, Annie didn't say a word.

"Mommmmm," Merry drew the word into the same pathetic plea employed by teenagers everywhere in the world.

"Oh, all right," Annie relented. "Pop quiz. Are you ready?"

"I'm ready."

"This is going to be a tough one."

"I'm tough. You and daddy made me that way."

"Very well. Question number one. Who are you?"

"My name is Meredith Bly. Or, at least it used to be. I'm seriously considering changing my name and my attitude to 'Merry.'"

"Question number two. What are you going to do with your life?"

"I'm going to dance."

"Question number three. Why do you want to dance? Is it because Larry, Curly, and Moe convinced you once that your mother was a Russian ballerina?"

"No. It's because dancing electrifies my soul. Dancing gives me joy."

"Me? 'Me' as in who? 'Me' as in what? What are you, Meredith, a.k.a., Merry Bly?"

"I'm a person. I'm a human being."

"What does that mean?"

"It means that I have choices."

"What kind of choices?"

"All kinds. I can choose to become something. Or I can choose to be nothing. I can accomplish great deeds with the genetic raw material I was given by two despicable strangers. Or I can ignore all of life's breathtaking possibilities and spend the rest of my days slumped on a sofa."

"Who determines which of those choices you are going to make, Merry?"

"I do. But because of my family... because of what you and Daddy and Uncle Billy did for me, I can make the right choices."

"What if you suddenly found out that we weren't really your family? What if we had never adopted you? Or the adoption wasn't legal? Or it turned out that instead of being nice people, we're really a gang of drug smugglers or thieves? What about all your wonderful choices then?"

"I would still have them."

"I thought you had to know where you came from to know who you are and what you could become."

"I've since discovered that rule only applies to maps and street signs."

"Which means what in terms of your limitations?"

"It means that the sky's the limit."

"And what does it mean to be adopted, Merry?"

"It probably means that you're an amendment to the Constitution of the United States," Merry said solemnly. "Oh, Mother, how could you have come up with that one?"

Annie sniffed. "If you were really my daughter, you would understand about the Bill of Rights."

"I *am* really your daughter, and I can prove it." She took her mother's hand, rested it for a moment against the side of her face and said, "Pop quiz."

Annie raised an eyebrow. "That's *my* line."

"Nevertheless," Merry insisted. "Pop quiz."

"Okay." Annie shrugged. "I'm ready."

"What's yellow and dances?"

"I don't know, Merry. What?"

"Banana Pavlova."

Annie's eyes widened in surprise.

"What barks when it gets room service at the Plaza Hotel?"

"I don't know. What?"

"The Muttcracker Suite. What wants to dance ballet, but weighs too much?"

"I can't wait to hear this one."

"The Lead Shoes."

Annie laughed. "Those are truly abominable. Where in the world did you find them?"

Merry raised her chin and grinned proudly. "I made them up."

"Honest?"

"Honest."

"Well, I'll be darned." Then Annie put one hand on either side of Merry's head, tilted it forward, and kissed her firmly on the brow.

"Good kid," she said. "Maybe you really are my daughter after all."

chapter 44

MANY THINGS TRANSPIRED the day that Annie got out of the hospital—the day Meredith performed her debut solo as a dancer with the Armand Delacourte School of Ballet.

Four tickets were, indeed, waiting for Annie at the box office. Billy, when they found their orchestra seats, waited for his sister and brother-in-law to file in first, so that he could take the aisle seat next to Arabella McKenzie. During the forty minutes that followed, some silent and subtle interchange must have occurred between the fire marshal and the ballet dancer because when the curtain closed for intermission, they practically leaped out of their seats and hurried up the aisle.

Neither Annie nor Sebastian could help but notice that Billy and Arabella were holding hands.

"How did *that* happen?" Annie whispered urgently. "I didn't even see them talking to each other."

"You didn't see me circling the block three times the day I set my sights on you, either."

"You didn't set your sights on me. You were lost."

Sebastian laughed. "Yeah. Sure."

Annie punched her husband on the shoulder.

"Face it, Annie," he said. "Not everything is under your control."

AFTER HER WILDLY SUCCESSFUL performance, after Merry had hugged her parents and blotted her mother's tears, after Armand Delacourte had kissed her on both cheeks and invited her to join his Ballet Theatre as a principal dancer, after she had put away her bouquets of flowers, removed her makeup, changed to her street clothes and gone home, Merry slept the sleep of an exhausted teenager who did not have a smidgen of space left in her psyche for one more emotional high or one more emotional low.

ANNIE AND SEBASTIAN took Billy and Arabella to a restaurant following Merry's recital. It was a very special restaurant that they had happened upon that very night. It was on the west side of Manhattan, in the vicinity of the John Jay College of Criminal Justice.

When Annie spotted it, she grabbed Sebastian's hand.

He took two steps toward the door and shook his head in disbelief.

"It can't be."

"But it is."

"How can ...?"

"Maybe it just reappears every eighteen years like Brigadoon." Annie turned to Arabella and Billy. "Or when two good people fall in love."

VERY EARLY THE NEXT MORNING, Annie, Billy, and Merry waited outside the house for Sebastian to pull his car up to the curb. Merry opened the door to the back seat, dropped her ballet bag on the floor, and pulled her uncle in beside her.

"I'm proud of you, Marmalade," Billy Nightingale said, looking into his niece's eyes and seeing with mesmerizing clarity the soul of the stoic, unhappy, and unsmiling infant she had once been. As if Merry knew, although she couldn't know exactly what he was seeing, she threw her arms around the man whose stubborn belief in her existence so many years before had saved her life, and she said, "I love you so much, Uncle Billy."

Uncle and niece sat hunched very close to each other for the entire ride to Brooklyn. They didn't separate until Sebastian drove through the gates of Washington Cemetery and stopped the car when he arrived at an area that looked vaguely familiar.

Then they all got out of the car together.

It took them half an hour of zigzagging through a bewildering complexity of unfamiliar gravestones before Billy said, his eyes still searching, "I think..." He took two steps to his right. "I think it's around here somewhere. It's..."

He stopped and motioned the others over.

Merry was the last to arrive. When she approached the headstone, Annie, Sebastian, and Billy moved aside.

"Yelizaveta," Merry read aloud. "It's such a pretty name."

She knelt to study the cameo-like portrait at the center of a rose etched into the stone and stared at it quietly. Several minutes later, she smiled and said, "Thank you, Yelizaveta."

"Daddy?" She turned to her left.

"I have it right here, sweetheart."

"Give it to me, please."

Sebastian Bly handed his daughter a shoe box. It had been old seven years ago, when her parents had first given it to her. It was very, very old now. Merry rested the box on top of Yelizaveta's gravestone and removed the lid. She reached into her ballet bag and took out a pair of size five, pink satin toe shoes. She unwrapped the ribbons and held them in one hand. With her other hand, she unclasped the necklace she had worn since she was eleven years old and dropped it into the toe of one of the shoes. Then she pressed the two shoes against each other, wrapped the pink ribbons around them, and bound them in a tight embrace. She repositioned the ballet slippers in the shoe box and handed it to her father.

It took Sebastian and Billy only a few minutes to dig a deep hole and bury the box.

Annie put her arm around her daughter, and they started to walk slowly away from the grave.

"What do you think she really was?" Merry mused aloud.

"I don't know, darling. Except that she died young, she had a sweet face, and in the final analysis, she did us one hell of a favor."

Billy slapped his hands against each other to brush off the dust and threw an arm over his sister's shoulder.

"Does anyone want to know what I think about Yelizaveta?"

Sebastian caught up with his family, linked arms with his daughter, and said, "What do you think, Billy?"

"I think that she really was a ballerina."

"Or an opera singer."

"Or an actress," Merry threw into the mix.

"And that long ago, an astronaut, or a concert pianist, or a playwright was once..."

"Madly, passionately in love with her, and..."

"One day, maybe in the middle of the summer, during a blackout, she..."

And that is how they left the cemetery, their arms around each other, walking slowly, thinking extraordinary thoughts about, perhaps, extraordinary people.

Speculating.